They needed a distraction. Fast.

Suddenly setting both the Desert Eagle and Beretta on the ground in front of him, Bolan jerked the ASP laser flashlight from his belt. His thumb found the button as he rolled to his side, keeping his head as low to the ground as possible. Pressing the button at the last possible second, he threw the flashlight as far away from them as he could.

Bolan rolled onto his belly, lifting his pistols once more. Almost immediately, all rounds coming from the Handsmen in the tunnel began flying farther over his head. A hard smile covered the Executioner's face. They were keying on the light, thinking Bolan and Harsey were a hundred feet deeper into the tunnel than they actually were.

Bolan waited, his aim ready, as the first wave approached.

MACK BOLAN ®
The Executioner

DON PENDLETON'S

THE EXECUTIONER®
PRECISION PLAY

A GOLD EAGLE BOOK FROM

WORLDWIDE®

TORONTO • NEW YORK • LONDON
AMSTERDAM • PARIS • SYDNEY • HAMBURG
STOCKHOLM • ATHENS • TOKYO • MILAN
MADRID • WARSAW • BUDAPEST • AUCKLAND

First edition April 2000
ISBN 0-373-64257-1

Special thanks and acknowledgment to
Jerry VanCook for his contribution to this work.

PRECISION PLAY

Printed in U.S.A.

Our deeds determine us, as much as we determine our deeds.

—George Eliot

Brute force without judgment collapses under its own weight.

—Horace

Intelligence is only as good as the man using it. If the man has no honor, then his decisions will reflect that.

—Mack Bolan

For Tibbie and Virginia

Prologue

Randall "Buddy" Holly had never liked the nickname that seemed to attach itself to him wherever he went. He'd been born long after the rock-and-roll musician by that name had died in a plane crash, and he didn't even particularly like the man's music when he heard it on the golden-oldies stations. But he had picked up the appellation from the mother of a grade-school friend who had been a big Buddy Holly fan, and it had stayed with him until he'd graduated from high school. Then, during his first year at Harvard, his freshman computer teacher—another fan—had begun calling him Buddy. Again, it had stuck, followed him all the way through law school and then right into the U.S. Secret Service.

Holly adjusted the earpiece connected to the walkie-talkie clipped to his belt and stared into the woods. He wondered where Vice President Winston Bass, and his seventeen-year-old daughter, Samantha, might be. Winston Bass was a nature freak—at least on the surface. But Holly, and the other Secret Service agents assigned to protect him, had realized early on in that assignment that the vice president's sensitivity to the wilds wasn't particularly genuine. It was merely another of the many vehicles that served to project an image of caring. Like most of the politicians Holly had met since joining the Secret Service, Bass seemed to feel people's pain only when it furthered his own political ambitions.

Holly scanned the trees again, looking for anything out of

place—anything that might mean trouble. He saw nothing out of the ordinary.

In any case, Holly thought, Bass often took walks in the forest so he could "commune with nature," as he called it. And while the vice president insisted that his walks be private, Holly and the other agents had noticed there were always video cameras handy in the event that footage was needed for the nightly news.

This day was a little different, however. The vice president's walk wasn't entirely private. Bass had Samantha with him so he could give her some last-minute advice before she left for her first year of college. She was scheduled to leave in less than a week, the day after the elaborate birthday party the White House was planning.

Holly shifted the leather holster on his belt and wondered how a vice president would give such advice. When you were the vice president of the United States of America how do you tell your daughter not to drink too much beer, use drugs or get pregnant? How do you explain the dangers of AIDS? Do you do it the same way other parents did, or does it have the same official ring to it that Bass often used when telling one of the Secret Service agents he'd like a glass of Perrier?

Holly wondered how Samantha would get along at college, and the thought made him wince. Thinking of her in bed with some fraternity boy caused his stomach to churn as if he might throw up.

A soft buzz sounded in his ear, shaking Holly out of his day-nightmare. He heard Mitchell's voice. "Unit Seven to Five," Mitch said. "Come in, Buddy." Holly had only a brief moment to remember the Buddy Holly fan, Secret Service academy fire-arms instructor who had been the reason the nickname had even followed him to his current position before he said, "This is Five. Go ahead, Mitch."

"Bass and his daughter are crossing out of my sector into yours. They're at point D-4. Moving southwesterly."

Holly glanced down at the grid map in his left hand and

nodded to himself. "Affirmative, Mitch," he said. "Five out."
He looked up through the trees to see movement twenty yards
in front of him. Branches and leaves rustled, then Winston
Bass, dressed in the finest Cabela's and Banana Republic had
to offer, stepped into a small clearing and held a tree limb back
so his daughter could walk through.

The young Secret Service agent felt the old familiar tightening in his groin as Samantha Bass appeared. She, too, was
dressed stylishly—looking for all the world as if she'd just
stepped out of an Eddie Bauer catalogue. Her khaki cargo
slacks matched both her vest and blouse, and he noticed that
she'd left the top two buttons open at her throat.

Randall Holly shook his head. He needed to keep his mind
on business. If anyone found out about his secret crush on the
young girl, he'd be removed from the VP's protection team
immediately and find himself chasing counterfeiters somewhere
in North Dakota.

Bass and Samantha stopped in the clearing, facing each
other, conversing in low tones. Holly tried to read their lips,
but they stood at an angle that made it impossible. The Secret
Service agent caught himself focusing on Samantha's hair.
Long and reddish brown, it had been styled into tiny curls so
tight it almost looked frizzy. It made him draw in his breath.
He wondered what it would feel like against his—

"Unit Seven to Five. You see them, Buddy?"

"Affirmative, Seven," Holly said. "They've stopped at
E-4. No movement."

"Seven out."

Holly forced his eyes away from the girl and scanned the
trees around him. At twenty-five he was the youngest man on
the VP's protection team. Many had been against his getting
the assignment, and now he knew why. Mitchell, Keating,
Lamb and all of the other agents on the team were well into
their forties, and they looked on Samantha like a daughter. But
only a few years separated him and the girl, and the physical
attraction had been almost instantaneous.

Had the others noticed? Probably. He was pretty sure Mitchell had, at least. But he wouldn't say anything unless it started to affect Holly's performance on the job. Mitchell was a good man—he'd become a sort of mentor to Holly.

Holly heard movement behind him and did a 180-degree turn, seeing a squirrel break from the bushes and dart up a tree ten yards to his rear. His hand, which had moved to the Glock beneath his jacket, relaxed. He stayed facing the rear for a few moments, grateful for the break. It was torture watching Samantha, trying to keep his mind on the business of protecting her, and wondering if the little looks she sometimes returned meant she had the same attraction to him.

The young agent turned back to Bass and his daughter, and saw Samantha looking his way. The breeze drifting through the trees lifted her chestnut ringlets off her shoulders for a moment, then let them fall back over her khaki vest. A faint smile appeared on her face as she looked at him, and Holly thought he might just jump right out of his skin then and there. He did, in fact, shiver where he stood.

And that shiver saved his life.

The sudden involuntary shudder jerked his body at an angle, and the crossbow bolt caught him in the shoulder rather than the middle of the back where it had been aimed. The force knocked him to the ground, where he found himself facedown with a mouth full of soggy leaves. The radio receiver had been knocked from his ear but lay a few inches away, and he could hear excited babble coming from the tiny piece of plastic. Blood spread from the shoulder wound down his side, and he felt the sticky wetness on his ribs beneath his clothes.

Still stunned, Holly heard the sound of footsteps—many footsteps—moving through the forest. He tried to roll to his side but his body had gone into shock; his muscles ignored the orders from his brain. Then, rough hands suddenly grabbed both his arms. More hands patted him down, ripping the Glock from the holster on his belt as well as finding the Smith &

Wesson Chief Special backup weapon in his ankle rig. He felt a jerk, and suddenly he was standing.

Holly peered across the clearing through hazy eyes and saw Winston and Samantha Bass surrounded by men wearing woodland camouflage. Several carried crossbows. Others bore small arms such as Uzis, M-16s and AK-47s. Two of the men were securing the vice president's and his daughter's hands behind their backs with cuffs.

"Take the bolt out or leave it in?"

"Leave it. He'll bleed to death if you don't, and we can use him."

Holly was pushed to the center of the clearing where he could now see close to thirty cammie-clad men conversing. In his peripheral vision, he saw Mitchell on the ground, an arrow through his back. Farther out and to his other side lay the body of Lamb. Randall Holly had no doubt that all of the rest of the VP's protection team had met similar fates, ending their lives of service on the ground of the forest with crossbow bolts in their bodies.

For the first time, Holly noticed that the men in camouflage all wore masks. Some looked like the Lone Ranger or Zorro, others as if they were getting ready to go trick-or-treating for Halloween. A man wearing the face of Dracula stepped forward.

"We'll be taking Mr. Bass and his daughter with us," Dracula said in an accent Holly could only describe as country. "You go back and tell your lords and masters that the Hands of Heaven will be in touch." The man reached forward and ripped the walkie-talkie from Holly's belt. He nodded to someone behind the agent, and a moment later the agent felt the blow to the back of head.

The woods were quiet when Holly regained consciousness; the only sound was the breeze rustling through the leaves. He struggled to his feet, grabbing a tree for support as he almost fell again. This time, he did throw up, retching and gagging until dry heaves racked his chest and abdomen.

Twilight had fallen over the forest as Holly staggered through the woods toward the cars that had brought them there. He passed Mitchell and Keating and a half-dozen other dead Secret Service agents, and was glad that he had already emptied his stomach so he wouldn't have to do it again. When he reached the vehicles, he noted that the tires had all been slashed. The radios in the first six cars he tried were dead, their wiring having been ripped from the dashboard.

But the radio in the next car was intact, and Holly knew that was by design. He took one last look back into the forest and thought of the men who had given their lives to protect the VP and his daughter. Then he thought of that daughter and wondered where she was, what her fate would be and if he would ever see Samantha Bass again.

It was at that precise moment that Randall Holly felt the crush he'd had for Samantha become full-fledged love.

With bloody fingers, the Secret Service agent unclipped the radio mike from the dashboard of the vehicle.

1

The big man in the black skinsuit battle-dress uniform opened his eyes and shook the sleep from his head. The roar of the jet engines buzzed in his ears, the resultant vibrations resonating through his body. He looked down through the window of the PacAero Learstar and watched the city of Boise, Idaho, zip beneath the wings. He turned to at the pilot. Jack Grimaldi, Stony Man Farm's ace pilot, glanced back and nodded, acknowledging that his passenger was awake. But neither man spoke, and they remained silent as the plane passed over several smaller villages before the waters of the Snake River finally appeared.

The Learstar cut north, following the winding twists that had given the Snake its name. Grimaldi, wearing a faded brown leather flight jacket and suede bush pilot's cap, which had seen better days, finally turned to face his passenger. "Good morning, Striker," he said. "Although it's actually early afternoon."

"Good whatever."

"See anything below?" the pilot asked.

The man who had been called Striker shook his head. "We're too high, Jack," he said. "Besides, they'll have the site hidden. I didn't figure we'd spot it from the air. But it was worth a try."

The pilot nodded, glanced at the controls, then said, "About fifteen more minutes."

The passenger nodded. He was a man of action rather than words, and the action he needed to perform now was a last-minute equipment check. With his hands, he made certain that the Beretta 93-R select-fire machine pistol, sound suppressor threaded into the barrel, was still tucked securely in the nylon shoulder rig under his left arm. It would spit three 9 mm hollowpoints with one pull of the trigger, making only a low coughing sound in the process. Opposite the Beretta under his right arm, the machine-pistol's weight was balanced by a pair of 15-round ammo magazines and the point-up sheath which held his Applegate-Fairbairn commando dagger.

The knife was a silent killer, a close-combat favorite, and could serve as a utility blade if it had to do so.

The big man tapped his side, reassuring himself that his trademark .44 Magnum Desert Eagle rode at belt level on his right hip. Unlike the Beretta, the Eagle roared with enough noise to bring down the walls around him when it unleashed its 240-grain semijacketed hollowpoint rounds.

The man in black glanced back at his pilot as he continued the equipment check. Grimaldi had just recovered from a killer bout with the flu. His face was still pale, and he looked as if he'd lost several pounds during the ordeal. The illness prevented the pilot from being his usual talkative self.

On the left hip, the man who had been called Striker adjusted the Hell's Belle Bowie knife in the cross-draw sheath. With its twelve-and-a-half-inch blade, it weighed nearly as much as the Desert Eagle on his other side. And it was a toss-up at close range as to which weapon could down a man faster. At close quarters one back cut with the Belle could sever a man's wrist. One thrust and pump to the chest ended a threat as quietly as the Applegate-Fairbairn and as decisively as the .44 Magnum, sometimes combining the best of both worlds.

The big man finished checking the rest of his equipment, slid the backpack, which contained his parachute, over his shoulders.

"Five minutes," Jack Grimaldi said, glancing to the controls of the Learjet again. He coughed.

"You need some more rest."

Grimaldi laughed and the laugh turned into another coughing spell. "You're one hell of a good example to follow, Sarge," he said, adding yet another name to the man's list of appellations. "When was the last time you rested?"

The man called Sarge grinned. "I slept all the way here."

"Yeah, what, an hour, hour and a half?"

"However long it took you to fly this bucket of bolts."

The pilot feigned hurt and patted the control panel lovingly. "Don't listen, girl," he said. "He's delirious from lack of sleep. He doesn't know what he's saying." Turning back to the man he'd just called Sarge, he went on. "And you'd been up what, three or four days without sleep when I picked you up?"

"I don't remember," he answered. It was true. He had been up so long finishing off a drug cartel on the Atlantic Seaboard that the days had begun to run together and he'd lost track. But it didn't matter. He'd gotten the job done.

With another glance in front of him, Grimaldi said, "One minute."

Striker began to stretch his stiff muscles. He disconnected the seat belt around his waist. He was ready to be launched when a feminine voice suddenly came over the radio.

"Stony Man Farm to Stony Man One. Farm to One. Come in One."

Now answering to Stony Man One, the big man unclipped the mike from the radio. "I've got you, Barb," he said.

"What's your 10-20?" asked Barbara Price, the mission controller at Stony Man Farm.

Striker glanced down again. "Thirty seconds from the drop site."

There was a pause at the other end. Then Price said, "Hal wanted to talk to you. But go ahead and drop. He says he'll catch you on your way down."

"Affirmative," said Stony Man One.

Ten seconds later, Grimaldi looked over again. "You ready?"

The big man nodded.

Grimaldi began the countdown. When he reached zero he pressed a red button on the control panel. "*Sayonara,* Bolan-*san!*"

The man in the passenger's seat felt himself catapulted upward as the roof of the plane parted. A split second later, he was free-falling over the Snake River and watching the PacAero move away from him in the sky. His hand went to the rip cord of his chute. He counted to ten, then jerked open the canopy.

Striker flipped a switch on his belt, then spoke into the microphone in front of his mouth. "Stony Man One to Stony Man Farm. You still there, Hal?"

The voice of Hal Brognola, the director of America's most top-secret counterterrorist institution, Stony Man Farm, came back to him as he began to drift downward. "I'm here," Brognola said. "Just wanted to let you know there hasn't been much change. Our best intel on the Hands of Heaven is that they've got at least one compound in Hell's Canyon. That's it."

The man nodded as he tugged at the steering controls, manipulating the risers and suspension lines toward a small flat area on the ground. In the center of the drop zone just off the highway, he could see a small speck he assumed to be a vehicle. Beyond the zone, in the distance, stood the city of Lewiston, Washington. "Is General Harsey in the car below?" he asked Brognola. The retired U.S. Army general, an old friend of Brognola's, was to be his local contact.

"Negative. I didn't know it but the general's been in a wheelchair the past two months. His son, Rick, is picking you up. He'll take you to Harsey's place." There was a pause, then Brognola added. "Rick assures me that the old man's mind is still sharp. And if anybody has local intel on the Hands, it'll be him."

The man in the black fatigues felt the wind shift as he dropped through the air. He readjusted his flight pattern, guiding the chute toward the drop zone.

"Refresh my memory once more," he said into the face-mike. "What exactly is it the Hands want in exchange for the VP and his daughter?"

"Oh, not much," Brognola said sarcastically. "Just ten billion dollars, the repeal of the Brady Law and all other gun-control laws back to, and including, the 1930 restrictions on fully automatic weapons, suppressors, minimum barrel length, and that sort of thing."

"But kidnapping the vice president and his daughter is hardly the way to go about changing laws," Striker said. He felt another gust of wind and readjusted his flight pattern once more. "What's the situation with the Feds?"

There was a long pause on the other end of the radio. Then Brognola drew in a deep breath and said, "I told the President I was sending you in and tried to get him to stall the other agencies." He paused again, and this time when he spoke his voice held the tinge of an efficient man who had seen politics get in the way of effectiveness for too many years. "He refused. The story is all over the press, and he can't afford to look like he's not doing anything."

The man in black tugged the controls harder as he neared the ground. The winds were changing rapidly over the canyon and he'd have to pay attention if he didn't want to end up on the ground miles from the drop zone. Turning his attention back to Brognola, he said, "It's the kind of behavior I'd expect out of him, Hal. Polls outrank principles. Symbolism over substance. What does he care if there's another Ruby Ridge or Waco? It won't be him or his family getting killed."

"Again, you'll get no argument out of me," Brognola said. "So you'd better get in, find the hostages, and get them out of there before the FBI and BATF decide to nuke Hell's Canyon."

"Okay. Just one suggestion, Hal."

"I'm listening."

"At least try to get the President to give command to the

Secret Service. It'll be better than some of the other hot dog cowboys running the show.''

"I'll do my best," Brognola said. "But I can't promise anything."

"Stony Man One clear."

"Stony Man Farm clear."

The man who had been called many names continued to descend through the air. As he neared the ground, he could make out the vehicle waiting below—a late-model Lincoln. General Richard Harsey, retired U.S. Army, had come from a wealthy Washington state family. But he'd been a good businessman himself since retirement, and the family fortunes had multiplied.

Two hundred feet above the Lincoln, the man felt the sudden gust of wind shoot him almost straight upward again. A split second later, he felt himself being sucked down once more as the wind created a vacuum. He looked down to see himself heading straight toward a sign that read Bonneville Power Administration. The small building behind the sign was surrounded by electrical wiring.

The man in black tugged on the static lines but the chute continued to be drawn toward the electrical lines as if by magnetic force. He took a deep breath, yanking harder on the lines, then letting them out again, hoping to catch a gust of wind that would send him sailing back up over the threat.

It didn't work. When he pulled once more, one of the toggles jerked off in his hand.

He was less than thirty feet from electrocution when he drew the Hell's Belle Bowie from its leather sheath. The mirror-finished blade flashed under the sun over his head before severing the lines holding him to the canopy in one clean stroke. Suddenly unattached to the parachute, he felt himself falling fast through the air. With a quick flip of his wrist, he tossed the giant knife away from him, to the side of where he knew he'd hit the ground.

Striker hit the pavement on his feet, rolled to his side,

then curled into a ball and began tumbling off the cement onto the dirt alongside the roadway. He felt dust bite into his eyes and mouth, and heard the snapping of electricity above his head. He came to a halt in the eye of his own self-made dust devil, looked up and saw that the canopy had wrapped around the high wires.

Rising to his feet, he dusted himself off as a tall muscular figure pushed away from the side of the Lincoln and walked forward. He stopped long enough to lift the Hell's Belle from the dirt, glance approvingly at the blade, then wipe it on his black T-shirt as he continued forward. He held out the knife hilt first. "Now that's what I call a dramatic entrance," the man said.

Striker took the Bowie, slid it back into his sheath and shook the man's extended hand.

"I'm Rick Harsey, General Harsey's son. What do I call you?"

"Belasko," said the big man. "Mike Belasko."

Rick Harsey chuckled. "Good a name as any," he said, indicating that he knew it was an alias. "Ready to go?"

Striker took a final glance overhead at the parachute canopy flapping in the wind around the high wires. It was a good reminder that in his line of work death could come at any time, in a variety of different ways. He followed Rick Harsey to the Lincoln and opened the passenger's door.

Rick chuckled again as he pulled the vehicle onto the highway. "Nice name. Make it up yourself?"

The man smiled back. "Among others," he said.

Rick nodded. They drove on.

The man in black took a moment to reflect as he choked more dust from his throat. Yes, he had been known by many names over the years. Sergeant Mercy, Mike Belasko, Colonel John Phoenix, and others. But regardless of what name he used, he was always the same man.

Mack Bolan.

But some people knew him better as the Executioner.

COLONEL FRED MORELAND'S fingers tightened around the pistol grip of his Colt AR-15 as soon as he heard the helicopter above him. It would be Russell, he knew, along with the other guards, Winston Bass and Bass's daughter. He looked up to see the chopper descending through the narrow opening in the mountains and felt a strange mixture of pride and embarrassment. The pride came from the fact that his Hands of Heaven had been able to carry out the most successful act of American patriotism of the century. The embarrassment was the result of not being able to accomplish the act on his own.

The helicopter touched down amid a whirlwind of flying gravel and leaves. A moment later, Webber Russell stepped down. He turned back to the glass bubble and held out a hand. It was grasped by long elegant fingers, and a second later a young woman with frizzy auburn hair stepped out.

Samantha Bass. The VP's daughter. She was wearing the same clothes Moreland remembered during the abduction, when he'd been staring through the cut-out eyes of the Dracula mask. Nice looking girl, he thought.

Winston Bass, his eyes frightened and his step unsure, followed his daughter from the helicopter. Neither of the prisoners was restrained as they had been in the forest, and Moreland knew that had to mean they'd been cooperating with Russell. He wasn't surprised. Bass looked like the consummate yuppie in his high-dollar adventure clothes. He was the ultimate tree-hugging nature freak, and tried to make himself look like an outdoors man by being an outspoken environmentalist. But he was no real outdoorsman. He was no fighter. He was a damn liberal wimp.

Russell turned to Moreland, shouting over the noise of the whirling chopper blades. "Any problems, Colonel?" The helicopter pilot chose that moment to cut the power. The blades began to slow, and with them went the accompanying noise. Not sure he'd been heard, Russell shouted again. "Any problems?"

Moreland shook his head. After the abduction in the forest,

he and most of the men had headed directly back to the Hands of Heaven compound in Hell's Canyon. Russell had taken several of Moreland's Handsmen along with his own United States Freedom Movement men and flown the VP and his daughter all over the U.S. first, making sure they weren't being followed and giving the damn Feds time to bust the Hell's Canyon camp in case someone had snitched. Obviously, that hadn't happened.

Moreland thought of Waco, Ruby Ridge and a dozen other lesser-known battles in recent American history in which patriots had opposed the villainous federal government. The FBI, BATF, Marshal's Service—none of those bastards pulled any punches anymore. They shot their own fellow Americans without justification and without remorse. Killed their own brethren with the same lack of mercy Moreland would have shown the North Vietnamese army and the Vietcong. If he'd had a chance or if he hadn't been rated 4-F for some stupid undefinable psychological babble.

The Hands of Heaven leader looked up the river, seeing a fish jump. The canyon seemed like something out of a Norman Rockwell painting, reflecting peace itself. But he knew that if the Feds located them, they'd all die in a violent bloodbath just like their patriot predecessors. A sudden thought struck him: Maybe that was why the Army, Navy, Air Force and Marines had all rejected him twenty-five years before. Maybe he'd have been killed in Vietnam, and God was saving him for this more important war on home soil.

Moreland's eyes moved to the building that served as the Hands offices, where the prisoners would be kept in the back room. Webber Russell waved Moreland forward, and the two men fell in with the guards who were watching Bass and Samantha. The party moved wordlessly toward the little building Moreland thought of as the brig. They passed several desks strewed with paper and a simple kitchenette with a refrigerator, cabinets and a rough-hewn wood table. Entering the back room, Moreland saw the hole in the center of the floor. Dirt and gravel from recent digging was still piled next to it. It was covered by a wood-framed screen.

One of the other men unlatched the covering and pulled it back on its hinges. A short homemade ladder led downward.

Adair Conway, the Handsman who had opened the screen, turned to look at Winston and Samantha Bass. "Down you go," he said, taking the vice president by the arm and shoving him toward the opening.

"Wait...down...there?" the vice president asked incredulously.

Conway spoke again. "That's right, Nature Boy. We're going to help you become one with the planet." He cackled at his own joke, then shoved Bass forward again.

But the vice president dug in his heels. "No, no, I can't...this is preposterous...we won't—"

The stock of the guard's CAR-15 struck Bass in the kidney and sent him sprawling into the hole. He collapsed in a heap ten feet below the floor of the room.

"Daddy!" Samantha Bass called out.

"You aren't calling the shots anymore, Bass Boy," Conway shouted into the hole. He turned to Samantha. "Now, if you'd rather stay topside and keep me company..." His voice trailed off and a lecherous smirk covered his face.

Webber Russell stepped forward. He stared Conway in the eye, then suddenly backhanded the man across the face. "You're out of line, Conway," he said. He turned to the girl. "I'm sorry, Miss Bass. Below, you'll find it uncomfortable but livable. Please excuse this man. He isn't one of mine or he'd exhibit better manners to a lady such as yourself."

Moreland watched Samantha Bass stare back at Russell. Without a word she turned to the ladder and began to descend.

Russell pulled a metal screen over the hole and fastened it to the frame with hooks. "We'll have men stationed here round-the-clock, " he said into the hole. "If you need anything Miss Bass, just let them know. You too, Mr. Vice President."

He got no response from Samantha and only a whimper out of Bass.

Moreland felt the embarrassment in his chest outweigh the pride, now. Russell was in charge now, that was obvious. Maybe not in charge officially but for all practical purposes he was calling the shots. But dammit, this was *Fred Moreland's* compound, and the Hands of Heaven were his militia. It was time he showed some authority.

Looking at Conway and the other men, Moreland said, "Conway, you, Eggers and Buxton take the first watch." He saw a faint smirk twist Russell's lips for a moment, then disappear. Russell didn't speak. He simply nodded his approval.

Turning on his heel, Moreland marched back out into the sunlight feeling his face redden and burn. Russell was laughing at him—laughing at his show of command. The man knew he was no longer in charge, Russell knew it and so did all of the men Russell had brought with him from the United States Freedom Movement. What was worse, all of the Hands of Heaven would soon realize he had been usurped, as well.

Moreland kept going when he got outside, feeling Russell's smirk on the back of his neck. He cut through the trees, then descended the mountain trail, not stopping until he reached the bank of the river, where he let his CAR-15 fall to the end of its sling as he squatted on the grass. Picking up a loose stone, he tossed it into the water and watched the turbulent currents gobble it up.

Moreland shook his head. He was the stone, Russell and the United States Freedom Movement were the river. They had swallowed up the Hands of Heaven in one swift action as soon as Moreland had agreed to join forces with them.

Colonel Fred Moreland, who had never been in the regular Armed Forces and owed his rank to this militia of his own creation, stood back up. Where would it lead? When this operation was over, where would he be? Forgotten? Cast aside as he had been in every other thing he'd undertaken throughout his fifty-five years? Perhaps, but so be it. His goal wasn't self-glory but freedom. Freedom for the United States of America. Freedom from the politically correct liberal assholes who had taken over this country and were doing their best to turn it into a twenty-first Century version of the Soviet Union.

"Freedom," Moreland said under his breath as he walked back from the river. That was what this war, *his war,* was all about.

THE LINCOLN roared down the highway, then turned onto an asphalt road. A few minutes later Rick Harsey and Mack Bolan drove along a gravel path. In the distance, the man known as the Executioner could see a twenty-foot chain-link fence topped by razor wire. Two large structures—the main house and what appeared to be a smaller guest house—stood within. A large sign on the gate warned trespassers that the fence was electrified and that their presence would not be tolerated.

Harsey pulled the vehicle to a halt in front of the gate. Bolan got out in time to see six Ridgeback dogs suddenly appear on the other side. They stood quietly in formation, side by side, eyeing the Executioner. As he watched, two snow-white German shepherds trotted up and took a position just to the rear of the larger dogs.

Bolan chuckled. "The Ridgebacks call for backup?"

Harsey returned the laugh. "Dad's trained them well," he said. "They'll stay just like that until I either tell them you're a friend or tell them to eat you."

"Then tell them I'm a friendly," Bolan said.

Harsey wasn't kidding. He snapped his fingers and the eyes of all eight dogs turned away from Bolan toward him. "This is Mike Belasko, boys," Harsey said. "He's our friend."

The Ridgebacks and German shepherds broke formation and ran off to chase their tails and play like any other dogs.

Harsey pushed a button on a remote-control device attached to his key chain and the gate swung open. He waved Bolan through, then followed and pushed the button again to close the gate. Harsey led the way around the corner of the main house to the rear of the property. Bolan looked out over one of the most beautiful river views he'd ever seen. Little islands dotted the wide water and driftwood floated in the current like something from a postcard.

Harsey noticed the Executioner's interest and paused. "This place has been in the family since the 1850s," he said. "Soon after great-great-grandpa Creighton Harsey and his brother, Ezekiel, came up the Oregon Trail. They had a falling-out over something or other in southern Oregon, and Creighton moved north to Washington along what's now called the Harsey Trail. This is where he stopped."

Bolan nodded. Brognola had told him that the Harseys had been one of the first families to settle Washington state. Many of the first generation had been instrumental in setting up state government, and four generations later they were still a political force to be reckoned with.

Harsey led the way up the steps behind the house to a cedar porch. Tables, chairs and loungers covered the hardwood floor. The door to the rear of the house stood open in the pleasant temperature but a screen door still covered the opening. Through the screen, Bolan could see an elderly man in a wheelchair at a computer terminal. A huge oak desk was positioned at a forty-five-degree angle to the side of the computer hutch and strewed with papers and other odds and ends.

Lying on the corner of the desk, and readily accessible regardless of whether the man in the wheelchair was at the desk or computer, was a large-frame revolver. Bolan recognized the weapon as a .45-caliber Colt New Service. The gun, which he knew would have begun life with a five-inch barrel, now sported a snubby two-inch nose. The hammer spur and the front half of the trigger guard had been removed, and while it appeared to still bear the original wooden factory grips, grooves had been cut on the left side for the fingers.

The Executioner smiled. Such customizing had originated from Colt's own J. H. Fitzgerald, and was known as the "Fitz

Special.'' It was the father of all of the snub-nosed combat-ready revolvers on the market.

General Richard Harsey held a cordless phone to one ear with his left hand while he tapped the keyboard with his right.

''Dad?'' Rick Harsey called out as they neared the open door. Before he could get a response, he turned to Bolan and whispered. ''You don't want to sneak up on him without warning. Damn good way to catch a bullet, if you know what I mean.''

''I saw the Fitz,'' Bolan said.

Harsey smiled. ''A present from Fitzgerald himself,'' he said. ''And the old man can still use it.'' He shrugged. ''Dad still outshoots me, anyway. His only problem besides the stroke is that his hearing is going. You may have to speak a little louder than usual.''

Bolan nodded his understanding.

Clearing his throat, Harsey stepped up to the doorway and knocked on the screen. ''Dad,'' he called again, louder this time.

The general turned slightly in his wheelchair, held up a hand in recognition, then waved them inside the house. ''Yeah, Hal,'' he said into the phone. ''Yeah, looks like they just got here.'' He paused. ''All right. You want to talk to him?'' The elderly man frowned. ''Okay, I'll tell him.'' He hung up, twirled his chair to face the Executioner and held out his hand. ''Richard Harsey, senior, Mike Belasko,'' he said.

Bolan grasped the hand, noting that the grip was still strong. General Harsey had suffered a stroke that left him without the use of his legs but it hadn't seemed to have affected much else. His eyes were clear, and Bolan's initial take was that he was every bit as sharp as Brognola had promised.

''Grab a chair,'' Harsey said. ''Can I get you something to drink?''

Before Bolan could answer Harsey rolled from the computer terminal to his large oak desk and pushed a button. ''Madeline,'' he said. ''You mind coming in for a minute?''

A moment later a beautiful young blonde wearing a maid's uniform entered the den with a big smile on her face. *"Ja?"* she said with a Swedish accent.

"How about a little scotch. Neat. And a glass of water," the general's son said.

"Beer?" Bolan asked.

"Ja," Madeline said smiling. "The general has very good beer."

"Bring me one, too, Madeline," the man in the wheelchair said.

The beautiful blonde frowned. "General, you are not supposed to be drinking," she said.

General Richard Harsey's eyes twinkled for a moment. "Yes, you're right, Madeline," he said. "Bring me a diet 7Up. But bring Mr. Belasko *two* beers, please."

Madeline put her hands on her waist, shook her head and sighed. Then she laughed and disappeared.

The general got down to business. "Don't know exactly who you are, Belasko, but if you're Brognola's man then you're mine, too. Anyway, with that out of the way, you think it was the Hands of Heaven who snatched the VP and his daughter?"

Bolan nodded. "They openly took credit for it. Why? You don't think it's them?"

The general shook his head. "No. At least I don't think they did it by themselves."

The soldier leaned forward slightly. "Why not?"

"Because they aren't that smart, that well trained or that disciplined," Harsey said simply.

The Executioner was about to speak when Madeline appeared again. This time the beautiful Swedish housekeeper carried a tray. She lowered it so Rick Harsey could take his whiskey and water, then turned to hand Bolan one beer and the other to the man in the wheelchair.

"Where's my 7Up?" the general asked innocently.

"Oh, General," Madeline said and laughed. "I get tired of that game. Just drink your beer and shut up."

Harsey laughed and took his beer off the tray.

"Not bad," Rick Harsey said as Madeline's hips swayed out of the room. "I meant the whiskey, of course."

Bolan laughed. His eyes had involuntarily followed the woman as well.

"Dad always did have an eye for the ladies," the younger Harsey said in a slightly louder voice. It was obvious he had wanted to make sure his father heard.

General Harsey lifted his beer can to his lips, then set it down on the desk. "Madeline has proved to be an excellent employee, Belasko," he said. "I don't hold the fact that she's attractive against her as my son seems to do."

Rick laughed. "I don't hold anything against her, Dad," he said.

General Richard Harsey turned back to Bolan. "My wife— Rick's mother—died fifteen years ago. When I was in my early seventies. I've never remarried and don't intend to do so."

"Yes, Dad," Rick said with a gleam of mischief in his eye. "But I've noticed you don't hire any male house employees or ugly females." He downed his Scotch in one gulp and turned to Bolan. "You should see his physical therapist."

General Harsey gave his son a disgusted scowl.

Bolan returned the subject to business. "General, you were about to tell me why you didn't think the Hands of Heaven were behind the kidnapping," he said. "At least not by themselves."

"One reason is that I'd never heard of them before Bass and his daughter got nabbed," the general said. "I found out why. They haven't done anything noteworthy—ever. After the abductions I finally found some intel in my data bank. They're like almost all of the militias, Belasko. Good old boys. Drugstore cowboys. Grown men playing at being tough. They're a bunch of beer-bellied middle-aged men who took up shooting automatic weapons as their hobby instead of golf."

Bolan nodded. Regardless of what the left-wing media tried to promote, such men really did account for ninety percent of what was being called militias in the U.S. Perhaps another nine percent were true patriots who wanted to be ready if America was invaded by a foreign power. In any case, less than one percent were hard-core right-wing extremists willing to blow up buildings with innocent men, women and children in them. Or kidnap the Vice President of the United States and his daughter.

And when they did, they were no longer militiamen under any stretch of the definition. They had become terrorists, pure and simple.

Bolan took a sip of his beer. "You have a theory, then?" he asked.

"Dad always has a theory," Rick Harsey said.

The general smiled. It was obvious to Bolan that beneath the hard exteriors of both Harseys lay a lot of love for each another. For a brief moment, he remembered his own father, and then for another second wondered what it would have been like to have a son.

Bolan pushed the thoughts from his mind. This wasn't the time or place for them. "I'd like to hear your theory," he said.

General Harsey shrugged. "Like I said, it's hardly developed. Nothing more than a simple hypothesis—somebody is using these guys as a scapegoat."

"Another, better trained and organized group?" Bolan asked. "Men who don't want to take the fall when it goes down?" And it would go down, one way or another. There was no way the United States would let someone get away with kidnapping the vice president.

"That would be my initial guess," Harsey nodded. "But like I said, the theory needs developing. We need proof."

Bolan took another swallow of his beer, then nodded toward the computer. "What did you find on the Hands?" he asked.

General Harsey snorted. "Their leader is a Colonel Fred Moreland," he said. "Salesman at a Best Buy or Sight and Sound or some such place. The rank is honorary. He's never been in the military."

Bolan frowned. It did sound as if someone else was behind the abductions. "No military experience at all?" he asked.

Harsey shook his head. "Just another good old boy like the rest of his pack, living in a fantasyland in which they're all patriotic heroes. But they're pretty harmless."

"Then somebody else has to be running the show," the Executioner agreed. He leaned forward and set his beer on a magazine atop the coffee table in front of him. He was about to ask the general if he had any idea where the Hands might be keeping their prisoners when the explosion blasted from the front of the house.

2

Bolan and Rick Harsey vaulted from their chairs as automatic gunfire sounded from both the front and rear of the house. Overhead, the general's alarm system kicked in and a loud siren threatened to deafen them all. The Executioner drew the Desert Eagle at his hip. In his peripheral vision, he saw Rick Harsey jerk a Browning Hi-Power from under his shirt. With a speed of hand that contradicted both his age and physical condition, General Richard Harsey snatched the Fitz Special from his desk.

From all sides of the house now, steady streams of automatic gunfire pounded the outer walls. Between bursts, Bolan could hear the barking of the general's dogs. Then came a low, menacing, canine growl. A moment later, a man screamed.

"Cover the back, Rick," the general ordered, nodding toward the open door through which Bolan and the younger Harsey had entered the house.

Rick Harsey sprinted to the door, hitting the floor as rounds penetrated the screen. Bolan dropped next to him and returned the fire blindly through the screen door and over the porch. A lone round from the Fitz Special exploded behind the Executioner and the room suddenly fell into darkness.

Bolan twisted back. The shadowy form of the general's revolver was still aimed upward at the overhead light.

For a moment, there was a pause in the attack.

"How many men, Dad?" Rick asked.

Harsey wheeled his chair closer to the door with one hand,

the Fitz Special in the other. "Impossible to tell," he whispered. "But there are more than three."

The Executioner understood the implication. The general didn't know how many men were attacking the house. But he knew they'd be vastly outnumbered.

"General, do you have any heavier arms?" Bolan asked.

In the moonlight drifting through the windows, General Harsey nodded. "Yeah," he growled in a disgusted voice. "But they're all locked up in the armory in the guest house." He paused. "Some of my great-grandchildren visited this afternoon."

"We'll have to go for them," the Executioner said as the volleys from outside resumed. Forced to speak between the explosions, he added, "We'll never hold them off with pistols."

Before anyone could speak again, a foolish man sprinted up the back porch steps toward the door. Bolan aimed through the opening and added more of his .44 Magnum holes to the screen. The hollowpoint bullets exploded in the man's chest, sending him flying back down the steps even faster than he'd come up.

"What about the girl?" Bolan asked.

"Girl?" Rick said.

The Executioner glanced at the ceiling. "Madeline," he said. "The housekeeper."

The general answered. "There's a saferoom upstairs," he said. "Steel door, concrete walls. She knows to head straight for it and lock herself in if something like this happens."

"How do we get to the guest house?" the Executioner asked.

"Follow me," the general said. He wheeled toward the door.

"Dad..." Rick Harsey started to protest.

General Harsey looked up at his son from the wheelchair. In the moonlight, Bolan saw a hard smile curl the elderly man's lips. "What?" he almost growled.

Rick shook his head slightly. "Nothing," he said.

What had just passed between father and son couldn't have been more clear had it been painted on the wall. General Richard Harsey had been a warrior all of his life. Advanced age, wheelchair and disability didn't change that fact one bit. But invalidism didn't set well with a man of his nature. At eighty-four years of age, he knew he was nearing the end of his life, one way or another. And if given half a chance, that end would come as it should for a man like him.

As a warrior. Given the opportunity, the old man intended to go out with sword in hand.

Bolan shoved the Desert Eagle back into the holster and drew the Beretta 93-R. Quickly, he unscrewed the sound suppressor and dropped it into one of the pockets of his fatigues. He needed the Beretta's autofire but not the silence. The noise of return fire would be almost as important as the bullets themselves in what they were about to attempt.

Bolan turned back to the general. "Lead the way, sir," he said.

General Harsey reached to his side and pushed a button on the wheelchair. Between the rounds exploding into the walls, Bolan heard a loud motor kick in. It sounded more like a car engine than the soft purr that usually came from motorized wheelchairs.

Bolan looked to Rick.

The general's son shrugged. "What can I say?" He chuckled and shook his head. "The chair didn't have enough juice for him so he had one of the CIA mechanics rewire the whole thing."

"Get the door for me, will you, Belasko?" General Harsey said.

The Executioner rose to his feet next to the screen. Taking a deep breath, he reached out, grabbed the doorknob and twisted. A second later he bolted though the door, opening it wide and cutting loose a 3-round burst from the Beretta at some shadowy forms between the house and the river. One of the figures dropped, the other took refuge behind a tree.

Rick Harsey sprinted through the doorway and took up a position next to Bolan, sending a steady stream of semiauto fire from his Browning in the same direction. The resulting explosions were too loud to be 9 mm, and the Executioner realized Harsey's Hi-Power had to be chambered for the newer .40 S&W round. Behind him, Bolan heard the general's souped-up wheelchair bump over the threshold onto the porch.

A shadow appeared to the Executioner's left. He turned, but before he could fire, the Fitz Special jumped in the general's hand and a .45 Colt slug split the attacker's breastbone.

"Let's go!" General Richard Harsey growled.

Drawing the Desert Eagle with his left hand, the Executioner laid down a blanket of cover fire. In the semidarkness, more shadows fell. General Harsey motored his chair along the porch, firing the Fitz selectively as he went. Two of the Ridgebacks and one of the German shepherds raced to the porch, taking up positions next to the wheelchair. Bolan and the younger Harsey made their way behind the procession, walking backward and returning fire as bullets whizzed past their heads. At the corner of the house, the general halted. "Lift me," he ordered.

The three dogs turned to face the rear as Bolan and Rick sprinted between them. The Executioner saw two steps leading upward to a wooden walkway, which led to the guest house. Firing a quick triburst over his shoulder, he grabbed one side of the chair while Rick took the other. A second later, the general was motoring toward the guest house.

The Executioner ran the Beretta dry, fired the Desert Eagle twice, then dropped the empty 9 mm magazine, replaced it with fifteen fresh rounds, and worked the slide. He tapped another burst into the chest of a man clad in woodland cammies, then turned and followed Rick Harsey and his father along the wooden path.

New figures appeared between the two houses from the front of the property. From the shoulders down, they were dark and blurry. But their faces and hands hadn't been covered with camouflage paint and glowed in the moonlight.

Flipping the Beretta's selector switch to semiauto, Bolan took three of the men out with lone hollowpoints. The Desert Eagle exploded in his other hand, accounting for a fourth. Rick's Browning popped away in front of the Executioner, downing two more men while the general emptied the last of his six .45 rounds into the final shining face. From his shirt pocket the elderly man produced a speed-loader and dropped more fresh rounds into his Fitz.

But the attackers seemed endless, and another half-dozen men rounded the corner shouting and firing. Bolan turned his Desert Eagle to the man in the lead and let 240 rains of copper-jacketed lead speak for him. With the Beretta in the other hand he downed a third gunner.

Rick Harsey pumped two rounds into a fourth hard man but was slowed when the man kept coming. He lost valuable time raising the weapon to head level but his third .40 S&W round split the attacker's face in two.

The general fired his Fitz until the firing pin clicked onto an empty chamber. He was out of ammo once more.

But he had other weapons.

Holding two fingers to his lips, he whistled shrilly over the gunfire. Both Ridgebacks and the shepherd shot from his side and lunged for the remaining two men. The shepherd in the lead caught a bullet in the chest as he leaped for the throat of a man wearing a floppy boonie hat. But his momentum carried him forward, and he died with a dead man's severed jugular in his teeth.

The Ridgebacks growled as they left the ground, knocking the remaining gunner down as a team. The larger of the two clamped his canine teeth into the soft flesh beneath the screaming man's chin. The other chomped a mouthful of groin.

A second later, Bolan, Rick Harsey and the general were at the door to the guest house. Rick Harsey had pulled his key ring from his pocket but Bolan didn't wait. Sprinting between the man and his father, the Executioner lowered a shoulder and slammed into the door. Lights flew on around him and another security alarm screeched amid the gunfire.

"Second door, left!" the general shouted as Bolan raced into the house. A bathroom on his left and a small bedroom to the right registered in the Executioner's brain as he ran. Straight ahead, he saw the main room of the house. Roughly thirty feet by thirty feet, it was more museum than house. Weapons of every size, shape and type were displayed along tables and on the walls. Cardboard placards identified each.

But Bolan had no time to read. And these weren't the weapons he was looking for.

Lowering his left shoulder, the Executioner executed a three-point turn, knocking the door to the armory open like he'd done to the one leading inside the guest house. He rose, flipping on the overhead light to illuminate two long racks of assault rifles and submachine guns. Behind him, he heard Rick Harsey sprint into the room. Lifting a Heckler & Koch MP-5 from the rack, he tossed it over his shoulder and heard the man catch it.

Bolan's hand fell on an M-16 and he swung his right arm into the sling. With the weapon suspended from his shoulder, he grabbed an AK-47 and turned in time to hand it to General Harsey as the man wheeled into the room.

Rick had already moved back out into the hallway where he was sending bursts of 9 mm fire from the H&K into anyone foolish enough to come through the door. Four bodies already lay in the hallway when Bolan jumped out of the armory to join him. The Executioner was surprised to see that one of the men was dark-skinned. Either Hispanic or Middle Eastern, by his looks.

Bolan frowned as he raised the M-16 and sent three 5.56mm slugs into a burly bearded man wearing a plaid lumberjack shirt with his cammo pants, sending him spilling back out the door. The Executioner glanced again at the dark-skinned man on the ground in front of him.

He had assumed it was the Hands of Heaven who were attacking. But the Handsmen were hardly known for allowing minority group members into their ranks.

This was no time for speculation into the militia's ethnic policies, however. An arm appeared around the side of the doorway, and a Government Model colt .45 began to spit rounds. One of the heavy bullets singed the thigh of the Executioner's black skinsuit, ripping a hole across his leg. Then the arm disappeared.

Bolan raised his rifle to shoulder level and sighted down the barrel. Rick Harsey had taken cover behind one of the display tables just to his rear. As the Executioner waited for the arm to reappear, as he knew it would, he heard General Harsey motoring toward the hallway. He turned long enough to say, "Wait." Then the arm with the colt emerged into the doorway again.

It was right where he'd expected it. Right where he already placed the sight.

The man with the pistol had dropped to one knee, following the age-old philosophy that you never reappeared around a corner at the same level from which you had last fired. Nine times out of ten, the technique worked.

But nine times out of ten you didn't face the Executioner.

Bolan squeezed the trigger. The Government Model went flying from the unseen man's hand and a screech of pain issued from outside the guest house. The Executioner hurried forward, the M-16 leading the way. He stopped at the doorway and dropped to his knee. A quick glance outside told him the man was alone. Another told him the attacker was struggling to get a Ka-bar blade out of its sheath with his good hand.

Bolan stuck the rifle around the corner and sent a single round through the man's nose.

Outside, the gunfire stopped. The alarm system had run its course minutes before. An eerie silence fell over the compound, broken now and again by the whimpering of a wounded dog.

Were all of the intruders dead? The Executioner couldn't be sure, but his gut told him no. Something had caused them to halt the attack. It was far more likely that he, Rick and General Richard Harsey were in the eye of the tornado; the quiet before the storm.

But the storm would break again. Soon.

The sound of a vehicle arriving along the gravel road soon shattered the stillness. The Executioner looked both ways through the door, then crept outside the guest house. He walked swiftly and silently between the two buildings until he could see the gate where they'd left the Lincoln. Pulling in behind the vehicle was a flatbed truck.

And in the back were at least twenty more well-armed cammie-clad men.

Bolan nodded in the darkness. So that was what had caused the lull in the battle. The Hands of Heaven—Bolan thought of the dark man on the floor of the guest house and wondered again if they really were the Handsmen—had signaled for reinforcements. The survivors were waiting for their comrades before resuming the attack.

It wasn't over yet. Not by a long shot.

BACK IN THE FRONT house, Bolan saw that both Harseys had crept to the door. The only chance they had now was for him and Rick to circle out and attack the Handsmen from the rear. "Rick," he whispered. "Grab all the extra magazines you can carry and get ready. General, I need you to stay here, sir."

General Harsey misread the Executioner's order. "I can move as well as half the pansy-assed twenty-year-olds out there," Harsey growled. "I'm going with you."

Bolan shook his head. "I'm not being condescending, sir," he said. "And I wasn't kidding when I said I needed you here. Your armory is a mixed blessing. We'd all be dead now if it wasn't here. But if those weapons fall into the hands of the enemy..." He didn't bother to finish the sentence.

The general understood. But Richard Harsey had his own ideas. "Rick," he said. "Cover the door for a minute. Belasko, come with me. I've got more toys you might find interesting."

He twirled the wheelchair and motored back toward the armory. Bolan followed.

Several canvas tarps covered boxes beneath the rifle racks. General Harsey threw one back to reveal a box filled with Israeli gas masks. He pulled three of them out of the box and tossed two to Bolan. "Give one to Rick," he said. Wheeling to another of the tarps, he pulled it back and leaned forward, lifting a heavy cardboard box into his lap. "Here," he grunted. "I'm sure you can figure out what to do with them." He turned the wheelchair again and shoved the box toward Bolan.

The Executioner let the M-16 fall to the end of its sling and looked into the box. What he saw made him smile. The box was divided into six sections, and each held a riot-control-sized canister of OC.

Oleoresin Capsicum. Pepper gas.

Bolan was screwing the sound suppressor back into the barrel of the Beretta when the general wheeled over to a drawer. He pulled out a High Standard .22 rimfire with a similar suppressor attached. "Give this to Rick, too," he said.

The Executioner shoved the pistol into his belt.

"The wind's from the south." The general grinned. "Coming up from the river."

Bolan turned out of the armory and met Rick in the hall. "I was just going to suggest that," the younger Harsey said when he saw the pepper canisters.

"I'll go to the west end and work along the river," Bolan said. "You go east. We'll meet in the middle."

Rick Harsey nodded and took off.

Bolan slipped the gas mask over his face and broke the seal on the filter. He exited the guest house and stopped long enough to see the men in the flatbed begin dropping to the ground. Moving between the houses, he cut to his right on the river side and began moving toward the water.

There was no fence along the rear of the property, the river serving to discourage all but the most dedicated attackers and thieves. But these men were dedicated, and some had crossed the water in small rubber rafts. Two men still sat in the crafts, guarding the shore.

A pair of quiet rounds from the Beretta ended that.

The Executioner stopped near the corner of the property where the fence ran into the water. He dug a shallow hole in the soft earth with his Applegate-Fairbairn knife, stabilized the pepper gas canister with dirt and broke the seal.

The powdered pepper shot into the air, caught the breeze and started drifting back toward the houses.

Bolan hurried along the shore, watching the buildings through the triangular eyepieces of his gas mask. He repeated his performance with the other two canisters, and by the time he spotted Rick near the center of the property he could hear excited voices nearer the houses. Shots rang out.

"Let's get some distance between us and move in," the Executioner said through the mask. "See if we can take somebody alive. I want to know who they are and what they're up to."

Bolan began moving up the hill toward the houses. Coughs, choking sounds and screams of fear and pain drifted down to the river as the pepper gas saturated the air. Two gunners spun blindly as he neared them. They shot each other.

The Executioner heard the soft swish of Rick's suppressed .22 pistol several times as he made his way back to the house. Another man moved from behind a tree, crying in pain as he dug the fingers of his left hand into his eyes. Shots leaped from the barrel of his Colt AR-15 as he, too, fired sightlessly into the night. As the rounds neared Bolan, he had no choice but to end the threat.

More gunfire sounded from inside the guest house, and Bolan redirected his footsteps that way. He encountered more blinded men as he cut around several small buildings. Each time he was forced to shoot them, and each time he hoped Rick was having better luck taking a prisoner. He wanted someone left alive to talk.

A shotgun roared inside the guest house and a man in woodland camouflage fell out of the doorway clutching his chest. The Executioner stepped between the houses once more. Another man, whimpering in pain, darted around the front of the houses out of sight. Bolan sprinted past the doorway and caught a brief glimpse of General Harsey sitting in his wheelchair, pumping the slide of a short-barreled 12-gauge shotgun in his lap. A wisp of smoke curled from the barrel.

The Executioner turned the corner in time to see the man he had pursued hop aboard the flatbed just as it pulled away from the house. He lifted the Beretta and fired into the mass of men as the vehicle pulled away. In his other hand, the Desert Eagle roared. Three men fell from the back before the truck turned onto the road and disappeared.

Bolan turned to the guest house and walked past the scattered bodies of more men. Again, he noted one with dark features, and once more wondered if the Hands of Heaven was really behind the assault.

In the guest house, Rick Harsey held a damp washcloth to his father's face.

"It's only a scratch," the general protested.

"Dad, just once do what I tell you," Rick said in an irritated voice. "It won't kill you."

The general grinned for a second, then the expression vanished. "How can I be sure?" he said with a straight face.

Both men aimed their weapons at the doorway, then lowered the barrels when they saw Bolan.

General Harsey wheeled back into the armory and opened the door of a metal box on the wall. He flipped a switch, and the entire compound was suddenly flooded with light. "I'd have done this earlier," he said. "But I figured we knew the layout better than them, and the darkness would be to our advantage."

"*I* didn't know the layout, sir," Bolan said.

The general squinted at the Executioner. "You obviously create your own advantages," he said flatly. He paused, and for the first time Bolan saw the signs of fatigue on his wrinkled face.

"Let's check for survivors," Bolan said. "Then we'd better make sure Madeline's all right."

The three warriors exited the guest house and began checking the bodies. All who had escaped death had made it to the truck and were gone. And none of the bodies bore any identification.

"Dad," Rick said when they were still only half finished. "We can do this. Why don't you go up and check on Madeline?"

The general grunted, then nodded. "Don't fall down and hurt yourself while I'm gone, Junior," he said as he wheeled toward the main house.

Bolan and Rick checked the last body for signs of life but found none. They returned to the den, and the Executioner dropped into the same chair he had occupied earlier. Rick disappeared into another room and returned with a shot of whiskey and a bottle of beer for Bolan.

The soldier glanced around at the bullet holes and other damage to the house. Repairs would be costly, but the damage to the house wasn't what concerned him at the moment. "Is this going to cause your father any problems with the law?" he asked Rick as the younger Harsey took a seat.

Rick laughed. "I doubt it," he said. "Couple of years ago some thieves heard about all the stuff in the guest house and came across the river in a rowboat. Dad shot them both, then called the sheriff to pick them up. That was the last we heard of it." He paused. "The sheriff served under him in Nam."

The Executioner glanced over his head at the ceiling. "You suppose everything's all right upstairs?" he said.

Rick nodded. "If not, he'd have been back down."

"Still," Bolan said, "maybe we should go check."

Rick had the whiskey to his lips as he shook his head and motioned for the Executioner to stay put. Setting the glass on the table, he said, "We go up there right now, we'll just embarrass them and us both."

Bolan stopped. "You don't mean—"

"That's exactly what I mean." Rick laughed. "I wasn't kidding when I said Dad still had an eye for the ladies."

WHITECAPS rolled along as the Snake River continued its billion-year journey south out of Lewiston, Washington. Bolan, Rick Harsey and a man wearing a navy blue T-shirt bearing the words Lewiston Charters stood on a wooden dock overlooking the water.

The man in the T-shirt shook his head. "All my speedboats are already booked, Rick, " he said. "You should have known that. It's peak season."

Bolan watched Rick Harsey grin. "I do know that, Tom," he answered. "But I worked for you for three summers when I was in high school, if you remember right. Which means I also know old Tom Majors never rents them all—you always keep one of the boats back for your own use. And it's always the best one, too. That's why we want it."

Tom Majors blew air between his clenched lips, making them flutter up and down. He shook his head again. "That jet's for family only, Rick," he said. "And while you're near enough to call family, I still can't do it." He paused and glanced from the docks to the building on the hill. "Jackie's twelfth birthday is this weekend, and Deb and I promised to take him fishing."

Bolan had been silent during the negotiations but now he cleared his throat. When the two other men turned to him, he said, "I've got an alternate plan your son might like even better." He pulled a huge roll of money from his pocket, twisted off the rubber band securing it and began counting off hundred-dollar bills. The money was part of the spoils from the drug cartel bust he'd conducted just before Grimaldi had flown him west, and he was happy to put it to good use. When he reached ten thousand dollars, he looked at Tom.

The man's eyes had widened.

"Jackie can go fishing with you anytime," the Executioner smiled. "But has he ever been to Disneyland?"

Majors grinned. "No, but I'm sure he could live with it instead," he said, jamming the cash into his khaki pants. He pointed down the row of speedboats tethered to posts in the slips. "Number four," he said.

Bolan looked down at the point Majors had indicated. The name *Norma* was painted on the hull of the craft.

"Named her after a good friend's wife," Majors went on. "Both gas tanks are full and there are extra cans onboard. But if you need more, there's a pump at Beamer's about seventy miles down. Rick knows the way."

"That's why he's with me," the Executioner said. "We'll also need kayaks."

"All I've got left is a double," Tom said. "And this time, I mean it. There's nothing else."

"What kind?" Bolan asked.

"Libra XT," Majors answered. "And it's a beaut. Come on." He turned and began leading them past the long row of speedboats waiting to go out. "Twenty-one feet, eight inches," he said over his shoulder as he walked. "The beam's about thirty-two inches, weighs ninety-two pounds. Fast and maneuverable."

Bolan nodded behind the man. It would do. He wanted the boat for speed, but they might need the kayak for silence. And the Libra sounded as if it would hold sufficient equipment loaded off the *Norma* during silent probes along the shore.

Harsey turned to the Executioner. "I need to call Dad," he said. "I want to make sure he's okay."

Bolan nodded as Harsey pulled a cellular phone out of one of the pockets of his jacket. As the general's son took a few steps up the hill to get away from the sounds of the river, the Executioner took the opportunity to scrutinize the *Norma*. It was big, with roughly sixty seats for sightseers. For a moment, he considered removing some of the seats but then decided against it. Such modifications would take time, and there was plenty of room between the benches to store the equipment they were bringing.

Bolan walked up the hill to where they had parked the Lincoln, got behind the wheel and drove it down the ramp to the pier. They had equipped themselves for the journey from General Richard Harsey's personal armory. Concealed guns, ammunition and other accessories were in cardboard boxes or wrapped in blankets—out of sight of curious eyes for when they shifted the equipment to the boat. He parked the car as near as he could get it and, as he began transferring the gear, his thoughts drifted to the general.

Like Rick, the Executioner had been worried about leaving the elderly warrior alone at the compound. Even in a wheelchair, the general was far from helpless but he would be one man against many if the Handsmen—if it was the Handsmen who had attacked—returned. So Bolan had suggested calling in men to guard the place.

General Harsey had scoffed at the idea. He would call in a few favors until the mission was over.

Bolan and Rick Harsey finished carrying the equipment from the Lincoln to the speedboat, then Harsey drove the car back to the parking area and met Bolan and Majors at a rack of kayaks. Majors pointed out the Libra, and the men carried it back to the *Norma*, lashing it to the rail with bungee cords on one side of the craft.

"You said you worked three summers for Tom?" Bolan asked as they moved to the pilot's area at the fore of the craft.

Harsey nodded. "Took tourists out on day trips mostly. You know…" his voice took the practiced tone of a tour guide "…on your left, you see the spot where the steamship, the *Imnaha*, sank during her fourteenth voyage, November 9, 1903. There have been rumors ever since that a conspiracy between mining promoters—" He stopped speaking abruptly. "You get the picture. Got where I could recite that stuff in my sleep."

"Good," the Executioner said. "You steer. I'll be keeping

a lookout for anything that might indicate where the Handsmen's compound is.''

"We ready then?" Harsey asked.

"We're ready," the Executioner said. Without another word, Harsey fired the jet engines to life, backed the boat out of the slip and the two warriors started down the Snake River into Hell's Canyon.

RANDALL HOLLY followed Secret Service Deputy Director Aaron Curtis into the conference room where the two men took the last seats at the table. Holly's shoulder hurt like hell where the crossbow bolt had struck him. He was also tired, nervous and scared. He and Curtis, along with the members of the vice president's personal protection team who hadn't been on duty during the kidnapping—the only members of the team still alive—had flown to Seattle less than an hour after the VP and his daughter had been abducted.

Holly knew he'd been lucky—damn lucky. The bolt had passed within a quarter inch of his subclavian artery, also missing all bones, major tendons and ligaments. Had it been slightly lower and even nicked the artery, he knew he'd have been unconscious two seconds later and dead a second and a half after that. As it was, he'd been treated in the White House clinic. His shoulder was now bandaged, and his arm was in a sling. The wound had been stitched but was in a difficult spot. It hadn't closed as well as might have been hoped, and blood still occasionally seeped between the stitches.

Holly had quickly removed the sling and made sure to keep the spots that occasionally crept through his shirt hidden by his sport coat. He was determined to be part of the search for Winston and Samantha Bass.

The young Secret Service agent looked around him as more men filed into the room. The suite housing the Seattle FBI field office was a cold, stark place filled with desks, chairs and shelf after shelf piled high with paper forms. The walls were covered with enough tiny reminder signs that it was obvious that Washington wanted nothing, absolutely nothing, left to the discretion of the individual agents assigned there. The signs appeared to spell out official procedure for everything from interrogating suspects to taking a piss. Had it not been for all the walkie-talkies, guns and other law-enforcement equipment, which also crowded the conference room, Holly knew the suite might be confused with any other federal government agency that was long on paperwork and short on results.

Other men, some dressed in business suits, others in outdoor gear, joined Holly around the long table. With all of the seats occupied, they took places against the wall until the room couldn't possibly have held even one more human body. The men were quiet, solemn. But Holly knew that was about to change. The fight for control over who would lead the search for Winston Bass and his daughter was about to begin.

The Secret Service man didn't have to wait long.

A drab-looking man in a dark gray suit Holly recognized as D. Elliot Strektuyu, the special agent in charge of the Seattle FBI office, suddenly cleared his throat. "All right, gentlemen," Strektuyu said. "Let's get started. We'll—"

A murmur suddenly rose from around the room. Then one of the local Secret Service agents shouted over the rest, "No, Elliot, this is a Secret Service case. You and the others are here as support. What we're going to do is—"

A man dressed in full woodland camouflage, his face and hands already painted to match, shot to his feet across the table from Holly. "Dammit!" he yelled. "The Hands of Heaven are already wanted on more firearm violations than you can shake a stick at," he almost screamed. "The Bureau of Alcohol, Tobacco and Firearms has decided—"

"BATF, my ass," Donovan shouted a voice from the other end of the table. "The Federal Marshal's Service is clearly in charge here, and what I propose is—"

Holly noted that his own deputy director had remained silent throughout the bickering. He could be wrong, but he suspected he knew why. Aaron Curtis already knew who was going to run the show on this one. The Secret Service man kept glancing at the phone on the table.

Holly had been wrong about something else, however. The door to the outer offices opened and one more body did squeeze into the room. He wore a Montana peak cowboy hat, a western-cut khaki uniform and hand-tooled gun belt. "I'm the sheriff here," said the man in the uniform. "And according to the constitution of the United States of America, the duly elected sheriff is the chief law enforcement officer within his county."

Holly looked down at the table as the arguing continued. All he could think about was that while this roomful of egomaniacs argued over who got to play boss, Samantha Bass might be getting tortured, raped and might even be dead already.

The childish debate, Holly was sure, would have continued if the telephone on the table hadn't suddenly rung. At least six hands shot toward it simultaneously. Strektuyu was the winner. "Yes?" the FBI man said into the receiver as the yelling around him lowered to a dull roar. "Yes, sir, it's Strektuyu, sir." There was a pause, during which his face began to darken. "But, sir...yes...yes, sir...but sir, I've got to say...certainly, sir. I'll tell them." He hung up and turned to the men. "That was the President. The Secret Service will be leading the investigation. Some of you may not like it. I don't like it. But that's the way it is." He turned to Curtis. "Tell us what to do, Aaron."

Curtis opened the briefcase on the table in front of him and pulled out a large stack of papers. Several sheets had been stapled together into individual units. He dropped one to his side, then handed the rest to Holly who took a copy and passed them on. Holly glanced down as the rest of the stack made its way around the room.

The top page was a geographical map of Hell's Canyon, which looked as if it had come off the Internet. Holly had turned to the page beneath it and saw a topographical map of the same area when Curtis spoke up again.

"If you'll look at page two," the deputy director said,

"you'll see that we've divided the canyon into sectors. These sectors are not of equal size. They've been determined, rather, by the terrain and the estimated geographical difficulty each team is likely to encounter. In other words, they're divided according to time. The sectors that contain arduous—" he glanced to the sheriff and rephrased the sentence "—the sectors that contain difficult terrain—"

"Go on, Mr. Deputy Director," the sheriff grinned. "Believe it or not, I had a little schooling. I know what the word *arduous* means."

Curtis cleared his throat, reddening slightly. "Sectors in which search progress is likely to be slower are smaller," he said. "As are those in which the land offers multiple hidden valleys and other potential hiding places. In addition, each sector was chosen to have a number of distinguishing landmarks that can be identified easily while on the ground."

"That's so you city boys in your Armani suits don't get lost," the sheriff said.

Curtis shot the man an exasperated look. The sheriff just continued to grin.

"Air and satellite surveillance has turned up nothing," Curtis went on, "which leads us to believe the Hands of Heaven compound must be in one of the many valleys hidden by overhanging mountains." He paused to clear his throat. "We have a total of roughly five hundred men. Fifty search parties, ten men each. Turn to page three."

Holly turned the page as papers rustled around the room.

"As you can see, each sector has been broken into subsectors of ten. Assign one man to each subsector. When he's finished, rotate him with another member and search again."

The BATF man named Donovan looked up. "Where are we getting all these men?" he asked.

"Simon, all federal agencies are sending personnel. But we're also using local deputy sheriffs and other local law enforcement officers who are familiar with Hell's Canyon."

FBI SAC Strektuyu glanced over the top of his glasses.

"Aaron, are you sure it's wise to bring in...well...amateurs?" he asked. "We've got Hostage Rescue on the way. And our regional SWAT teams are sending men. Wouldn't it be better to wait and get professionals?"

Holly glanced to the sheriff in the cowboy hat. Instead of being offended, the man looked more amused than ever. "I understand your concerns, gents," he said. "Very few of us local yokels have been through the extensive training you've had. But for all our shortcomings, we probably *do* know the Canyon a little better than you."

The grumbling started again and began to rise as each of the various agency men expressed their dissatisfaction with one another.

"All right, shut up!" Curtis screamed at the top of his lungs. "The next man who speaks out of turn will be ejected from this room."

The voices came to a halt. The sheriff just continued to smile and tipped his hat.

"Get out of here," Curtis said in exasperation. "All of you. And try to keep one thing in mind: The vice president of the United States of America and his daughter have been kidnapped. Call me crazy if you like, but I think that might be just a little more important than our inter-agency jealousies." He looked down at the table and shook his head. "Now go get your teams together."

The men filed out of the room, grumbling in low voices, until only Curtis and Holly were left.

As soon as they were alone, Holly turned to his boss. "Sir?" he said.

Aaron Curtis looked up from the papers on his desk.

"Sir, I haven't had a chance yet...there's something I've been wanting to ask you...."

Curtis anticipated the question. An almost fatherly look came over his face as he looked into the younger man's eyes. "No, Buddy," he said. "Nobody's blaming you."

"Yes sir," Holly said. "It's just that—"

"You got lucky, Buddy," Curtis said. "Fate decided it wasn't your day to die. Don't let it make you feel guilty. Do you feel up to joining one of the search parties?" He glanced at Holly's shoulder.

"I want to go," Holly said, nodding his head enthusiastically. "I've...I've *got* to go."

Curtis frowned as if trying to decide whether he should permit it. Finally, he said, "All right. I'll put you with one of the teams." He glanced toward the doorway. "Whichever one that camouflaged-clown ATF asshole, Donovan, is with." Turning back to Holly, he said, "Under one condition—If the pain gets so intense you're hindering the search, you drop out. Immediately. Is that understood?"

"Yes sir," Holly said. "Consider it done." He stood and started to leave the room.

"Oh, Buddy?" Curtis said.

When the young man turned back, the deputy director was looking at the pages in front of him again.

"Yes, sir?"

"There's one other condition."

"Sir?"

"The safety of the vice president must be our primary concern. That takes precedence over capturing his abductors. I'm not sure the FBI and ATF people fully understand that. They're out for blood."

"Yes, sir," Holly said, nodding.

"But I want to make sure you understand all of the other implications of the vice president's priority, Buddy," Curtis said.

"Sir?" Holly said, frowning. It seemed a strange question. The safety of the subject over apprehension of an attacker was a basic premise of bodyguard work. It was drilled into Secret Service candidates all through the academy and reemphasized in advanced training before anyone was allowed to join any of the protection teams.

"You see, Buddy, there's another very real aspect to this, as well."

"I'm sorry, sir," Holly said. "I'm not sure I understand."

Curtis continued to look down at the papers. "There's an old story, Buddy—sort of a joke, actually. It goes like this— A newlywed wife awakens in the middle of the night after a nightmare. She rolls over and wakes her husband. 'Honey,' she asks, 'if your mother and I were both drowning, and you could only save one of us, which one would it be?'"

Holly waited, more confused than ever.

"The husband is still half asleep," Curtis went on. "So he says, 'Well, I've known my mother longer.'"

Holly smiled uncomfortably. "It's a good story, sir. But I'm sorry, I'm not sure I see the correlation."

Curtis finally looked up. "The correlation, Buddy, is that in this case the vice president is the mother. Samantha Bass is the wife. Therefore his safety takes precedence over that of anyone else should it come down to that."

Holly felt a cold chill run down his spine. Curtis was saying that if only Winston Bass *or* his daughter could be saved, Samantha would have to be sacrificed. And at the same time he came to understand what Curtis meant, he wondered if the deputy director also knew how he felt about the girl.

"Yes, sir, of course," Holly said.

He had turned to leave again when he heard Aaron Curtis say, "That's good, Buddy. Because none of us can ever allow our personal feelings to stand in the way of the job."

Which erased any final doubt that word was out concerning his feelings for Samantha Bass.

3

Created during the last ice age, when receding glaciers, floods of devastating proportions and other geological forces sliced through the land, Hell's Canyon gained the honor of becoming the deepest gorge in North America. Surrounded by three separate mountain ranges and the same number of states, its northern boundary lies on the Washington state line. The eastern rim is guarded by the coarse Seven Devil Mountains of Idaho, and towering to the west are the Wallowa and Eagle Cap ranges of Oregon.

On many of the mountains' rocky walls, faded from the countless rains and winds of the centuries, petroglyphs can be found, estimated to have been carved by human hand three thousand years ago. A mile and a half off the Snake River, up Kirkwood Creek, remnants of a pit village twice that age have been found. Both are reminders of ancient visitors whose identity has been long forgotten—if indeed it was ever known. Other artifacts dating back hundreds of years have been discovered, scientifically dated and deeply meditated over by countless anthropologists, geologists and archeologists. These scientists assume the early visitors to the canyon came for the mild winters and abundance of game animals, fish and digestible vegetation. But these theories are just that—theories. Nothing can be proved.

It was simply too long ago.

By the mid-nineteenth century, Europeans had entered the canyon in search of gold. But by the 1870s focus had shifted to hard-rock mining, and tunnels and shafts were drilled through the mountains to the side of the Snake. The modern era of Hell's Canyon had begun.

Mack Bolan scouted the sandy shores as Rick Harsey guided the *Norma* through the water at close to sixty miles an hour. The Executioner had instructed the general's son to put as much distance as quickly as possible between them and Lewiston. They wouldn't slow the pace and scout the banks more thoroughly until they reached the old Mountain Chief gold mine. The site was marked on the map, which was tucked into the pocket of his bush jacket. There was a possibility that the Hands of Heaven wouldn't have set up camp close to Lewiston.

The Mountain Chief's six-hundred-foot tunnel ran from the Snake River to its tributary, the Imnaha. It had been abandoned since the early part of the twentieth century.

The Executioner shielded his eyes with his hand and stared up into the white pines and towering Douglas Fir trees dotting the mountainsides. The Hands of Heaven were somewhere in Hell's Canyon. They might even be in the Mountain Chief mine, itself. But that was unlikely. He seriously doubted they would keep their hostages at such a well-known site or that close to the river when there were so many more remote areas available in the canyon.

The Executioner liked beautiful scenery as much as the next person, but his work rarely allowed him to indulge in it. Though he often spent time in some of the world's most enchanting and exotic places, he was most often trying to look through the panoramic landscapes for the more sinister forces hiding within them. Until they reached the old mine, there was little chance that he'd overlook any telltale signs of the Hands of Heaven. So he allowed himself to succumb to the stunning vistas passing on each side of the boat.

The water had been thick with fishing boats and jet skis when they'd left Lewiston. Here and there, small herds of sheep had grazed in green valleys between the craggy foothills along the banks. At the speed the boat was going, Bolan felt more like he was watching the docile animals in a pasture as he raced down the highway in a car. Roughly five miles from Lewiston, they passed a riding stable in the distance. A few mounted tourists were preparing to follow their guide. But as they drew farther away from the settlement, all signs of domestic life began to disappear. The backpackers walking the trails became fewer and farther between, and the mountain bikers and motorcyclists in the foothills vanished.

A lone fisherman, his rod and reel resting in the fork of a tree as he cupped his hands and drank from the river, was the final person the Executioner saw. Soon after, telephone lines and all other indications of humanity disappeared and Bolan knew he was seeing Hell's Canyon much the same way it had been seen by its first visitors years earlier.

For a fleeting moment Bolan thought he was experiencing one of the few periods of total peace he had ever known. The moment ended quickly, however, as the speedboat rounded a sharp curve in the river and the gaping entrance to the Mountain Chief mine suddenly appeared to the right. The Executioner turned to Rick Harsey.

Harsey nodded. This was it.

Bolan had to shout over the roar of the wake and the jet engines. "Pull in and tie her off!" he said. "Keep the boat this side of the entrance where she can't be seen from inside!"

Harsey nodded again. He cut the engines, reduced speed and angled the *Norma* toward the gaping mouth of the mine. The boat began to purr its way through the water, rocking slightly back and forth.

"Tell me about the mine," the Executioner said as they made their way slowly toward shore.

"Must have been through it a million times when I was a kid," Harsey said. "Tunnel runs all the way through to the Imnaha—about six hundred feet. About a third of the way inside, there's a basalt dike. Maybe halfway are a couple of winzes...shafts. Then it opens up again."

"Enough room for the Hands to use it?" the Executioner asked.

"Yeah," Harsey said. "But it's unlikely. Everybody knows it's there. Too much tourist traffic."

Bolan nodded. They'd still have to check it out.

The boat continued to slow until the bow bumped against the rocky embankment in front of the tunnel entrance. Bolan grabbed a line coiled on the deck and fashioned a quick lasso. Tossing it over one of the sharper rocks, he pulled until the *Norma* came abreast of the bank.

The soldier jumped onto the rocks, tightening the noose in the line until the boat was secured and bobbed gently in the current. They had seen their last human being fishing along the bank a good half hour earlier. Now, only the mountains loomed above them on both sides of the river.

The scene couldn't have appeared more docile. But that didn't stop the cool chill of anticipation that suddenly shot up the Executioner's neck.

Bolan took note of the mental warning. He had experienced it too many times, in too many places just like this, to let it go unheeded.

The soldier glanced quickly back at the boat. They had hidden the long arms, ammunition and other supplies onboard to keep from drawing suspicion on the dock at Lewiston, and left the tarps covering them to keep them dry. It would take several minutes to reboard the craft and outfit themselves—minutes he didn't want to take. If any of the Hands of Heaven were inside the mine, they might have heard the boat arrive. For all he knew, the Handsmen could have scouts in the mountains watching them this very minute.

Bolan's hand dropped to the Desert Eagle on his hip. He had it, the Beretta under his left arm and several extra magazines for both weapons. In addition, the Hell's Belle Bowie knife was hidden beneath his bush vest in the leather sheath. Backing it up was the Applegate-Fairbairn dagger carried under his right arm opposite the Beretta.

He turned his attention toward Rick Harsey. Earlier, Harsey had added a second pistol—an eight-shot .357 Magnum Taurus revolver—to his carry arsenal. At Bolan's suggestion, he had also brought along the sound-suppressed High Standard .22. The general's son wore a vest similar to the Executioner's, and beneath it Bolan knew the man also carried a Wicked Knife Air Assault blade in a shoulder rig. As he watched, Harsey sniffed the air like a bird dog, then drew his Browning Hi-Power.

He had sensed the threat in the air, too.

Both men had lapsed into a sudden silence as the feeling deepened in their chests. Bolan nodded to Harsey as he drew the Desert Eagle. Harsey nodded back.

Turning to the mine, the Executioner led the way to the opening, taking up a position against the rocks to the side. Harsey followed.

Dropping to one knee, Bolan grabbed a handful of damp reddish earth from the ground. Quickly, he rubbed it across his face and neck to blend with the rock, then peeked around the stony wall. The sunlight from outside allowed visibility roughly twenty feet into the tunnel, then grew blurry, gradually fading into total darkness ten feet further.

The Executioner pulled his head back around the rock and felt himself frown. There were two ways to approach the situation. One was to shine his strong ASP laser-flash down the tunnel before entering. If the Handsmen were waiting, and they weren't beyond the beam of the light, he would see them. But the flashlight would tip off the Handsmen to *their* presence as well.

If they hadn't already been tipped off by the sound of the *Norma* pulling into shore. If any of the Handsmen were even in the deserted gold mine.

Taking a deep breath, Bolan considered the other alternative. They could enter the tunnel with lights off, try to stay against the wall of the tunnel and make their way blindly through the old mine to the exit on the Imnaha. But if the Handsmen were close enough to the entrance to see them enter, it would be like knocking off ducks in a shooting gallery.

More to himself than for Harsey's benefit, the Executioner shook his head. He'd use the light, shining it down the tunnel while still around the corner, then determining his next move from what he saw. After another deep breath, he turned to Harsey again. They repeated their nods of understanding as Bolan pulled the ASP laser flashlight from his belt. Holding it in his left hand, the .44 Magnum Desert Eagle in his right, he started to lean back around the rocks.

Just as his thumb found the button, another sixty-seat speedboat rounded the curve carrying a full load of armed men.

Then, before Bolan could think further, automatic rounds from at least ten rifles were ricocheting off the rocks all around them.

THE BASE STATION of the two-way radio on the table crackled with static. Then a voice said, "Freedom Three to One. Come in One."

Seated in a frayed armchair in the compound's main office building, Fred Moreland, a plastic bottle of caffeine-free Diet Coke clenched between his thighs dampening his camouflage pants, listened intently.

"One here," said a second voice. "Come in Three."

"What's your 10-20 One?" the first voice asked.

There was a momentary pause. "About six klicks south of the Mountain Chief mine," the second voice then said.

"Any sign of them?"

"Negative."

"Three out."

Moreland raised the bottle to his lips and took a drink. The Hands of Heaven had three speedboats scouting the river, both to look for Rick Harsey and the big man he'd teamed up with and to alert them to any other federal search parties.

The pilot of Boat Three was Jesse Davis, a strange man. Davis had been something of a hermit in the canyon for years, trapping and hunting for a living. Everyone had heard of him but few had actually seen him. Then the Hands had stumbled upon his camp one morning while picking the site for their compound. It had been a case of either kill him or convert him, but Davis had convinced Moreland and his men that he agreed with the Hands of Heaven mission statement and could be trusted. And he knew Hell's Canyon like the back of his hand. They had taught him to steer speedboats, and now he was among the best of the Handsmen's river pilots.

Yeah, Moreland thought, Jesse Davis had turned out to be a good man. But there was still something mighty strange about a guy who had spent the vast majority of his life in the isolation of Hell's Canyon. And sometimes, when he looked past the wrinkles around Jesse Davis's eyes, what he saw there frightened him. He couldn't put his finger on it but it was as if somehow Davis, well, knew things from living so long in the canyon that no human being should ever have learned.

Moreland took another sip from the bottle. Boats One and Three were made up of both Moreland's Handsmen and United States Freedom Movement troops brought in by Webber Russell. Boat Two was manned by Handsmen alone, with Hiram Spencer and his two brothers in charge. He squeezed the bottle between his legs again. The condensation had soaked all the way through his pants now, and sent uncomfortable shivers up his legs and back. He left it where it was. Training. Training and toughness.

Everything depended on training and toughness, Moreland reminded himself, but couldn't remember where he'd read it. You had to train hard and right. And that training had to lead to toughness. Even after it was achieved, you couldn't allow yourself to get soft again. You had to stay tough for what might come. What would come.

Webber Russell saved him from the reverie by pushing open the door to the main office and walking in. The Hands of Heaven leader fought the temptation to leap to his feet and salute. No, dammit, *he* was the colonel. *He* was still in charge of the Hands of Heaven. The Hands and the USFM had formed an alliance. He wasn't subordinate to Russell, they were equals. He didn't have to stand or salute.

"Had any radio traffic?" Russell asked, moving to the cupboard and pulling out a glass and a bottle of Scotch.

"Yes, sir," Moreland blurted out before he could stop himself. "I mean, yeah, there's been a little." He felt himself redden. And although Russell was facing away from him, the man's bobbing shoulders told him he was chuckling.

Moreland felt his face grow even hotter. Not only had he slipped and verbally demonstrated the subservience he felt toward Russell, he had compounded his humiliation by trying to hide it.

Russell moved to the refrigerator, opened the door to the freezer and began dropping ice cubes into the glass. "Had any more trouble with the generator?" he asked.

This time, Moreland was careful to keep his reply casual. And although he rarely used foul language when he spoke, he suddenly thought this was one of those times when he should. "Nope, Web," he said. "I think Willy's finally got the son of a bitch fixed right this time."

Russell looked at him strangely, condescendingly, as if Moreland's rare cursing was some demonstration of his brawn. The USFM leader walked to the sink and filled the glass almost full with water. Then, pouring just enough Scotch into the drink to give it flavor, he set the bottle on the counter and pulled out one of the chairs at the table.

"How many men did we lose last night at the general's?" he asked.

"Close to forty," Moreland said. "Only eight came back. One of them yours."

Russell shook his head in amazement. "Buffoons," he said under his breath. "Fucking buffoons." He looked at Moreland. "Hard to believe. Forty-some men can't take out three? And one of them's an octogenarian in a wheelchair." He paused, then turned away. But beneath his breath, Moreland heard him say, "And your idiots got six of my troops killed."

Moreland hesitated answering. Octogenarian meant somebody in their eighties, he was pretty sure. But it didn't matter. Russell's meaning was clear no matter what it meant. Finally, he said, "There were more than the three of them, Web. The guys who made it back said there had to have been at least twenty. And defending is always easier than attacking."

Russell shook his head. "They lied," he said simply. "There was the old man, his son and the guy I wish had hit that fucking electrical line when he fell from the sky. My man who came back—my only man who came back—told me the truth."

Several seconds passed. Moreland took another drink from his bottle of Diet Coke. "Web, do your people have any more word on who he is?"

Russell's mind had moved on. He frowned. "Who?"

"The guy who almost hit the line. The big guy. The one Harsey picked up."

Russell shrugged. "No, but it doesn't matter—FBI, ATF—whoever. What it means is they're hitting us from two angles. The main force met this morning in Seattle. They'll have begun their search by now. But they've sent this guy on his own. Which means he's some kind of specialist." He paused to sip at the watered-down whiskey. "But whoever he is, he's good. He already proved that at Harsey's place. He has to be good to take out that many men." He turned to Moreland and a cruel smile covered his face and twinkled in his eyes. "Even your men."

Moreland shifted uncomfortably in his chair. Finally, he said, "Web, there's one part of this plan I'm not clear on."

Russell turned to him with the face of an adult about to be questioned by a child. "Yes?" he said.

"Well, they—the Feds—are coming. They know we're in the canyon. Isn't it just a matter of time before they find us?"

Russell looked like he'd anticipated the question. "Of course it is," he said.

Moreland frowned. "Well…what do we do then?"

The USFM leader chuckled. "Why Fred," he said. "You sound worried."

Moreland shifted uncomfortably again. "No, it's not that, it's just that I don't know…."

"Don't worry, Fred," Russell said, taking another sip of whiskey-flavored water. "We want to draw them in. We've got close to forty choppers waiting to attack, wipe them out, then evacuate us before the Feds can bring in more troops."

"Where do we go?" Moreland asked. "After they evacuate us, I mean?"

Russell shrugged. "Don't know, Fred. I just follow orders like a good soldier."

Moreland nodded. The plan seemed like it might have some flaws in it, but he'd have faith in Russell's superiors just like Russell did. He, too, would follow orders like the good soldier he was.

Russell changed the subject. "Fred, how many more of your men can you call in?" he asked.

Moreland shrugged. "I don't know. A couple dozen. They'd have been here before now but some of them couldn't get off work."

The contempt flickered in Russell's eyes again for a moment. "Perhaps you could tell them it's important," he said sarcastically. Then his face went deadpan. "I want the land perimeter guards doubled. Even though we want them to locate us, we've got to have enough advance warning to get Bass and his daughter out of here before the choppers attack." He paused long enough for another sip. "But it's this big guy with Harsey who worries me. He's the wild card we hadn't planned on. He's hitting this from a completely different angle. And there's something about him…like I said before, he's good." He turned to Moreland again. "When was the last time your men had him in sight?"

"When he and Harsey rented the boat. By the time our guys got into position to follow, they were gone."

Disdain covered Russell's face once more but he didn't comment on the fact that the Hands of Heaven had lost Harsey and the big man. Instead, he said, "Well, at least your men saw which way they went. So it's only a matter of time before they come up on them."

As if in response to this statement, the radio scratched again. Then Jesse Davis's voice echoed over the airwaves. "Boat Three to Base. Come in Base."

Moreland's hand shot to the microphone on the table next to the radio. He depressed the button and said, "Base to Three. Come in Three."

"We've spotted them," Davis said. "They're at the old Mountain Chief mine. We're moving in."

Before the boat pilot let up on his own mike key to silence the radio, Moreland heard the sound of gunfire over the airwaves.

BOLAN FIRED .44 magnum rounds from the Desert Eagle, dropping two men at the front of the speedboat. Next to him, he saw Rick Harsey's Browning Hi-Power leap repeatedly in his hand as .40 S&W hollowpoint slugs spit from the barrel. Another man slumped over the rail as the boat continued to speed forward.

"Inside!" the Executioner shouted. He spun toward the entrance of the mine and dived into the shadows. A second later, Harsey came flying in on top of him.

Bolan rolled from under Harsey, and both men rose to their knees on the hard rocky floor. The Executioner thumbed the button on the flashlight, letting the beam shoot down the tunnel. Just because there were Handsmen outside the tunnel didn't mean more weren't waiting inside. And if that were the case, they were trapped between the devil and the deep blue Snake River.

Squinting along the beam of the light, the Executioner could see all the way to where the tunnel took an abrupt turn. He suspected many such twists existed before the dark shaft emerged at the Imnaha River. But at least for as far as he could see, no sign of human activity was visible.

Automatic fire, some of it 5.56 mm from either M-16s or CAR-15s, other rounds louder and heavier from 7.65-caliber weapons, continued to pepper the outside of the mine. Bolan knew that firing the Desert Eagle, or any major caliber handgun, within the confines of the mine tunnel would be comparable to driving ice picks though his eardrums. He could switch to the sound-suppressed Beretta. But Harsey's .40 S&W Browning would deafen them both almost as quickly as the thunderous Desert Eagle. He turned to the man across the tunnel from him. "You have any earplugs?" he shouted over the roar outside.

Harsey shook his head.

Bolan fished inside his vest and came up with two small plastic vials, each holding a set of foam-rubber plugs. He tossed one across the tunnel.

Harsey caught the tiny canister with his left hand. Inching forward, closer to the mouth of the tunnel, he pressed his chest against the left side of the rock wall. "When they hit the shore they'll split up," he yelled over the gunfire still coming at them. "I'll take the left. Anybody to the right is yours."

Harsey chuckled under his breath. "There are still about fifty of them left," he said. "Give or take a few. That's twenty-five-to-one odds. Good plan."

"If you have a better one, I'd be glad to hear it."

"Unfortunately," Harsey said, "I don't."

"Then I guess we better play the cards we were dealt," Bolan said as he put the plugs into his ears and watched Harsey do the same. He extended his arm through the opening, and fired two more .44 Magnum rounds. Another man at the front of the speedboat slumped to the deck.

The boat roared on, in spite of the fact that another pair of men fell—one to the Desert Eagle, the other to Harsey's Browning. Perhaps a half dozen of the attackers at the front of the boat dived over the side and began swimming for shore.

The rest continued to lay down cover fire as the boat continued to near.

Then, at the last possible second, the engine suddenly went silent. The boat's bow rose suddenly, causing the Executioner to miss a man he'd had in his sights a second earlier. The .44 Magnum entered the lower portion of the hull.

Bolan swung the Desert Eagle toward the motor. A few well-placed rounds would incapacitate the boat. He started to fire, then stopped.

When outnumbered and defending a position, it was important to leave the enemy an escape route. They might take it. As Harsey had pointed out, the odds were long against them. Each of them killing twenty-five men or more before being struck dead themselves was highly unlikely. But if they could kill enough of the Hands, the men might decide to cut their losses and take off. At least that had been what they'd done at the general's house.

The speedboat hit the shore fast enough to throw two men over the rail and onto the rocks. Before they could recover, one wore a .44 Magnum hole in the chest, the other a .40 S&W from Harsey. The rest held on as the boat screeched onto the rocky bottom, then began diving over the rails.

As the Executioner had predicted, half of them went to the right, the other half to the left. All of them lay down cover fire as they moved. Bolan drew the sound-suppressed Beretta with his left hand, flipped the selector switch to 3-round burst and moved farther into the mouth of the tunnel. He could afford to present a little bigger target now—the men from the boat were firing recklessly as they made their way to cover in the foothills to the sides of the mine's opening. They weren't aiming, and if he or Harsey took a round before the Handsmen made it safely to concealment, it would be by nothing more than accident.

While the roar thudded dully into his ears through the earplugs, Bolan felt the pressure of the blasts from Harsey's Browning as they rebounded off the rock walls of the mine tunnel. He opened fire at the men running toward the right of their position, the Desert Eagle dropping a man wearing a khaki BDU. Three smaller sound-suppressed rounds from the Beretta ended the run of a man in camouflage. The pressure the Executioner felt from Harsey's return fire suddenly increased, and Bolan glanced to his side to see that the general's son had jammed the Browning under his belt buckle and drawn the .357 Magnum Taurus eight-shooter. Harsey fired the revolver with his left hand as his right jerked a fresh .40-caliber box magazine from the carrier under his arm and jammed it into the butt of the upturned Hi-Power.

The Executioner couldn't help but watch Harsey, even as he fired again, downing a pair of Handsmen running side by side. What the general's son was doing was an advanced combat reload technique of which few men were capable. It required hours of practice and superior dexterity, but most of all the ability to separate the right hand from the left in the brain—working both hands independently at the same time. It wasn't easy to perform, even on the practice range, and few men could accomplish the task while under fire. One mistake—one lapse in which the right and left hands got confused with each other's tasks—could be disastrous.

Bolan fired again as Harsey completed the reload, jerked the Browning skillfully back out of his pants and let the Taurus roll out of his grasp and dangle from his index finger on the trigger guard. His fingers now free, he used them to rack the slide of the Browning and chamber a round.

Another pair of attackers fell to the Beretta 93-R and a third to the Eagle, as Harsey resumed firing to the right of the mine. Bolan was impressed with the general's son's skill. Rick Harsey had performed the complex reload as if he'd been doing it all his life. And he probably had. He hadn't learned that trick in the military, of that the Executioner was certain. He had learned it from his father.

As best he could determine, Bolan had dropped roughly a half dozen of the men as they raced from the boat for cover at the sides of the tunnel. But there had been too many to get them all, and fifteen, maybe twenty, had gotten past his line of vision. The only men who remained in sight were the ones who had leaped overboard early during the boat's approach to shore. They were running through the shallow water toward the rocks.

Between the Executioner and Rick Harsey, they got them all.

Suddenly, the gunfire in Hell's Canyon stopped. An eerie silence reigned. Even through the plugs, Bolan's ears had taken a hammering inside the rocky tunnel, and his head rang like the bells of Notre Dame. The heavy odor of cordite filled his nostrils.

The Executioner hadn't forgotten the other end of the tunnel. They faced the probability that at least some of the Handsmen would make their way through the mountains to enter the tunnel from the Imnaha. He thumbed the button on the ASP laser light and let the beam dance down the tunnel once more. Nothing. At least not within range of the flashlight.

Turning back to the opening in front of him, Bolan jerked one of the plugs from his ear. The pounding had ceased, and he edged closer, trying to listen now that the enemy was out of sight. The chirping of the birds, which had been so prevalent when he and Harsey had first arrived at the mine, was absent. The rushing water of the Snake River was the only sound.

Bolan turned to Harsey, who was less than three feet away against the opposite wall. He motioned for the man to remove an earplug. When the general's son had done so, the Executioner kept his voice low. "They'll come from both sides," he said. "Just as soon as they regroup. A few at a time. If that doesn't work, they'll rush us."

Harsey frowned, contemplating the soldier's words. "What makes you so sure?" he said. His tone didn't reveal any distrust in Bolan's judgment. Just curiosity.

"Because it's what I'd do in their shoes," the Executioner said. "And I can feel it."

Harsey nodded his head slowly. That seemed good enough for him. "So, what do we do?" he asked.

Bolan glanced over his shoulder into the darkness again. He didn't like their current position. While he had seen no sign of anyone behind them in the mine, he couldn't be sure no one was there. And even if the tunnel had been vacant when they arrived, he couldn't help believing that some of the Handsmen were heading for the Imnaha entrance in an attempt to trap them in the middle.

Drawing a deep breath, the Executioner said, "Let's stay where we are until the first ones come. They'll be scouts—trying to get a read on our position as much as take us out. Make sure we let at least one man escape so he can tell the rest we're still here."

Harsey's face took on a quizzical look. "I get the feeling there's more to this plan?"

"As soon as the guy we let go is gone, we start moving back. Far enough into the darkness we can't be seen from the entrance. We've got to watch both ends of the tunnel, and we have no cover—just concealment. But that's better than nothing."

Harsey drew in a breath. "If they rush us we still won't be able to hold them off. Too many of them. And as soon as we return fire, they'll see the muzzle-flashes and zero in on us. There's not much room to move after each shot in here."

"Like I told you before, Rick," he said. "If you have a better plan, I'm ready to listen."

The general's son laughed, and again Bolan was impressed with the man's coolness under stress. There was every chance in the world they'd both be dead within the next half hour, but Rick Harsey hadn't lost his sense of humor. "Short of Scotty beaming us back up to the Enterprise, no, I don't have a better plan. Just playing the devil's advocate, you know."

Bolan turned back to the opening. "Plenty of devils around already," he said, his mind shifting to a more immediate problem. With the Handsmen out of sight, making their way toward the entrances to the mine from the sides, he and Harsey would be forced to rely on their auditory senses as their primary alarm system. And while the plugs had saved their eardrums earlier, returning them to his ears now would block any telltale sounds of the attackers' approach. So the earplug he had taken out would have to stay out.

Which led to another, equally dangerous situation. After the first shot from any of their weapons except the Beretta, they'd both be temporarily deaf again. He turned to Harsey. The man seemed to have read his mind.

Harsey had holstered his Browning. As the Executioner watched, he dumped the .357 Magnums rounds from his Taurus into his hand, then dropped the loose rounds into a breast pocket of his vest. Another speed-loader appeared and the new cartridges went into the eight-shooter. Harsey snapped the cylinder back into the frame and held the revolver in his left hand. With his right, he drew the Air Assault blade. Glancing at the Executioner, he said, "Changed to some light .38 hand loads. And they're only for emergency." He holstered the Taurus again and drew the sound-suppressed High Standard. "Sorry, but I don't put a lot of trust in .22s if I don't have to."

"Don't be sorry," the Executioner said. "This is one of those times you'll have to."

Harsey held up the Wicked Knife Company steel in his hand and smiled. "It's been a long time since I cut anybody. Are you going to use the suppressor?"

Bolan nodded. He had already holstered the Desert Eagle and now drew the Hell's Belle Bowie with his left hand. The Executioner and Rick Harsey stood silently, awaiting the inevitable.

Seconds turned to minutes. Minutes became a half hour. They heard nothing but the river.

Then, finally, somewhere outside the mine to the left, the snapping of a dry twig broke the stillness in Hell's Canyon.

SAMANTHA BASS'S legs were beginning to cramp. She pressed her back against the dirt wall of the hole and stretched them as far in front of her as she could. In the dim light, she stared across the pit at her father.

Winston Bass's eyes were closed. He appeared to be asleep. Samantha watched his chest move in and out as the muscles in her thighs began to relax again.

The vice president was only forty-eight years old but right now he looked ninety. He was in terrible physical condition, and the stress and physical exertion had exhausted him. Samantha glanced at the screen over their heads. Actually, she realized, there was no reason to keep them imprisoned. The terrain of Hell's Canyon would keep them right where they were.

The vice president's daughter turned her eyes back to the aging face of the man across from her. She had an almost classic love-hate relationship with her father, and had realized that fact several years before. She loved him for the kind, gentle and caring parent he always was when they were together. But she hated him for the fact that those times had always been so few and far between. To Winston Bass, family would always come second to his political career—a very distant second. And she hated him for the phony she had known him to be ever since she'd been old enough to recognize the duplicity in the man.

A snore shot from the vice president's nostrils and Samantha continued to stare at him. The man who had pushed him down into the hole—Conway had been his name, she remembered— had called him "Nature Boy." Which was exactly the image he had worked so hard to obtain. Winston Bass, Nature Boy. Winston Bass, Defender of the Planet. Winston Bass, Captain Ecology. She had heard them all. But not before his second term in the U.S. Senate when her father had realized that the "tree huggers" had become a viable voting block. Before that, he had owned stock in tobacco companies, strip-mining operations and the lumber business. But in one gigantic change of heart, suddenly, Winston Bass had come out against all such enterprises and had begun using ecology as one of his primary stepping stones toward the White House. Samantha supposed she could have accepted the dramatic reversal in her father except for one thing: Winston Bass, she knew, still owned stock in all those operations. He was a silent partner. His involvement with the corporations he worked against was just so far buried in holding companies and other covers that it would never be exposed.

Winston Bass was seen on TV in a Banana Republic safari vest almost as often as he was wearing a suit and tie. But it was all show, and for all she knew the man had never even urinated outdoors.

The thought of urination made the vice president's daughter close her eyes tightly. She had been so scared during the kidnapping that she'd been afraid she'd wet her pants. The horror had expanded during the crazy plane ride all over the U.S. the terrorists had taken them on. But for some reason, it had left her as soon as they'd arrived at this hideout in Hell's Canyon. She didn't know why but there was no longer fear in her chest.

Samantha Bass had recognized Hell's Canyon from the air because she had visited the Snake River with her parents two years earlier on a well-publicized, well-guarded family canoe trip. She remembered the virtual flotilla—her mother and father in one canoe, she in another, both paddled by Secret Service agents while other bodyguards floated along beside them with machine guns ready, looking like some bizarre cross between modern federal agents and ancient warriors preparing to attack a village. Her father never paddled—except when the cameras had been on him. Each time it appeared his picture might be taken, Winston Bass had grabbed the paddle out of the hands of the nearest Secret Service man and posed.

The sound of men moving above them met her ears, and Samantha opened her eyes and tried to look through the screen. It was nothing, she decided. Just the feet and blunted voices of the pigs who had kidnapped them going about their business. She wondered again at her lack of fear. Was it because she had given up hope? No, she didn't think so. If that had happened, she would have expected the fear to be replaced by despair. Actually, no emotion at all had replaced the fear. She felt, well, nothing. Maybe she'd been through so much that her well of emotion had simply gone dry.

The voices above her quieted again. Samantha Bass closed her eyes once more. Her mind drifted back to the talk she and her father had been having as they walked through the woods. He had wanted to caution her about the dangers of college boys, and the memory of how awkwardly he had approached the subject brought a faint smile to her face. It was nice that he cared, and he did, she supposed. But it would have meant so much more if he hadn't made sure there were television cameras around to document the event. She wouldn't be surprised if the front page of the *Washington Post* read "Vice President Warns Daughter about the Perils of College Life."

No, she thought, old Winston Bass never missed a trick when it came to publicity. He still had his eyes on the White House for the next election. When you were the vice president's daughter, she supposed, you had to take what you could get and learn to mix politics with family life and everything else.

Samantha's thoughts returned to her father's warnings about college boys. He called them college men but that's not how Samantha thought of them. She caught herself smiling again. Her father was so naive. She had figured out what most boys wanted by junior high, and she'd had plenty of practice blocking their hands ever since. College boys couldn't be much different than high school and junior high boys. Basically, until they reached the age of about twenty-five or thirty, she guessed, boys were just cocky, immature, little creeps whose brains resided in their penises.

Rumbling sounded overhead and Samantha looked up to see the screen being lifted. A face peered down. Conway—the one who had leered at her. Talk about a case of arrested adolescence. He was forty if he was a day, old enough to be her father. Some men never grew up.

Conway checked her out again, one of his lecherous smiles covering his face. Then the man let his eyes drift briefly to her father before he lowered the screen and disappeared from sight once more.

Her train of thought exhausted, Samantha's mind finally turned to the one thing she had tried hard not to think about. Randall Holly. She had been afraid if she thought of the young Secret Service agent, she'd break down in tears. Now, it was too late. He had invaded her mind like he did so often, even under normal circumstances. Would she ever see him again?

The vice president's daughter pictured Holly in her mind. He was so different than the other young men she was used to. He was a man, not a boy. Oh, she could tell he had the same thoughts and desires as any other normal young male. But he kept them in check, didn't let them rule his life. He wanted sex, she knew, and he wanted it from her. Women could sense these things. But he wanted more. He wanted a relationship. He wanted love.

Which he didn't have, Samantha knew. At least he didn't have a steady girlfriend. She knew he went out with one of the criminal analysts who worked at the FBI, but it was an off-and-on thing. She had checked that out with a well- planned series of roundabout questions to different Secret Service agents without anyone being the wiser as to what she wanted to know or why.

She thought of Holly now; pictured his face. They had never been alone together. But when they had been together in a group, she had always felt the chemistry between them. She had caught him looking at her more than once, then watched him shuffle his feet uncomfortably when their eyes met. She had seen in his eyes that he wondered if she was attracted to him, as he was to her. She had sensed right away that while the others called Holly Buddy, he didn't like the name. So she had always referred to him as Randy, and he had always smiled when she did so.

Across from her, Samantha heard her father snort, then jerk. His eyes opened, and for a moment, she could see that he didn't know where he was. Then memory set in, and his face took on a long, dark look of resignation.

Samantha knew that her father's political talents were useless under these conditions. Even if a miracle happened, and the terrorists decided to release them, Winston Bass would be helpless in Hell's Canyon. He didn't know which side of a tree moss grew on, he couldn't even read a compass and he probably couldn't walk two miles without becoming winded and having to stop. If the terrorists dropped her father a mile from here and told him he was free, his best bet for survival would be to try to find his way back to this very camp and throw himself on their mercy.

Samantha shook her head. Escape, she was sure, hadn't even crossed Winston Bass's mind. That would involve courage, risk and fighting, and he was certainly no fighter. Maybe with words, but not with guns or knives or fists. While he played the part of outdoorsman for the sake of the voters, she knew that in reality he considered such activities barbaric. Beneath him. Beneath the interests of all "civilized" men.

Suddenly the screen opened above them again. Conway looked down, grinning. "Feeding time at the zoo," he said, then laughed as if it had been really funny. A second later, he dropped a loaf of white bread and a package of lunch meat into Samantha's lap.

Conway grabbed his groin. "Boner petite," he said and grinned.

Samantha smiled sweetly up at him. "I'm sure it is," she said.

Conway's expression didn't change, telling her he didn't understand what he'd just said or that his paraphrase of the French term had actually ridiculed himself.

The screen closed once more. Samantha offered the food to her father.

Winston Bass just shook his head.

Samantha wasn't hungry either but she forced herself to open the bread and meat. And in doing so, she realized, she had made a vital decision. She would eat not because she wanted to, but because she needed to keep up her strength. If the opportunity to escape arose, she would take it. Unlike her father, she was in top condition from running, tennis and aerobic dance. As a member of her high school's trekker club and graduate of Outward Bound—her father had pressured her into both experiences and gotten good press out of them—she had experience in basic woodcraft. That could be put to use as well.

Samantha Bass looked across the hole at her father as she absentmindedly made a dry sandwich out of the bread and meat. She and her mother had always come second to Winston Bass's career. She suspected that her father loved them in his own way, and, she supposed she loved him, too.

The vice president's daughter took a bite of the tasteless food. As soon as she had eaten, she would begin working on a plan of escape. That plan wouldn't include a middle-aged, unfit man who would only slow her pace. She would have to leave her father behind, Samantha realized. But that would be no more than he'd do to her and her mother.

She would simply be doing what she'd been taught at home.

4

The snapping twig sounded as loud as a gunshot in the silence which had fallen over Hell's Canyon. A soft curse followed, and the Executioner inched closer to the opening, his sound-suppressed Beretta held at a forty-five-degree angle in front of him ready to be raised into action.

Mack Bolan smiled. Again, the Handsmen were proving that what little strength they had lay in numbers rather than professionalism. Stepping on a twig in broad daylight was the sign of a rank amateur. But compounding the sound warning with words of irritation afterward was the mark of a complete idiot.

These men could be taken. And the Executioner would do it.

The smile on Bolan's face slowly faded. Yes, at least some of the Handsmen were amateurs. But they weren't being led by novices. Such men simply wouldn't have been capable of kidnapping Winston and Samantha Bass—the U.S. Secret Service was made up of the world's best bodyguards, and pulling off the abductions of the Vice President of the United States and his daughter had taken strategic genius.

Again, Bolan remembered the dark-skinned bodies he had left at General Harsey's house. Whoever was actually pulling the Handsmen's strings on this operation was an expert. They might run the rookie Handsmen out front, but they weren't held back by the same bigotry and racial prejudices that marked the Hands of Heaven. They took advantage of manpower regardless of race, color or creed.

Like a stone statue, the Executioner waited. He felt, rather than saw, the gunner round the corner. Raising the Beretta, he pumped a lone round through the man's mouth as it fell open in surprise.

Bolan's hand shot out, and he pinched the lapel of the Handsman's camouflage shirt. He jerked, and the already dead body flew behind him and into the tunnel, out of sight.

Again, he waited silently, listening. But the next Hands of Heaven scout made no warning noise. The man was just suddenly there, three feet outside the tunnel entrance, the rifle in his hand rising toward Harsey on the other side of the tunnel. Bolan swung the Beretta that way, but at the same time another Handsman, wearing a black T-shirt, appeared directly in front of him.

At the same time he fired, the Executioner heard four near-silent .22 slugs choke from Harsey's High Standard. Bolan lunged forward, his Hell's Belle lashing out in a vicious backhand slice, which caught the Handsman between the wrist and elbow. The man's hand stayed clenched around the forend guard of the rifle; the extra weight of the dead hand and half the man's forearm pulled the rifle barrel earthward, and the round he triggered with his other hand blew harmlessly into the ground.

The Handsman's eyes glazed over in shock. He stared uncomprehendingly at his severed arm.

But he didn't stay in shock long.

Bolan brought the Beretta around and drilled another sound-suppressed round between the Handsman's eyes. The man slumped forward. The Executioner reached out and caught the Handsman under the arms, dragging him back into the tunnel and dumping him on top of his fallen comrade. He turned in time to see Rick Harsey doing the same with the other man.

The two men returned to the mouth of the cave and resumed their wait. They were relying on superior speed, reflexes and the surprise the Handsmen experienced by not expecting them to be right at the entrance to the mine. But that surprise wouldn't last forever. There were bound to be more men acting as scouts for the main group, and they would see what was happening. If they hadn't already.

And there were always the men the Executioner knew by now would have entered the Imnaha end of the tunnel.

Bolan was about to order Harsey deeper into the mine, when a head suddenly appeared above him. An arm clad in camouflage shot downward from over their heads, a Colt Government Model clutched in its fingers. Bolan raised the Beretta, the sound suppressor actually making contact with the frame of the .45. He pulled the trigger and another 9 mm coughed from the weapon.

The pistol flew from the Handsman's fingers as the man screamed in pain. The Executioner reached up, wedged the man's wrist between his thumb and the grip of the Hell's Belle and jerked.

The Handsman screamed again as he fell to the rocky ground in front of the tunnel entrance. He landed on his face but quickly rolled to his back and started to sit.

The Executioner brought the Hell's Belle around in a wide-sweeping arc. The blade first made contact with the side of the man's neck near the hilt. Drawing the knife toward him as he continued the swing, Bolan severed the man's head from his shoulders.

The head rolled down the embankment and plopped into the river, turning to face the mine as it floated, eyes open but no longer seeing.

Bolan dragged the rest of the body into the mine. He turned to Harsey. "If they didn't know what we were doing already, they do now," he whispered.

Harsey glanced at the river. "Yep," he said and smirked. "Severed heads bobbing in the water are almost always a hint that something's amiss."

Bolan ignored the joke and began stacking the bodies on the ground just inside the entrance. He wanted to block the pathway as best he could. Now that the Handsmen knew that he and Harsey were close to the entrance, they'd know their only chance was to swarm the mine in numbers. How well they did that would depend on their dedication to their cause; how willing they were to die for it. The bodies blocking the entrance wouldn't stop the attack, but it would at least slow it. And slow men were easier to shoot.

"Ever study psychology?" Harsey asked as they went about their work.

Bolan didn't answer.

"Me either," Harsey said. "At least not much." He pulled the headless man to a sitting position, using the other two bodies as a back support to keep him in place. The still-bleeding stump would be the first sight the Handsmen saw when they entered the old mine. "But you don't need a Ph.D. to be pretty sure this will freak them out when they see it," Harsey went on. "It sure would me."

The Executioner led the way back into the mine. When they reached total darkness, he stopped. He could hear no footsteps or other sounds coming from the Imnaha end of the tunnel. Dropping to his knees, he pressed an ear against the ground. Again, nothing. Either the Handsmen he suspected had headed for the other entrance hadn't yet reached it, or they'd decided to stay along the Imnaha and simply seal off that avenue of escape.

Pulling the ASP from his belt carrier, the Executioner risked a quick flash down the tunnel. From where they were, he could just make out the dike of fine-grained basalt, which ran across the tunnel. Beyond that, the beam stopped at a twist in the underground pathway. He killed the light as soon as he'd seen all he could see.

Leading the way, the Executioner moved another two hundred feet into the darkness, glancing over his shoulder every few seconds. Finally, he stopped and turned back toward where the river could barely be seen around the piled bodies in the entryway. Dropping to one knee, he used his sleeve to wipe the sweat from his brow. There wasn't much of it. It was cool, almost cold, inside the tunnel.

Bolan turned to Harsey. "We've got to watch our backs as well as our fronts," he said.

Harsey nodded. He had dropped to one knee too, and pressed his back against the wall of the mine across from the Executioner.

Sound carried well inside the tunnel, and when the first voice whispered, "Oh shit!" Bolan and Harsey could hear it almost as plainly as if the man who'd spoken the words stood directly in front of them. But the headless monstrosity at the entrance to the Mountain Chief didn't stop the men. To the sides of the piled bodies, the Executioner saw shadows appear in the entryway. He raised the Beretta. Thumbing the selector switch to 3-round burst, he pulled the front handgrip down from under the barrel, grasping it in his left hand.

A second later, three quiet 9 mm hollowpoint rounds shot down the narrow tunnel.

Two shadows dropped. Someone screamed. There was a flurry of movement at the mouth of the tunnel, and then suddenly the blue water of the river could be seen again beyond the bodies on the ground, which now numbered six.

The last two just hadn't been as carefully stacked.

"They've gone back outside to regroup," Harsey whispered.

Bolan nodded in the darkness, knowing he couldn't be seen. They had learned one thing, at least: Most of the Handsmen weren't anxious to become martyrs for their cause. While they knew they had enough men to flood the mine with more firepower than any two defenders could resist, they also knew that the first ones through the mouth of the tunnel would be committing suicide. No one seemed to want to take on that role. And if they continued these half-hearted attacks, rather than go balls-to-the-wall in one sudden assault, they knew he and Harsey would keep picking them off. One by one. Two by two. Already, he figured they had decreased the Handsmen's numbers by roughly a third.

How the Handsmen behaved now would depend on two things vital to any military attack: Leadership and the courage of the men following that leader.

"Time for earplugs again," Bolan said. He pulled the plastic vial from his pocket and stuck the foam rubber back in his left ear. Though he couldn't see, he knew Harsey would be doing the same thing.

The Executioner switched the Beretta to his left hand and drew the Desert Eagle. He shifted to his other knee and settled in to wait. This time, they didn't have to wait very long. Suddenly, a wild war whoop sounded just outside the tunnel. The light around the bodies on the ground disappeared altogether.

Then the tunnel lit up with the muzzle-flashes.

EVERY SIZE and shape of bullet suddenly seemed to fill the deserted Mountain Chief mine. Lead poured past Bolan and Harsey in blankets, forcing them to the dirt-covered rock floor of the tunnel.

Bolan returned fire, sending bursts back at the Handsmen and each time rolling as soon as he'd pulled the trigger. The sound suppressor hid some of the 9 mm muzzle-flash. But not all of it. There was more than enough flame leaping out the end of the barrel for the Handsmen to target, and that's exactly what they did. Normally, he would have rolled to a new position after each burst of fire. But there was little room to maneuver within the narrow confines of the tunnel, and at the same time he emptied the magazine in the Beretta, he felt himself roll against Harsey.

Harsey was pulling the triggers of both his High Standard and Browning Hi-Power as fast as his fingers would move.

Bolan fired two rounds from the Desert Eagle, then speed-loaded another 9 mm magazine into the 93-R as he rolled back to the other side of the tunnel. Their return fire had slowed the men streaming into the tunnel. But not enough. Rounds continued to fly past the Executioner, striking in front and behind him on the rocky ground, or zinging along the walls of the tunnel over his head. It was only by the grace of God, he knew, that he and Harsey hadn't been hit yet.

They needed a distraction. Fast.

Suddenly setting both the Desert Eagle and the Beretta on the ground in front of him, Bolan jerked the ASP laser flashlight from his belt once more. His thumb found the button as he rolled to his side, keeping his head as low to the ground as possible. With his left hand cupped over the beam, he drew his right arm back. Depressing the button at the last possible second, he threw the flashlight as far into the tunnel behind them as he could make it go.

Harsey must have seen his actions in the dim light that flowed from around his hand. And the general's son knew what to do. He immediately quit firing.

The Executioner rolled back to his belly, lifting his pistols once more. Almost immediately, all rounds coming from the Handsmen in the tunnel began flying farther over his head. As Bolan had hoped they would, they were keying on the light. They thought he and Harsey were a hundred feet deeper into the tunnel than they actually were.

Bolan, waited, flat on the ground, as the first wave of the assault drew nearer.

Four shadows—four men abreast were as many as the narrow walls would allow—suddenly appeared in front of the Executioner. Still prone, he rested the side of his hand on the ground, raising only the barrel of the 93-R. With the selector switch on semiauto, he pumped one round each into three of the men. It took Harsey's little .22 five rounds to drop the fourth.

Directly behind the falling bodies, Bolan saw three more men sprinting their way. Before this second wave of Handsmen could understand what was happening, he and Harsey had downed them, too.

The rest of the Handsmen were a good 150 feet away, when they pivoted back toward the river. Bolan aimed carefully, dropping another pair as they attempted escape. Harsey's

Browning ended the career of one more. The rest disappeared around the sides of the entrance to the Mountain Chief mine.

The roar of the gunfire inside the tunnel began to die. Once again, Hell's Canyon was quiet.

The Executioner rose to his feet, glancing over his shoulder toward where the flashlight had rolled to a halt. Far away in the darkness, the bright laser beam shone against the stony wall of the tunnel. "Can you hear me?" he whispered to Harsey.

"Barely," the general's son said. "Even with the plugs in…" He let the sentence trail off.

"We've got to move deeper," Bolan said. "Let's go." He took off jogging toward the flashlight. Behind him, he heard footsteps as Harsey fell in step.

Reaching the flashlight, the Executioner scooped it from the ground and then slowed to a walk as they neared the slight bend in the tunnel. Just before rounding the curve, he put up a hand to stop Harsey, then killed the beam. For all he knew, some of the Handsmen had entered the mine during the gunfight.

Using his hand to follow the wall of the tunnel, the Executioner rounded the curve, then halted. He held his breath, listening, using every battle sense he had honed to perfection over the years to determine if he and Harsey were alone. He could see nothing but darkness. He heard nothing. He smelled nothing. Most of all, he *felt* no other presence.

Finally satisfied, the Executioner thumbed the ASP's button once more and aimed the light down the tunnel. They were near the first shaft, and training the light downward he could see the depression dug into the ground. He glanced over his shoulder once more but the mouth of the tunnel was now out of sight around the curve. "Take a look," he whispered to Harsey.

The general's son stuck his head around the curve, then shook it. "Not yet," he said.

"Stay there," Bolan ordered, "where you can see them when they come." The Executioner killed the light once more.

As the darkness surrounded him Bolan thought they were trapped. And sooner or later, he and Harsey would face attack from both ends of the tunnel.

A drop of moist condensation dripped from the ceiling of the mine and landed on Bolan's cheek. He reached up, wiping it away with his sleeve as he continued to ponder their predicament. There was a way out of this. There always was. For the man who could stay cool under pressure, plan under stress and then have the courage to carry out that plan regardless of the odds against him, there was always a way out. Sometimes it just took a little time to find it.

But Bolan knew they had no time.

In the darkness, he heard Harsey's feet shuffle slightly. Then the general's son whispered, "I hear something." There was a short pause, then, "They're back. Looks like a couple dozen of them creeping in the entrance, from what I can make out."

The Executioner nodded, and the tunnel became quiet once more. Then, as he listened, trying to pick up the soft footsteps of the men approaching from the Snake River, he heard something else.

Footsteps, all right. But not the ones he had expected to hear. These footsteps came from the opposite end of the tunnel.

The Hands of Heaven Handsmen who had entered the Mountain Chief from the Imnaha side of the mine had finally arrived.

"OH SHIT," Rick Harsey muttered under his breath.

He'd heard the footsteps, too.

Harsey tried to look through the darkness to where he knew the big man who called himself Mike Belasko was standing. Belasko was good at what he did. Damn good. But he'd better be more than that if they expected to get out of the mine alive. He'd better be great.

Because Rick Harsey knew he himself was good. And he didn't have a clue as to what they could do to survive.

Harsey heard a faint clicking sound. Ten feet away, he saw the flesh of Belasko's hand turn red. Belasko had switched the

ASP flashlight back on but kept the bulb pressed into his palm to diminish the glow.

"Come on," Harsey heard Belasko whisper.

Harsey followed the other man's quiet footsteps toward the Imnaha end of the tunnel. Belasko had already shown a tremendous creativity in his approach to combat, but tackling the devil they didn't know instead of the one they did? But Harsey doubted he'd deviate that far from conventional wisdom under these circumstances.

No, the general's son thought as they traversed the rock floor, Belasko had something else in mind.

Harsey followed Belasko to the first of the two winzes dug into the ground. Due to the immense number of tourists who explored the old mine, the shaft had been boarded over decades earlier. In fact, Harsey realized as they neared the rotting wooden planks, he had never actually seen the shafts—either this one or the one farther down the tunnel. They had been closed before his birth, shortly after the mine had shut down nearly a century earlier.

Belasko reached the shaft and stopped, squatting next to the wooden cover. He kept his hand over the laser-flash, but angled it downward, removing his fingers just enough to send a sharp beam onto the cover. "Come here," he whispered in the semidarkness.

Harsey hurried to squat next to him, the sounds of footsteps from both ends of the tunnel growing louder. Neither group of Handsmen could completely conceal their approach.

Belasko pressed the ASP against his thigh with one hand and reached down to the wood with the other. Harsey watched him pry up one of the boards, then set it on the ground next to the hole. Careful not to release the beam until it was below ground level, he shone the light into the shaft. A rickety old wooden elevator, secured to the frame by rat-chewed ropes, still hung in the center of the hole. Belasko shifted the beam slightly, shining it around one of the edges of the platform.

The hole seemed to drop without end.

"You've got to be kidding?" Harsey whispered. When he got no reply, he said, "I know, I know. If I've got a better idea, you're willing to listen."

"You want this one or the other one?" Belasko asked him.

"Oh, this one's probably much safer," Harsey said, sarcastically. "I'll take it." He pried off another of the boards and gingerly stuck a foot through the opening, pushing against the platform with his foot. It held. But would it support all of his hundred and ninety pounds? There was only one way to find out. And he supposed death from plummeting into the bowels of the earth wasn't any worse than taking a few bullets from the Handsmen.

Rick Harsey climbed carefully into the hole, the creaks of the ancient wood sounding as loud as explosions in his ears. He wondered if the Handsmen were close enough to hear. He sat down and the elevator shifted slightly, sending his heart leaping up through his throat. Pressing his back against the side of the frame above the platform, he did his best to dig his shoulder blades into the rock along the side of the shaft, hoping it would take some of the stress off the frazzled ropes.

Above him, Belasko laid the boards back over the hole. Then Harsey heard the man's voice whisper down through the cracks. "Stay put until my cue," he said.

"Which will be…?" Harsey whispered.

"I don't know yet."

"Well, that's encouraging."

A moment later, he heard Mike Belasko move quietly down the tunnel. Harsey hadn't been inside the deserted gold mine for years but he remembered the other shaft as being around thirty to forty feet away. In the stillness, he heard the distant footsteps from both ends of the tunnel continue to near. Then the muted sounds of wood being pried from rusty nails met his ears. A moment after that, the footsteps were all that remained.

Rick Harsey moved carefully, slowly, as he ejected the magazine from his High Standard .22 and filled it with loose ammo from one of his vest pockets. He had lost count of the rounds he had fired from the Browning, so he traded what he knew had to be a partially empty box magazine with a fresh load. The Taurus had been replenished earlier and now held eight rounds.

But would it be good enough? Would he be fast enough? He didn't know.

And suddenly, strangely, he didn't care.

Harsey let his mind drift as he waited for whatever was going to happen. He was no longer the same kid who had explored this mine. He was forty-six years old and he had survived Vietnam as an infantryman and later as a Special Forces small arms expert, then gone on to U.S. Army Intelligence where he'd taken part in clandestine ops all over the world. After that, he had spent several years as a U.S. Forest Ranger before finally taking over the management of the Harsey family business holdings. Surprisingly enough, he had come as close to death as a forest ranger as he ever had in the army. Now, as he waited, Harsey couldn't help but smile as he remembered the grizzly bear who had refused to succumb to the five .44 Magnum slugs that had hit the animal squarely in the chest. They had sure made him mad, though. And the last desperation round, aimed between the bear's eyes, had instead glanced off the top of the creature's skull. The bear still had more than enough fight in him to chase Harsey up a tree and keep him there for two days before finally loping off into the woods again.

A sudden thought finally struck Rick Harsey. Was this what they meant when they said your life flashed before your eyes before you died?

The footsteps heading toward him were still soft, but growing louder. Harsey could tell that the men approaching from both ends of the mine were nearing. In fact, it sounded as if they might meet right about where he and Belasko had hidden.

THE BIG HELICOPTER flew low over the Seven Devils Mountains, weaving in and out of the ascents and depressions in the hopes of spotting some sign of the Hands of Heaven camp. It was a semifutile hope, however, somewhat like casually walking past a roulette table and dropping a chip on a random number.

None of the members of Search Team Six were counting on it, particularly Randall Holly. He had lived only twenty-five short years, but during that time he had learned a few things. One of those lessons had been that few of life's worthwhile endeavors came easily, and he didn't expect to just look into Hell's Canyon and see Samantha Bass waving a rescue flag in the air.

The chopper descended just north of the mountains, its rotary blades slowing imperceptibly as it finally came to rest on top of Hell's Canyon Dam. The door slid open and the men began to drop to the ground. Holly was second-in-command of Search Team Six, which was made up of four Secret Service agents, three FBI men, two local reserve deputy sheriffs and, unfortunately, the same Bureau of Alcohol, Tobacco and Firearms agent who had been at the meeting in Seattle—Simon Donovan. Donovan had attended the meeting already dressed in full battle gear, complete with camouflage makeup, Holly remembered. He was the special agent in charge—or SAC—of the Seattle BATF field office. He was also the leader of that Bureau's SWAT team, which was famous for the rough treatment they rendered to all suspects, guilty or innocent.

Holly watched Donovan jump out of the chopper with a loud "Geronimo!" as if he might be bailing from twenty-thousand feet instead of four. He didn't like the ATF man—hadn't liked him at the meeting, and Donovan had done nothing to change Holly's opinion during the flight from Washington into Oregon. The ATF agent had spent most of the time boring the hell out of them with stories of how he'd gotten by with civil rights violations. One of his favorite yarns was how he'd confiscated several dozen rifles from a man suspected of dealing fully automatic weapons, only to discover that the gun shop owner was legitimate—the rifles were semiautomatic only. It had taken him and his team two days, he said laughingly, to convert them to full-auto and they had completed the task just in time for court. Donovan expected the other men in the helicopter to laugh along with him, and the FBI men had. But Holly, the other Secret Service men and the two reserve deputies had been horrified that a man sworn to uphold the constitution would do such a thing. And one of the deputies, a big man Holly had learned owned a plumbing supply by day, had looked as if he might have liked to wrap one of his arms around Donovan's neck and break it.

If he had, Holly was pretty damn sure he wouldn't have done anything to stop it.

Holly's leather-and-nylon combat boots hit the concrete of the dam and he felt a sudden surge of pain in his shoulder. He moved to the side to let the other men out as a wet, sticky feeling replaced the pain. He knew what had happened: The jump from the chopper had been short, but it had been enough to rip away at least some of the surgical stitches in his shoulder. The wound was bleeding again.

The Secret Service man looked out over the canyon as he waited for the call that would assemble the men. He didn't try to look at his shoulder, fearing such a move would draw attention to it and result in his being sent back on the chopper. Instead, he studied the scenery. To his left was Idaho, to his right, Oregon. The terrain was as rustically beautiful as anything he'd ever seen, and he wondered how it had gotten the appellation Hell's Canyon. Having spent the past six months in Washington, D.C., it looked more like heaven. He'd been born and raised in Montana, and this was more like the kind of country he could call home.

Butch Singer, the Seattle Secret Service SAC, broke into Holly's daydream as he called out, "All right! Everybody up!" Holly turned back as the men gathered around Singer as the helicopter lifted off. "You've got your assignments," Singer said. "I want you to search under every rock, every blade of grass and up the asshole of every grasshopper, flea and tick

you come across. When you've finished, move up to the area
of the man next on the list. In other words, Agent One will
then search Agent Two's assigned area. Two will take Three's.
Any questions?''

He got no response.

"Then let's move out."

Holly turned his injured shoulder away from the group, trying to keep it out of sight in case it had bled though his
T-shirt and the camouflage jacket over it. He pulled the detailed
map he'd been given out of his pocket and saw that his sector
was on the Oregon side of the river. He hurried down off the
dam, his M-16 banging against his side as the nylon sling bit
painfully into his injury. He winced slightly, then glanced
around to see if anyone had noticed. He couldn't act like it
was slowing him down. Not if he wanted to stay in the search.

The shoulder continued to hurt as Holly left the dam and
started through the weedy brush along the river. As he made
his way up the incline, his shoulder began to feel even wetter
under the bandages. Damn, he thought. The sling rubbing
against the stitches was making it worse, maybe ripping even
more of them from his skin. He not only had to get it stopped
before it bled through and gave him away to Singer, he'd have
to get it stopped if he didn't want to bleed to death right there
in Hell's Canyon.

A tall outcropping of rock stood twenty yards farther up the
incline, and Holly hurried that way. With a quick glance to see
if any of the other members of the search team were watching,
he stepped around the stony wall, out of sight. He dropped to
a sitting position and pulled the rifle from his shoulder before
sliding out of the chest straps for his backpack. Dropping the
pack to the hard ground next to him, he quickly slipped out of
his jacket and then the khaki T-shirt beneath it.

The blood had already soaked through the gauze bandage
and his T-shirt. He jerked the bandage off along with the adhesive tape securing it, and what felt like a good deal of his

own skin. From the Cordura backpack he pulled three fresh bandages and the roll of tape. He had no time to reclean the wound, so he simply applied a fresh coat of antibiotic cream to the mess already there, then stuck the bandages on top one after the other. The triple gauze made a hump on his shoulder but would act as padding between the rifle sling and his arrow wound. At least he hoped it would.

Holly's thoughts drifted back to ATF Agent Simon Donovan as he worked. Donovan had been at both Waco and Ruby Ridge and was proud of it. He had told of how the tanks at Waco had purposely knocked down the walls of the compound in strategic areas which would create the configuration of a pot-bellied stove.

Holly shook his head in disgust as he began slipping back into his T-shirt. Donovan was one of too many federal officers who had been allowed to run wild and, in the process, violate the rights of American citizens.

Holly shrugged into his jacket and began doing the buttons as he rose to his feet behind the rocks. Never before, he knew, had so many good American citizens literally despised their own leaders. And he wasn't sure he could blame them. Sometimes, he was ashamed to be part of it all.

The Secret Service man finished buttoning his camouflage jacket and slid the backpack on. He was a citizen first, a federal law enforcement officer second. He believed in the rights of the individual. He believed every citizen, be they man, woman or child, had a God-given right to freedom, privacy and the pursuit of happiness. He knew no cops—local, state or federal—could ever hope to protect citizens from personal criminal attack, and for that reason the government gave each individual the right of self-defense. The right to keep and bear arms.

Men like Donovan didn't think that way. And the public saw only the men like Donovan. They were the ones who made the news.

Holly slipped the rifle sling over his shoulder and let it rest on top of the triple-bandage. Pain shot through his shoulder and down his arm, but it wasn't as bad as it had been. He had more bandages in his pack and he would use them as he needed them. Right now, he had to get moving.

He was about to climb from behind the rocks when he heard the voice to his side.

"Buddy."

Holly turned to see Donovan and Singer standing just beyond the rocks. In a flash, he knew what had happened. Donovan had seen him drop to cover, guessed what was happening and hurried to snitch on him to the search team leader.

Singer didn't waste words. "The base camp is three miles south of here, Buddy," he said. "Just follow the river."

"But—" Holly started to protest.

"No buts," Singer said. "I don't have time to screw with you. I shouldn't have let you come along in the first place and I won't risk your life and the lives of other good men just because you want to be a hero." He paused. "How are you fixed for bandages?"

"Fine, sir," Holly said.

"Do you need someone to go along with you?"

"No sir."

"Then get going. If I see you again after I turn my back, I'll write you up for insubordination."

A smile had played at Donovan's lips during the brief conversation. Now the ATF man's cammo-painted face broke into a full-blown leer.

Holly turned and started along the river away from the rest of the men, his heart a confusing mixture of anxiety, anger and shame. He was worried that someone like Donovan would be the first to locate the Hands of Heaven, and one of the bloody fiascos for which BATF had grown famous would occur—a debacle in which Samantha might be hurt or even killed. He was angry that he'd been caught redressing his wound and that men such as Simon Donovan were even allowed to carry a gun and badge.

Holly suddenly stopped and turned back to see the rest of Search Team Six scattering across Hell's Canyon. He wasn't going to bleed to death—not if he was careful and didn't open the wound any farther. He had enough bandages in his pack to last a week, and there was a full bottle of antibiotics in there as well. To disobey a direct order from Singer would be more than enough to get him fired from the Secret Service. But he didn't care.

If Simon Donovan or others like him found the Hands, Samantha could die.

Randall Holly knew he was only one man, and that the chances of him finding Samantha were slim. But he wasn't sure he would ever again be able to look in the mirror if he didn't at least try.

The young agent waited until both Donovan and Singer were out of sight and the other men were far in the distance. Then he changed course, moving away from the river and into the mountains along the Snake River.

He might end up pushing a broom for a living before all this was over. But at the moment, he couldn't have cared less.

Bolan ripped three of the aged one-by-four boards from the shaft cover, shone the light down onto another wobbly elevator, then lowered himself slowly downward. The wood squeaked as he carefully distributed his weight across the platform, then replaced the boards as best he could over his head. Looking down, he shone the ASP through one of the larger cracks in the floorboards.

Like the shaft where Harsey had hidden, the bottom of the winze was too far away to be seen. If the wood split in the wrong place or the hundred-year-old ropes gave way, he was in for a long plummet downward. The Executioner breathed shallowly, trying to hear whatever he could above his hiding place. The two groups were still moving cautiously forward, one from the Snake River side of the mine, the other from the Imnaha.

The way he saw it, one of three things was about to happen. First, whichever group of Handsmen reached the winzes first might immediately realize where he and Harsey had taken refuge. The shaft covers were in plain sight, and anything more than a cursory glance would reveal that the boards had been recently ripped away, then replaced. If that happened, all the Handsmen would have to do was start shooting. They wouldn't even have to lift the boards away—their rounds would easily penetrate the rotten wood. It would be like shooting fish in a barrel—but without any water to get in the way.

The second possibility was that the two groups would meet,

then wonder briefly where he and Harsey had gone. But *briefly* was the operative word, and their confusion wouldn't last long. There were only two ways out of the tunnel, and the Handsmen had them both covered. That realization would lead the men eventually back to the shaft where the first possibility would be realized.

The third and maybe the most likely feasibility was that one or both of the elevators would fail before any of that could happen. One snapped rope or broken board in the wrong place, and he or Harsey, or both of them, would fall to their deaths deep within the earth.

The Executioner waited, listening. He was counting on, hoping for, the second possibility. It was their only chance. If the Handsmen met in the tunnel over their heads and paused, even for a moment, it would give him and Harsey a chance to knock away the boards above them and begin shooting from the relatively good cover of the holes. And if the Hands of Heaven reacted as they had before, a few deaths would send the rest scampering out of the mine to regroup.

But what then? Bolan wondered. There would still be plenty of the men left to return. And his well of strategy was in immediate danger of running dry.

Above him, Bolan heard the footsteps from both entrances grind to a halt. Whispered voices sounded from both sides of the tunnel over his head.

Then all hell broke loose.

Even below the ground in the shaft, with the earplugs jammed firmly in his ears, the sounds of automatic gunfire threatened to burst the Executioner's eardrums. With the Desert Eagle in one hand, the Beretta 93-R in the other, he reached up, pressing the heels of his hands against the sides of his head. Amid the almost constant explosions, he heard screams, moans and shrieks for help. Had the Hands of Heaven from the Snake River side and those from the Imnaha mistaken each other for Bolan and Harsey? It didn't seem likely. Even the Handsmen had shown more caution and common sense than to make such a mistake.

The autofire lasted for almost thirty seconds, then died. A single set of footsteps sounded, running toward the Snake River exit. With a deep breath, Bolan reached over his head and knocked away the loose boards, then rose high enough to peer over the edge of the shaft.

The tunnel was half lit by the beams of flashlights that had fallen to the ground. Visible in the light were the bodies of dead men lying along both sides of the tunnel. Seeing no movement, Bolan thumbed the button on the ASP. Toward the Snake River entrance to the mine he saw body after body of camouflage-clad Handsmen. He raised the flashlight higher but saw nothing beyond where the dead men lay. The distant running footsteps had already rounded a curve out of sight and grew fainter with each step.

He couldn't be sure but it sounded as if only one man had escaped in that direction.

Swinging the light back toward the Imnaha, the Executioner squinted along the beam. More bodies lay along the dirt-packed rock. But they looked somehow different, and it took Bolan a moment to realize what that difference was.

These men wore newer, cleaner camouflage. A few were even dressed in black rather than cammies. And unlike the uniforms of the Handsmen, all of the shirts sported shoulder patches of some sort.

Careful not to split the wood of the elevator or put undue stress on the ropes, the Executioner climbed out of the shaft. He had just reached the surface when he heard the screeching sound of breaking wood farther down the tunnel. A gasp shot up through the boards covering the other winze, and then the sound of the elevator banging against the stony walls of the shaft bounded down into the bowels of the earth.

As he scrambled to his feet, the Executioner heard the dull crash of the elevator hitting bottom. A sick feeling filled his belly as he trained the flashlight on the other shaft, forty feet away. He sprinted to the cover and ripped away the boards he had loosened earlier. He expected to see the dark bottomless pit as he aimed the ASP into the cavity.

Instead, a smile curved the Executioner's lips upward. Rick Harsey was there, in plain sight. The general's son was hanging onto the frazzled end of a hundred-year-old rope.

"Need a hand?" Bolan asked as he holstered the Beretta and Desert Eagle.

"Oh, all of them you've got," Harsey said.

Bolan knelt on the hard ground and reached into the shaft, grasping the collar of Rick's vest with both fists. The angle was awkward but he managed to raise the man high enough to slip a hand under his arm, then leaned back, pulling Harsey the rest of the way out of the hole.

Harsey collapsed on the ground, panting. "Well...that was...interesting," he said between breaths. "That's what I like about you, Belasko. There's never a dull moment when you're around."

The Executioner rose back to his feet and followed the beam of the flashlight back toward the men with the shoulder patches. Focusing the light on the arm of the nearest man, he saw the Federal Bureau of Investigation emblem. Next to him lay the body of one of the men dressed in black. His shoulder identified him as an agent of the Bureau of Alcohol, Tobacco and Firearms. Moving along the line, Bolan checked the rest of the men. Some were Secret Service agents. One wore the patch of a nearby county sheriff.

Bolan frowned. The representatives of so many diverse agencies could mean only one thing: A task force had been formed to search the canyon.

Hal Brognola had been unsuccessful in stopping such an operation, and it would now be a race between the task force and Bolan to see who found the vice president and his daughter first. A race to see if Winston Bass and his daughter could be extracted safely before another Waco or Ruby Ridge could occur.

Harsey was rested and on his feet now, and joined Bolan. "Who are they?" he asked. "They aren't Handsmen."

Bolan trained the light on the nearest shoulder patch.

"Search team?" Harsey asked.

Bolan nodded in the dim light.

"Shit," Harsey said. "Hope the wanna-be commandos from the FBI and ATF aren't running the show."

The Executioner nodded again. He hoped Brognola had at least been influential enough with the President to see that the Secret Service was in charge. They were known for using far more restraint, and restraint was exactly what was called for in this situation.

"This doesn't make a lot of sense," Harsey went on. "I mean, yeah, I can see forming a task force in addition to sending you. There's probably so much interagency rivalry going on that it sounds like a PTA meeting. But there had to be Handsmen who went around and came in from the Imnaha side."

Bolan didn't respond except to train the flashlight farther down the tunnel. Stepping over and around the bodies on the ground, he led the way through the passageway until light appeared at the other end. They stepped out to see the Imnaha river rushing by.

And six dead Handsmen lying scattered about the bank.

"They must have both gotten here at the same time," the Executioner said. "Looks like the Feds won."

"Yeah, I'd say so," Harsey agreed. He dropped to one knee and began going through the pockets of the nearest body. Bolan did the same with another man who had been shot repeatedly through the chest. They searched all six bodies but found nothing but weapons, survival equipment and a few personal items. Nothing to indicate where the Hands of Heaven might have their base camp, or where the vice president and his daughter were being held.

Turning back into the mine, Bolan and Harsey retraced their steps to where the battle between the Handsmen and search team had taken place. They resumed their search of the bodies but again found nothing of use. Moving back along the tunnel toward the Snake, they stopped at each dead man to repeat the procedure. Nothing.

Finally moving back out into the sunlight along the river, Bolan saw that the speedboat the Handsmen had arrived in was gone. Whoever that man was who had escaped had taken it. The soldier hurried immediately to the *Norma*, worried that it might have been disabled. It wasn't. In his frantic desire to depart the area, the fleeing Handsman had either overlooked it or hadn't wanted to take the time. Further inspection showed that a few stray rounds had hit the boat and some of their equipment. But nothing had been destroyed. Bolan inspected the kayak, in particular. It was fine.

"Let's go," he told Harsey.

"Any idea where?" the general's son said as he climbed behind the wheel of the boat.

Bolan stared down the river. The wake left by the Hands of Heaven speedboat was long gone, and he had no way of knowing which way the man had headed. But his gut instincts told him that the man had headed downriver, deeper into the canyon.

"Same way we've been going," the Executioner said. "Full throttle. My guess is that in a few miles whoever escaped will slow down. Which means we've got a chance of catching up."

The Executioner said no more.

He had to find Winston and Samantha Bass before some group from the task force did and decided the glory of their organization was more important than the lives of the vice president and his daughter.

JESSE DAVIS shook the water out of his steel-gray beard and pulled the speedboat into shore. He dropped the anchor over the side of the rail, checked to make sure it was secured, then climbed out onto the rugged shoreline. It took another moment to wipe the condensation from his eyeglasses, but as soon as he looked up at the grass and other vegetation on the slope beyond the rocky bank he smiled. There, just in front of a stack of firewood he had collected only last week, he saw the circular spot of bare earth and ashes where he'd built so many fires in the past. His smile widened. This was only one of many favorite campsites he had used during the forty years he'd spent as one of Hell's Canyon's few permanent residents.

Davis knotted the speedboat's line to a tall pillar of rock with a smooth groove indicating the countless thousand other times similar ropes had encircled it. He reboarded the boat and located the cooking griddle he'd welded together from an old smoke screen and some scrap steel, then found his frying pan before moving to the igloo cooler tied down in the stern of the boat. From it he took a small plastic container which had once held margarine and one of the sirloin steaks the Handsmen had iced earlier in the day before leaving the main camp.

Force of habit sent Davis's eyes skirting up and down the river again. His ears pricked, listening. Nope. Still no sign of anybody chasing him. And nothing coming from the other end of the river, either. But there was no point in taking chances. Carrying the bundle in his arms to the front of the boat, he pulled the .44 Magnum Marlin lever-action carbine from the holder by the pilot's wheel and slung it over his back.

Davis stepped back onto the rocks and walked the ten yards to the grass. He peered through his spectacles at the grayish scraps of wood and ash that were all that remained of the previous week's fire. Then, setting the items down, he left the Marlin slung over his shoulder as he moved up the slope to the stacked wood. Carefully gathering only the driest of sticks and logs, he looked up and down the river once more.

It didn't appear that anybody had bothered to follow him from the Mountain Chief mine. For all he knew, everyone had been killed. But there was no sense taking chances with a smoky fire. He picked up a handful of dry leaves on his way back to the fire site.

Arranging the wood on top of the leaves, Davis struck a

kitchen match on his thumbnail and held it to the pile. Almost immediately the leaves began to smoke, then tiny flames leaped upward. Davis dropped slowly to his knees and bent to blow softly on the flames. Not until several of the smallest sticks of kindling had caught fire did he rise painfully back to his feet. Prying off the lid of the plastic container, he stuck in his fingers and scraped out a liberal amount of bear grease with which he began coating the frying pan. The act brought a smile to his face and his mouth began to drool. Nothing like good old-fashioned bear grease to liven up the taste of a cow, he thought. That had been one of the first things he'd learned after he'd quit his job as a shoe salesman in Boston, disappeared from his wife and children and headed for the Snake River close to four decades ago. An old Indian—Bright Cloud, a descendant of one of the Nez Percé tribes that had once inhabited the canyon—had taught him to hunt bear. He had also taught him to ignore such frivolous things as hunting seasons, licenses and limits. Davis laughed as he set the frying pan down on the grid and began unwrapping the white butcher's paper that covered the steak. He was the son of a Methodist preacher and had been raised to honor and obey the laws of both God and man. Funny how quickly he'd taken to the life of an outlaw.

With the steak sizzling in the pan, Davis jumped back on board the boat and grabbed the aluminum folding chair off the hooks on the rail. His mind drifted back again to the old Nez Percé, and how the two of them used to sit cross-legged by their campfire at night. Those days were over, he knew. Bright Cloud was dead. And the arthritis in his knees and hips was a constant reminder of the fact that he wouldn't be sitting cross-legged anymore, by a campfire or anywhere else.

Unfolding the chair, Davis unslung the Marlin and set it carefully on the ground. He carefully positioned himself on the nylon webbing and grimaced slightly as the arthritis shot up through his lower back. He listened to the steak as it began to cook. Now and then, the bear grease popped in the pan, echoing up and down the river in the stillness of the canyon. He checked the river again, then turned in his chair, looking up at the mountain behind him. Somewhere beyond that peak was the cave where he and Bright Cloud had gotten snowed in during the winter of '84. Or was it '85? He couldn't remember. Time was of little importance in Hell's Canyon in those days.

Davis turned back around to face the water again. He had chosen this spot to bed down for the night for two reasons. First, he could watch the overhang to the north and get good advance warning of any boat that came from that direction. With the scope mounted on top of the rifle he'd have plenty of time to pump .44 Magnums into the craft. But his second reason for choosing this spot was just as important.

He didn't want to go back to the Hands of Heaven compound yet. He needed to get away from those damn Handsmen for awhile.

Jesse Davis sat back and closed his eyes as the smell of beefsteak and bear grease infiltrated his nostrils. He had left that damn wife—what was her name?—and the brats he had sired to get away from people. And coming to Hell's Canyon had gained him the solitude he wanted. At least, forty years ago it had. But now it seemed everybody wanted to get away from people and the canyon was getting crowded. Maybe not crowded by some folks' standards but it seemed crowded to him. There were few people in the canyon compared to most places, but too many damn tourists flocked through each season.

But as if the tourists weren't bad enough, then the Hands of Heaven had come.

The old mountain man's trained ears heard a sudden scraping sound from the direction of the overhang. His eyes popped open and shot that way. Squinting in what was fast becoming twilight, he saw a dark shadow drop back over the other side of the rocks. Probably a squirrel, he thought. His eyes might not be as sharp as they'd once been but they were good.

Looking back at the frying pan, Jesse Davis saw that the steak was nearly cooked. Pulling the skinning knife from the sheath on his belt, he leaned down and cut a piece from the corner, then stabbed it with the point. He held it in the air briefly to let it cool, then stuck it in his mouth and began to chew. Good. Damn good. The bear grease had soaked into the beef just the way he liked it.

The taste brought back another old memory and Davis turned back to glance at the mountain behind him. Yep, although he had never gone back after that long hard winter, he still remembered well the cave where he and Bright Cloud had nearly starved to death in their snowbound fortress. Lucky for them, they had had enough firewood to keep a small fire going most of the time.

His thoughts returning to the Hands of Heaven, the old mountain man turned back to the river. He had joined up with Colonel Moreland's group in self-preservation. He hadn't wanted to be part of any damn militia—didn't want to be part of any damn group. But he had awakened at another of his favorite campsites one morning to find himself surrounded by a dozen men wearing camouflage suits and aiming assault rifles at his head. He soon found out that they had chosen that remote site to build their compound, and he could either become one of them or die. Playing their game seemed the better part of valor. At least until he found some other way out of the mess.

Davis reached down with the knife again and stabbed the steak in its center, raising it to the breeze again to let it cool. He hadn't counted on the Hands of Heaven being any more than a bunch of nutcases playing soldier when he'd first met them. And that's pretty much what they had been. But then that Russell fellow had showed up with his own men and before he knew it, Jesse Davis was helping hold the Vice President of the United States of America and the man's daughter hostage. Now, he didn't see how he'd ever get away from them.

Then, as he held the steak in the air, a sudden random thought struck him and he kicked himself for not having thought of it sooner. His mind must be slipping along with his body—the answer to how to shed the Hands of Heaven had been right before his eyes all the time. Well, maybe not all the time. At first, they had watched him like a hawk, but after several months during which he'd helped commit robberies and other crimes to finance the group, he'd been accepted as trustworthy. Then he'd been allowed to go off on his own on various tasks, and it was during those times he'd usually retreated to places like this to get a little of the time on his own for which he thirsted. He'd thought then about reporting the Hands of Heaven to the police. But at that time they hadn't really done anything.

But now they had.

Jesse Davis's grin spread across his face again. The answer was simple. And he even had a boat.

He could turn them in for something now. And he would. First thing in the morning, he'd take the boat upriver toward Lewiston. By now government search parties were bound to be out looking for the hostages, and if he didn't bump into one of them during the trip, he'd seek out the Lewiston police. Then he'd lead them back to the compound and that would be that. Maybe he'd even collect a reward with which he could restock for the upcoming winter.

The dusk that had fallen over the canyon had now become night and was illuminated only by the half-moon in the sky and the light of his campfire. Davis took another bite and savored the taste. Yep, bear grease had turned just about every kind of game he'd come across during his forty years in the canyon into a delicacy—venison, rabbit, squirrel and, of course, bear meat itself.

Yep, Jesse Davis thought as he watched the river flow by in the moonlight, he owed old Bright Cloud a lot for teaching him how to stay alive in Hell's Canyon. And the old Indian had saved his life one final time with the ultimate sacrifice during that winter so long ago. A long-forgotten Bible scripture Davis remembered his father quoting came to mind: Greater love hath no man than he lay down his life for a friend. Something like that. Anyway, Bright Cloud had been a true friend, he guessed.

And the old Nez Percé had tasted pretty damn good with bear grease after Jesse Davis had slit the sleeping Indian's throat.

HARSEY PILOTED the *Norma* down the Snake, taking the twists of the river like an Indianapolis 500 driver bent on winning the race. Behind them, the wake extended a quarter of a mile, and to the sides, the water shot up over the shore onto the banks of both Oregon and Idaho.

Bolan held a set of binoculars to his eyes, scanning the trees, hills, nooks and crannies that made up the canyon. He saw few birds overhead and little wildlife elsewhere, and the animals who did appear peeked out from behind various hiding places, then ducked to cover as the speedboat neared. A hard smile curled Bolan's lips.

The animals were wary. That meant it hadn't been long since the other speedboat went by. They were gaining on the fleeing Handsman.

The Executioner dropped the binoculars to the end of the strap around his neck. A small but constant mist sailed up from the bow and Bolan lifted his shirttail, wiping the lenses clear. When he'd finished, he glanced up again. As they rounded a curve, the boat rose slightly and the Executioner looked past the bow to see the tail end of a wake.

Harsey had seen it too, and he immediately cut back the engines to reduce their sound. He turned to Bolan, a quizzical look on his face.

The Executioner thought hard as the *Norma* slowed. They needed to take the man piloting the Hands' boat alive, if possible. But if they cut back the power very long, they risked losing him. And if they roared on, the escaping Handsman was likely to hear them coming over the purr of his own reduced jets. They were damned if they did, and damned if they didn't.

Harsey answered the question on his own face, suddenly

killing the jets completely. He pointed a finger ahead. "Look at the wake," he whispered.

Bolan followed the man's arm. The wake had disappeared. The boat ahead had stopped.

"Pull her in," the Executioner whispered back. Harsey aimed the boat toward the rocky bank and the *Norma* glided through the water, finally bumping her hull against the wet stones. The Executioner jumped out holding the line but saw no trees or rocks sharp enough to secure the rope.

"Here," Harsey whispered up at him.

Bolan looked down to see the general's son's arm swing back holding a steel stake. The short metal bar came lobbing up to him and he caught it with his free hand, then set it quietly down on the craggy shore as Harsey lifted a small sledgehammer.

A moment later, the Executioner had tapped the stake into a crack in the rocks and tied off the *Norma*. He hopped back onto the deck of the boat and set down the hammer as Harsey finished dropping the anchor quietly into the water.

The men worked silently as they loaded the Libra XT Kayak with a pair of SIG-551 LB select-fire rifles and extra magazines from General Harsey's armory. The other equipment they might need had been stored in the kayak before they'd left Lewiston. As they boarded the craft, Bolan's nostrils picked up a faint scent of smoke.

"Cocky bastard must be damn sure he got away," Rick Harsey whispered as they paddled away from the *Norma*. "He's cooking dinner."

As soon as they'd cleared the bow of the speedboat, Bolan nodded toward the shore. Harsey understood. They needed to stay as close to the bank as possible, every turn they made might be the one that brought them into full view of the Handsman.

The Libra XT moved through the water a few hundred yards, the smoke getting stronger. Bolan and Harsey pulled in their paddles and reached out, grabbing the rocky bank and moving the small craft along by hand. That way, they hugged the shore-line even tighter, and both men's hands were free to move to the SIGs slung over their shoulders.

The man who had escaped the Mountain Chief mine in the speedboat knew his stuff, the Executioner had to admit, as they moved quietly on. Though the smell of burning wood and meat was thick in his nostrils now, no smoke could be seen. The Handsman was using dry wood rather than green for his fire.

Ahead, a long-dead tree, seeming to grow out of the rocks itself, appeared on an overhang of the jagged shoreline. As they neared, Bolan finally saw faint tendrils of smoke drifting beneath the tree in the light breeze. He grabbed hold of an outcropping in the rocks, stopping the kayak. "He's got to be right around that bend," he whispered to Harsey.

The general's son nodded.

Reaching into the forward hatch, Bolan's hand came out with a coiled length of yellow nylon rope. He quickly fashioned a noose, looped it over the outcropping he'd been holding and tied off the kayak.

The bank was steep, and both Bolan and Harsey were forced to sling their rifles over their backs as they hauled themselves up toward the tree. The Executioner's head was the first to rise over the top, and he inched it cautiously upward until he could see down to the shoreline below.

The Handsman's boat had been anchored and tied a hundred yards farther down the bank. The man had set up a quick campsite in the grass and dirt beyond the rocky shore. The legs of a small steel grid stood over the fire, and on the grid was a frying pan. Something too far away to identify sizzled in the silence of the canyon.

The man himself sat in an aluminum folding chair next to the fire. What looked like a lever-action rifle lay on the ground to his side.

Harsey was just finishing the climb to the top when the snaps on the pockets of his vest suddenly scraped against the rock.

Bolan saw the man in the chair start to turn toward the noise. The Executioner shot his head back down behind cover. Harsey saw the movement and froze in place behind the rocks.

"Did he see us?" the general's son whispered.

"I don't know."

Bolan and Harsey waited a good five minutes before the Executioner risked another look. The man still sat in the chair. The rifle on the ground lay in the same place it had earlier and didn't appear to have been moved. Even if it had, the fact that the Handsman had returned it to the ground and remained seated meant he had written off the noise as nothing of concern.

Harsey's head now came up next to Bolan's. The general's son grinned. "Smell's like beefsteak," he said in a low voice. "Lets try to take him before he eats it."

Bolan frowned at him.

"I'm hungry," Harsey explained. "And steak sounds a lot better to me than the stuff we packed."

Bolan turned his head back to the problem at hand. As far away as the Handsman was, there was little chance of reaching him without being seen first. Not if they followed the shore, at least. And being spotted too soon would lead to shooting, diminishing the chances of capture and interrogation. Bolan shifted his weight slightly on the rocks. No, if he wanted the man dead, he had an easy shot from where he was.

Turning farther inland, the Executioner saw that the rocky shore gave way to grass- and bush-covered terrain twenty yards away. If they could make it without being seen, it would be simple enough to circle behind the Handsman and approach from the rear. It was just the first few yards over the rocks that they would be in full view.

Bolan looked up at the sky. Already, the sun was beginning to fall behind the mountains.

In less than an hour, he estimated, darkness would fall over the Snake River and Hell's Canyon. He turned to Harsey. "Can you hold on here for an hour or so?"

Harsey looked up at the sky, understanding the reasoning

behind the question. He nodded, but said, "My arms and legs can. But he'll eat my steak, and I don't know about my stomach."

The Executioner shifted his weight again to begin the wait. Long seconds became even longer minutes as the time dragged by.

Then finally, the sun dropped far enough below the mountains and night fell over Hell's Canyon.

"You ready?" the Executioner whispered to Rick Harsey.

"Oh yeah," Harsey said. "More than ready."

"Then let's go." Bolan pulled himself over the edge of the rocks to the top of the overhang, staying low on his belly to avoid being silhouetted in the moonlight. He reached back, pulling the SIG-551 over his head, then began the painful crawl on his belly over the sharp rocks to the grass. Behind him, he heard Harsey doing the same in the near-silence of the canyon. The Executioner paused at the edge of the rocky shoreline, taking a final look down at the Handsman. His shadowy silhouette was again seated in the folding chair. He'd stood momentarily to remove the cooking grid from the fire while Bolan and Harsey had crawled toward the grass. The soldier had been grateful for the diversion during the period where, even at night, they might be noticed moving in the moonlight.

They were behind the man's line of vision now but Bolan and Harsey still kept to the ground as they moved onto the grass. They had seen the Handsman turn to look up at the mountains several times as if he were entertaining some memory about them, and there was no telling when he might wax nostalgic again. Not until they had reached a shallow arroyo forty yards from the river and descended out of sight, did they rise to their feet.

Bolan drew the ASP laser light from his belt and narrowed its beam with his cupped hand as he'd done earlier in the Mountain Chief mine. Following the reddish glow, he and Harsey made their way along the valley, circling behind the Handsman's campsite. Once they reached the area where the Executioner estimated they'd be directly behind the man, they'd move back up the hill to the top. They could make any positional readjustments necessary to an approach from the man's rear at that time.

Then they'd have to walk the fine line between speed and stealth as they left the concealment of the arroyo and made their way to the happy camper. They'd have to hope and pray that they could get to him before he heard them or decided to make one of his random surveys of the mountains at his back. If he spotted them with time enough to go for the rifle next to him, the chances of taking him alive were almost nil.

Moving quietly back up the hill, Bolan and Harsey resumed prone positions and pulled themselves to the crest with their elbows. With the moonlight reflecting off the river, the soldier could see that they had only slightly overshot the mark. They were approximately ten yards to the right of the aluminum chair. Perhaps twenty yards separated them from the man's back. He wasn't asleep yet. But his dark head kept leaning forward every few seconds, as if he was about to drift off in his chair.

Bolan and Harsey moved a few feet down the hill, out of sight from the river.

"Let's give it a few more minutes," the Executioner whispered to Harsey. "Looks like he's ready to fall asleep." Slipping out of his rifle sling, he set the SIG on the grass and motioned for Harsey to do the same. He started to draw the Desert Eagle, then switched to the sound-suppressed Beretta. There might well be other Handsmen nearby. The man in the chair might even be waiting for them at this prearranged meeting place. There was no sense alerting the enemy if they were near.

In any case, Bolan hoped not to use a firearm of any type in the next few minutes. He transferred the Beretta to his left hand and drew the flashlight from its carrier once more. But now, the light stayed off. This time around, he intended to make use of its hard plastic. A mere five inches long, it was capable of delivering blows that ranged from painful to lethal. It could also be pressed into nerve centers to assist in restraint techniques.

Bolan heard rustling behind him and turned as Harsey drew a weapon the Executioner hadn't even known he'd brought along—a lightweight collapsible baton. Rather than noisily snap the three-sectioned twenty-one-inch club to its full length, the general's son pried the ball-shaped end out with a twist of his fingers, then quietly extended the additional two lengths by hand. He jiggled the weapon several times to make sure it was locked in place, then drew his sound-suppressed .22 with the other hand.

The two men crawled back to the top of the ridge and peered over it once more. Little had changed except for the fact that the Handman's chin now rested permanently on his chest. Bolan rose silently and began creeping forward. Harsey followed.

They had covered the first ten yards when the Executioner heard the sharp snap of a twig directly to his rear. He didn't have to turn around to know what had happened. Harsey's boot had hit a stick hidden in the darkness. The general's son cursed softly under his breath.

The Handsman's chin shot up from his chest. His head and shoulders began to swivel in the chair.

Bolan and Harsey sprinted forward as the man lurched for the rifle on the ground next to him. The Handsman's pained-looking movements were nevertheless surprisingly fast, and he had the rifle in both hands and was rising to his feet by the time the Executioner had closed the gap.

The lever-action rifle was still pointed away from him, however, as Bolan brought the ASP laser light over his head and then down against one of the man's forearms. A sharp squeal pierced the night. A second later, Harsey struck with the collapsible baton, bringing it around in an arc on the Handsman's thigh, and elicited another sharp scream.

Dropping the ASP, Bolan reached down and extracted the

rifle from the man as the Handsman fell to his back on the ground, holding his leg and moaning.

The Executioner dropped to one knee, rolled the Handsman to his belly, and drew a skinning knife from the sheath on the man. He tossed it out of the way. A quick frisk found a well-worn Buck 110 lock-back folder in the back pocket of the old man's khaki work pants but no other weapons. Bolan locked the man's hands together behind his back with one of his own, then jerked him to his feet.

Bolan nodded to Harsey and looked down at the chair. Harsey grabbed the back of the aluminum frame to steady it, and the Executioner slammed the Handsman into the seat. "You got a name?" he asked the man.

The Handsman looked up at him coldly.

"Don't make the mistake of thinking I won't hurt you because of your age," the Executioner said, looking back even more coldly. "I'll ask you again. One more time. Who are you?"

Harsey stepped in, reaching out to grab the man's chin and tilted it in the moonlight. "Well, I'll be damned," he said. "Old Jesse Davis."

The Executioner turned to Harsey. "You know him?"

"Not really," Harsey said. He dropped the man's chin. "But I know of him. He's an old coot who's been living in the canyon for years."

Bolan was a little surprised when the old man's eyes suddenly cleared. He looked closer at Jesse Davis's face, now convinced that the cold stare had been more from fear and shock than resistance.

"You've joined up with the Hands of Heaven, have you Jesse?" Harsey asked.

"No, not really."

"Don't lie to us," the Executioner warned the man. "You were in the mine. And I remember you now from the Hands' boat. You were the pilot."

"No denying that," said the old man. He looked surprisingly calm now, and a grin was even starting to form at the corners of his mouth. "You boys with the government?" He pronounced the word "gubment." "FBI boys, maybe?"

"We're from the government," Bolan nodded. "That's all you need to know."

A smile spread across his face. "Well, good. You have saved me a long trip upriver to Lewiston."

Bolan leaned forward until his face was only inches from the old man. He frowned. "What do you mean?" he asked.

"Well, you boys are looking for the Hands of Heaven, right?"

"Right."

"You're wanting to find the vice president and his daughter, right?"

"Right again."

"Well, I'm the man who knows where they are. I was on my way to find some of you federal boys so I could take you to them."

"Yeah," Rick Harsey said from behind the chair. "And my friend and I are on our way to the Hell's Canyon Arts and Crafts show a few miles downriver. We've got some of our quilts entered and we think they might win a ribbon."

Jesse Davis half turned in the chair. "I ain't kidding, boys," he said. "I've been with the Hands, yeah. But it wasn't my doing. I've been living along this river for the past forty years. On my own, for the most part, which is how I like it. Then these fools in their you-can't-see-me tree-and-leaf suits show up. I joined up with them, all right. They'd have killed me, if I hadn't. But now I'm on my own, and I want their asses out of my canyon." He paused to take a breath, then went on. "To be honest, I don't give a rat's ass about the vice president and the girl. But I want my canyon back."

Bolan studied the man's face. Jesse Davis might well be telling the truth. He wasn't dressed in camouflage and he looked like a man who might have lived nearly half a century in this remote region. He smelled like it, too. But the man radiated an even stronger smell than body odor—the smell of evil. There was something intangibly decadent about the old man. As if during his years, he'd committed unspeakable acts that had gone unpunished.

The Executioner didn't like Jesse Davis. But he believed him.

"So you'll take us to where they're holding Bass and his daughter?" Bolan asked.

"Sure thing," Davis said. "Is there any reward?"

"Yeah," Harsey said. "You get a warm fuzzy feeling for having served your country. I'm sure that's all you want anyway."

Davis shrugged. "If that's all I get," he said. "You boys think we need to go get some reinforcements first?"

"Not for what we have planned," Bolan said.

"Well, you're the boss," Davis said. "But I don't really think the three of us can kill all the Hands of Heaven in that camp."

"We're not going to kill them," the Executioner said. "We're planning to get the vice president and his daughter out of there."

"But after that, there'll be more of you FBI and CIA or whatever types who'll go in and kill them?"

"We'll see," Harsey said.

"Good. That's all I ask. Get them the hell out of my canyon."

Bolan grabbed the old man's shoulder and hauled him to his feet. "Let's go," he said.

As they prepared to return to the *Norma*, another boat rounded the curve in the Snake River.

Loaded with heavily armed men in Hands of Heaven camouflage.

6

The stillness that had covered the Hell's Canyon night had been punctured first by the sounds of Bolan's laser-flash striking the old man on the forearm and Harsey's collapsible baton being drawn across the same man's thigh. But now that quiet was shattered as rounds of gunfire exploded from the speedboat a split second after the Executioner had seen it round the curve.

Bolan dived to the ground, returning fire with the Beretta in his left hand. His right whirled the Marlin by the lever, twirling the carbine in the air to chamber a round. He brought the weapon into firing position, wondering as he did how he and Harsey could have failed to hear the oncoming boat. Just as quickly, he answered his own question.

The pilot would have seen the *Norma* anchored while his boat was still far upriver. He would have killed the jets and let the craft drift quietly along with the current.

Bolan pulled the Marlin's trigger, then twirled the carbine once more as the Beretta spit 9 mm semijacketed lead toward the boat. He heard the jets fire to life again, and the boat suddenly shot forward in the water. Gunfire from the men at the rails continued to pelt the ground around him.

To his side, the Executioner heard Harsey's .40 caliber Browning Hi-Power explode into action with a fast burst of rounds. He turned long enough to glance at the aluminum folding chair. Jesse Davis still sat where he had been most of the evening, his shocked gaping mouth the only real change.

"Get down, you old fool!" Harsey shouted above the gunfire. The Executioner turned his attention back to the boat as it continued to race forward. Levering the Marlin's action yet again, he fired another big .44 Magnum round at the craft, wondering what it had hit, if anything, in the darkness. He levered again and pulled the trigger, repeating the process until the Marlin clicked on an empty chamber.

The oncoming boat hadn't even slowed.

Bolan dropped the lever-action to the ground and drew the Desert Eagle. He bolted to his feet as he jammed the Beretta into his belt. With his free hand, he reached down and grasped Jesse Davis under the nearest arm. "Let's go!" he yelled at the top of his lungs.

The man sat rigid, as if made of ice.

"Grab him!" the Executioner ordered Harsey.

The general's son yanked the old man by the other arm and together they dragged the lifeless form out of the chair. Davis seemed to find his feet and began to shuffle along as Bolan and Harsey led him away from the river and up the hill toward cover. Both men returned fire over their shoulders with their free hands, but in the confusion their rounds had little, if any, effect on the boat or the men occupying it.

Rifle rounds continued to pelt the ground around them as Bolan and Harsey half dragged Jesse Davis up the hill. Then, suddenly, the old mountain man jerked, almost folding in half backward. A soft groan escaped his lips, then his body went completely limp.

Bolan and Harsey dragged the drooping form the rest of the way to the top of the hill before dumping him on the other side. Shots sailed over their heads as they fell to the ground themselves, lunging for the Swiss-made assault rifles.

"See how bad he's hit," the Executioner yelled to Harsey as he swung the SIG around and cut loose with a full-auto stream of fire at the boat. The craft had been forced to slow as it neared the rocky shore, and he couldn't help but believe at least a few of his rounds had found targets.

Screams heard over the explosions strengthened his belief.

Bolan ran the rest of the magazine dry, then popped a fresh load into the weapon. The SIG-551 LB sported an eighteen-inch barrel—just long enough to keep the grenade launcher option like its "father," the SIG-550. But General Richard Harsey had had only two grenades in his armory, and the Executioner was determined not to waste them. He would wait until he had a stationary target.

"He's bad," Harsey said as the gunfire quieted for a few seconds. "It's through the spine."

"Going to make it?" Bolan asked, sending another firestorm into the boat. The only apparent effects were two rifles falling over the rail into the water.

"I doubt it," Harsey said, then paused. "No."

"Get directions to the compound, then," the Executioner ordered. The boat was only a few yards from shore now, and he emptied the rest of the magazine into it. He jammed another box mag into the rifle but didn't fire again until the boat had bumped against the rocks next to the boat Jesse Davis had piloted.

And this time, it was the grenade launcher he fired.

Men had already begun to leap from the boat as the Executioner ignited the small rocket-grenade. The missile sailed away dragging a smoky tail of light under the moon. A split second later, an explosion erupted from the speedboat.

Bodies and pieces of bodies went flying over and through the boat rails to land in the water and on the rocky shore. Wails of torment sailed into the night. A man who looked like a human torch, with flames encompassing his entire body, jumped over the rail and disappeared beneath the surface of the river.

But not all of the Handsmen on board the craft had been killed. A few rounds continued to fly up at the hill to burrow through the grass at the Executioner's side. And several of the men had gotten off the boat before the explosion. They now dropped to the ground, trying to squeeze behind whatever cover they could find in the craggy stone growths around the shore.

Bolan reloaded the grenade launcher. He aimed carefully this time, training the sights on the boat's gas tanks. A second later, another of the missiles swept down from the hill, through the night, to strike the steel container.

Flames shot through the night like some ancient funeral pyre, and for the men still on board that was exactly what the boat became. All of the bodies, alive and dead, burst into flames. Several more of the Handsmen leaped into the river. Others died where they stood, leaning bizarrely over the railings as their weapons melted in their hands.

A few of the men fell back into their seats to sit while they burned, becoming one with the upholstered benches. The leaping flames spread throughout the boat, melting both plastic and flesh until they were one. Then, looking like some giant finger, the fire suddenly jumped from the Handsman's boat to the craft Jesse Davis had anchored earlier.

The only remaining gunfire came from the men who had reached shore before the Executioner had employed the grenade launcher. As his finger moved back to the trigger, Bolan heard Harsey whisper to Jesse Davis. But the general's son's words were indistinguishable in the uproar.

The sickening odor of burning human flesh filled the Executioner's nostrils as he aimed down the hill. As best he could tell, there were only three Handsmen still alive onshore. And they had only partial cover in the rocks. The nearest man's boot was sticking out from behind a pile of stones. Bolan triggered a 3-round burst at the leather sole, and the foot inside it jerked. Another scream entered the chorus of shrieks still coming from the boat, and the man involuntarily sat up and reached for his leg.

The Executioner's next rounds took his head off.

The very top of the next man's head was visible above the only cover he could find. Bolan sent a lone round ripping that way, and the Handman's scalp peeled back. The impact sent him reeling back screaming, and the Executioner added two more rounds to silence him.

Next to him, Bolan heard Harsey curse softly.

The final man's shoulder was exposed. Bolan was preparing to send a round into it when a third explosion suddenly roared through Hell's Canyon. He lifted his line of sight enough to see that the gas tank on Jesse Davis's boat had finally been ignited, sending another fireball racing upward in the night.

The explosion caused the man on the ground to turn that way, and when he did he exposed himself from waist to head. A burst from the SIG entered the left side of his torso and exited the right. He sprawled to his side in death.

The boats continued to burn, illuminating the Snake River with their dancing flames for hundreds of yards in every direction. Bolan glanced to his side and saw that Jesse Davis was staring open-eyed toward the stars. He shook his head in disgust. The rest of the men were dead as well. The ticket to the Hands of Heaven had been his. But the wind had blown it from his fingers before he could get it punched.

The Executioner set the rifle on the grass and rose to a sitting position. He looked at Harsey. The general's son's face was black from the smoke, and Bolan knew his would be as well. "Did he tell you anything?" he asked.

"Nothing worthwhile," Harsey said. "He was out of his head. Just kept muttering some nonsense about eating bright clouds or something."

SAMANTHA BASS looked across the dimly lit prison at the plastic bedpan in the corner. She needed to use it badly. She'd been holding her bodily functions for almost twenty-four hours now, and she was afraid if she tried to keep it up much longer, her bladder would explode.

On the other side of the prison hole, his back still pressed against the dirty rock wall behind him, Samantha saw her father. He hadn't moved for hours. He had crawled to that same sitting position shortly after being thrown into the hole by the terrorists and had moved only once. That was when he had stood and walked self-consciously to the bedpan, a sheepish

stupid grin on his face. Turning away from her, he had unzipped his pants and urinated into the bowl.

The sound had echoed off the walls of their tiny dungeon as
if a firehose were aimed at a tin wall. Samantha had turned
away from him but that hadn't helped much. The acidic odor
of urine had filled the hole ever since. Winston Bass had been
embarrassed afterward, and returned to his sitting position,
closing his eyes to feign sleep.

Samantha had been just as embarrassed as her father. It
wasn't that she didn't know he was human. She did. But she
rarely saw any signs of it, and that made this sudden "crash
course" in Winston Bass's humanity a little hard to take.

Samantha had been trying to think of other things to take
her mind off her bladder for the past few hours. But as the
pressure got worse, those other thoughts had always drifted
back to her immediate problem. Sometimes those daydreams
had merged with the problem, as they did now as she forced
herself to think again about Randall Holly. She knew it was
only a fantasy and unlikely to ever happen, but what if she and
Randy got married someday? Would she be as uptight about
using the bathroom in front of him as she was her own father?
Maybe. There was no way to be sure. Did it matter? Maybe,
maybe not.

All that mattered right now was that she was very likely
going to wet her pants in the next few minutes.

The screen above her head rumbled and Conway's leering
grin peered down into the hole. "Doing all right down there,
sweetheart?" he asked lecherously.

His words seemed to double the pressure on her bladder.
Out of desperation, Samantha decided to take a chance. "No,
I need to go to the bathroom," she said.

Conway's eyes moved to the bedpan in the corner, then returned to her, the leer on his face widening. "Didn't think you
high-class girls on your way to join fancy sororities had to do
such things," he said. "But you got the means so go ahead."

Samantha closed her eyes. This was worse than any of her childhood nightmares.

Another voice, its words indistinguishable, could suddenly be heard above her head. Samantha opened her eyes to see that Conway had turned his face to the side and was saying something.

A second later, one of the leaders of the terrorists peered down into the hole. But at the moment, he looked like an angel dropped from heaven.

"Please," Samantha said. "I've got to use the rest room. And I don't want to do it down here."

The terrorist leader looked to her father and Samantha followed his eyes.

Winston Bass was pretending to be asleep again.

The man above her nodded. "I understand," he said. He turned to Conway. "Take her out where she can have some privacy."

"No!" Samantha blurted out. "Please! Not him."

There was a moment of silence, then the leader nodded again. A moment later, the screen was removed from the hole and the wooden ladder came sliding down.

Winston Bass opened his eyes and in them Samantha saw fear. "Be careful," her father said.

"What do you mean?" Samantha asked as her foot found the first rung of the ladder.

"I won't be out there to protect you."

The statement was so ludicrous that Samantha didn't even bother to answer.

Climbing to the top of the hole, Samantha's eyes squinted against the brighter lights of the room. But through the window she could see that darkness had fallen. Even during the short period of time she and her father had been imprisoned beneath the earth, she realized she had lost all track of time. She ignored Conway and turned to the leader. "Thank you," she said, forcing a grateful and subservient smile she didn't feel onto her face. "Sir...what should I call you?"

"I'm Colonel Moreland," the man said. He took her by the arm and led her out the door.

As soon as they were away from Conway and alone, Samantha said, "Please, Colonel, why are you doing this to us?" Her instincts had told her the man would enjoy being addressed with his title and shown respect.

"It's nothing personal," Moreland said.

Samantha felt the anger rise in her chest and threaten to come out her mouth. But already a plan was forming in her mind and she controlled her words. "With all due respect, Colonel," she said and felt the man's already light grip on her arm lighten even further, "how can I not take it personally?"

Moreland led her away from the building. Samantha glanced over her head at the half-moon, then looked down through its light to see that they were heading toward the edge of a thick cluster of trees. But it was too dark to see how far the brush extended. Without moving her head so he would see what she doing, her eyes searched her field of vision both ways. She couldn't see the river, although it might be behind her. She'd be able to look that way, though, once she entered the trees to go to the bathroom. A sudden thought struck her and she said, "You have a daughter, don't you, Colonel." It was phrased as a statement rather than a question.

Moreland's grip on her arm suddenly tightened again. He stopped her. "How did you know that?" he asked suspiciously.

The hand on her arm hurt but Samantha didn't let on. "By the way you're treating me," she said. "You understand how humiliating it would be for me to go to the bathroom down there in front of my own father."

Moreland nodded. They began walking again.

Samantha knew she was onto something and decided to play it for all it was worth. "I can also tell you are a family man," she said.

"How?"

"Because you're kind. I can see it in your eyes." The grip tightened slightly and she realized she was on shaky ground.

Quickly, she added, "You're tough, too. That's obvious. I mean, without being tough and smart, you could never have gotten to us. But you aren't mean. Not when you don't have to be."

The man holding her arm coughed nervously. "I don't like doing this, Miss Bass. But it's necessary. I hope you understand."

Words of warning from one of the Secret Service agents who had counseled the Bass family when her father first took office suddenly rushed through her head: *Don't pretend to agree with the terrorists' doctrine if you're ever taken hostage. At least not too soon. They'll see through it.*

Samantha caused herself to stiffen slightly. She made her voice sound less sympathetic to the man leading her toward the trees. She even let a trace of indignation enter her words when she said, "I don't see how kidnapping my father and me can help you."

They had reached the edge of the trees and stopped. "I don't expect you to understand," Moreland said. "But what we're doing is for the good of the country. For the good of all Americans. Whether you can see it or not, it's even for the good of you and your father."

Samantha looked into the man's eyes and let a sad smile cover her face. At the moment, she was happy for not only the experience she's had in her high school's trekker club but the drama club as well. "I'd be lying to you if I said I understood, Colonel," she said. "But I'm not afraid anymore. I know you won't hurt me."

The fact that the man who had called himself Colonel Moreland looked away from her when she said that didn't pass unnoticed. And it was at that moment that she realized the importance of the fact that she and her father hadn't been blindfolded.

The Hands of Heaven had no intention of letting them out of there alive.

"Don't go far," Colonel Moreland warned. "And don't take

any longer than you have to. I don't want to embarrass you further Miss Bass, but I'll come looking for you if I have to."

Samantha forced a good-natured laugh. "You think I might try to run off, Colonel?" she asked. "Where would I go? I don't know anything about the woods like you do. And how could I leave my father?"

Moreland smiled. "Go on," he said, waving a hand toward the trees.

Samantha Bass turned and walked into the trees. Every few paces she looked over her shoulder, knowing Colonel Moreland would think it was out of modesty and a desire to get out of his sight while she tended to her bodily functions. When the silhouette just outside the trees was finally out of sight, she stopped and made a point of rustling a bush. Just in case he could hear in the still night, she unzipped her pants as loudly as she could. Then, turning away from the Hands of Heaven compound again, she began to walk as quickly and quietly as she could. She had gone another fifty steps when she could control her fear no longer.

Her bladder still threatening to burst, Samantha Bass began to run.

HAVING LOST the opportunity to have Jesse Davis guide them to the Hands of Heaven camp, Bolan and Harsey had no other choice than to continue searching the Snake River, blindly hoping they'd spot some clue that would lead them to the compound. As the flames of the two speedboats still rose into the sky, they had paddled the kayak back to the *Norma*, which had been waiting where they'd anchored and tied her off.

The Executioner was the first on board, pulling the kayak out of the water and up over the side of the rail. He whispered a silent prayer of thanks that the Handsmen hadn't taken the time to disable or destroy her. They had undoubtedly planned to come back after killing him and Harsey to get the boat for their own use.

As Bolan bungeed the kayak back to the rail, Harsey boarded

and moved directly to the aft of the boat. The temperature in Hell's Canyon had dropped dramatically as soon as the sun went down. Harsey slipped the Gore-Tex top of a rubber rainsuit over his vest, then opened the top of an insulated cooler lashed to the deck. He pulled out a package of hot dogs, water dripping from the plastic around it, and looked up. "Wish we'd gotten the son of a bitch's steak." He grinned. "But I guess this is better than nothing. You want some?"

Bolan shook his head.

Harsey frowned in mock amazement. "You know, Belasko," he said. "Sometimes I wonder if you're human. Maybe you run on batteries."

Bolan didn't answer.

The general's son moved forward to take the wheel again as the Executioner unzipped one of the bags and took out a hooded camouflage sweatshirt. Slipping out of his cargo vest and the shoulder holster holding the Beretta 93-R, he pulled the sweatshirt over his head, then replaced the rig and covered it with his vest. Digging deeper into a ballistic nylon bag, he came up with a pair of lightweight Bushnell Yardage Pro 800 binoculars. The Yardage Pro utilized a laser ranging system that could measure up to eight hundred yards at the push of a button, and could be adjusted for rain, heavy foliage and moving targets. It also included scan mode and 6X permanent focus sighting system. But the option the Executioner was most interested in at the moment was the backlight LCD for low lighting. He slipped the leather strap around his neck and returned to the bow of the boat as Harsey pulled it away from shore.

The canyon was lighted as if it were still daylight as they passed the fiery boats. But as they moved down the river, the flames began to disappear. Their visibility was greatly diminished but Bolan was a little surprised at the way the moonlight reflected off the water.

Harsey had sliced open the hot dog package and was eating the raw wieners as he guided the boat down the river. He kept the lights off and the engines to a soft purr as the Executioner began scanning the shores with the binoculars. Progress was, understandably, far slower than it had been in the daylight. But the search was far from futile. Indeed, the night-vision binoculars enabled him to search the banks several hundred yards ahead of the creeping watercraft. He could only hope that his line of sight was also beyond the sound of the softly purring boat engines.

While the shores betrayed no signs of human occupancy as the *Norma* puttered slowly through the night, white pines and the mighty Douglas Firs, both so common to both Hell's Canyon and the Pacific Northwest in general, were silhouetted against the sky atop the mountains. Lower, the mountainsides were dark to the naked eye. But the Yardage Pro optics clarified every hole, crevice and arroyo in surrealistic gray tones. Still, none of the potential hiding places betrayed any sign of concealing human beings, and although the Executioner watched rabbits skirt from bush to bush and squirrels dart along the limbs of trees as the boat glided by, he saw no hint of the Hands of Heaven.

At one point during the night, Bolan spotted what appeared to be a campsite midway up one of the mountains. A tree had been cut down, the trunk still partially joined to the stump jutting out of the ground. The limbs, it appeared, had been stripped for firewood.

"Cut the engines," Bolan whispered to Harsey, turning to lift his SIG from where he had secured it to the railing behind him. Harsey complied, and the *Norma* drifted through the night toward a spot parallel to the site. The Executioner held the binoculars in his left hand, the rifle in his right, as they neared. He was about to order Harsey to flood the area with the boat's spotlight, when the picture through the Yardage Pro suddenly became more clear.

Yes, it was a campsite. Or at least had been. The remnants of the tree limbs were visible only as charred logs and sticks scattered across a shallow pit. He shifted the binoculars back to the tree. The cut marks—an ax had been used to fell the tree—had faded in the weather. The site looked weeks old. There were no other signs to lead him to speculate on a current human presence.

"Go on," Bolan said to Harsey. He dropped the binoculars from his tired eyes as Harsey fired the engine back to life.

The first hint that daylight was returning was the birds chirping at the tops of the trees. A few minutes later, the sky over the mountain crests changed from a dark black-blue to a deep purple. As the mountainsides themselves began to lighten, the crags, crevices and caves appeared once more. The Executioner dropped the binoculars to the end of the strap.

Rick Harsey yawned as dawn broke over Hell's Canyon. "You ever sleep, Belasko?" he asked.

"When I get the chance," he answered.

Harsey chuckled. "Just wondered," he said. "I mean, I found out last night that you don't eat, so I wasn't sure."

"You need a nap?" the Executioner asked. "I can pilot and watch the shores at the same time."

"No, I'm okay. At least for a few more hours."

Bolan nodded.

With daylight flooding into the canyon, Harsey increased the *Norma's* speed—but only slightly. The noise from their own engines was their worst enemy and would likely announce their presence long before they could be seen.

Earlier Bolan hadn't believed that the Hands of Heaven would risk a base camp too close to civilization. The Executioner had used the Mountain Chief mine as the landmark where the search would begin in earnest. But now they were deep within the region where the Hands might be, and every mile made the chance of finally running into them more probable.

Bolan rubbed his weary eyes as they moved down the river. They did have the advantage that the Handsmen were using speedboats similar to theirs. There was a good chance that if they were heard before they were seen, they'd be mistaken for one of the patrol boats that had attacked them. But that mistaken identity would be short-lived, allowing them only a slight advantage.

For a moment, the Executioner considered abandoning the *Norma* altogether. For the equipment they would need to carry out the surgical strike he planned, they had more than enough room on the kayak. But he dismissed the idea as quickly as he had considered it. The problem with that was speed. They had to find the vice president and his daughter before anything happened to them. And searching the canyon in the kayak was simply too slow.

Bolan finished rubbing his eyes and dropped his hands, grateful to see that the weariness he had felt when the sun rose was gone, and his vision had cleared. The bottom line was, he and Rick Harsey would have to continue along in the boat, keeping the engines as low as possible and praying that they spotted signs of the Hands of Heaven and had a chance to switch to the kayak before the kidnappers were alerted to them.

In a reversal of what he feared, it was sound rather than sight that first alerted the Executioner that there were men up ahead.

Above the purr of the their engines, Bolan suddenly heard a laugh drift through the canyon. Harsey heard it too, and the general's son didn't have to be told to kill the jets. At almost the same time, the faint odor of smoke met the Executioner's nostrils. He scanned the horizon above the mountains.

Tiny wisps were rising from somewhere in the rocks on the Idaho side of the river.

As they drifted through the water, the sounds of more laughter and voices came from the same area. Harsey turned the wheel toward the bank and let the *Norma* drift in. A moment later, they were anchored, tied off and on the move.

The acoustics of Hell's Canyon were strange, and the voices, which Bolan knew had to be far away, sounded as if they were right in front of him. He looked up at the sheer face of a cliff ten feet from the water, knowing the sounds had to come from somewhere behind it. Harsey had taken several steps to the left, and now the general's son was sweeping the limbs of a bush to the side. He looked past the foliage, then his head jerked toward the Executioner and he waved him that way.

Bolan moved softly across the rocky shore to where Harsey still held the branches back. The voices continued to speak as if they were right in front of the two men as the Executioner peered past the general's son to see a hidden pathway into the rocks. Looking at the ground, he saw that the weeds and stalks of grass growing out of the boulders on the path had been trampled flat.

Men, maybe Handsmen, had recently ascended the mountain using this trail. But where was their boat? How did they get there? Bolan had seen no watercraft anchored along the shoreline nearby. He supposed it could have been hidden, but he had searched both banks with the advantage of seasoning and experience, and he doubted he would have missed it. That left three possibilities.

Either the boat that had brought the men to this spot was tethered farther down river, they'd been dropped off or they had arrived by some other means on a land route hidden from the Executioner's view.

Bolan didn't speak. He and Harsey had both grabbed their SIG rifles as they disembarked the speedboat but now they slung them over their shoulders, out of the way. Harsey drew his sound-suppressed .22 pistol. The Executioner's equally quiet Beretta leaped into his hand.

Stepping past Harsey, Bolan led the way onto the stony path. He heard the soft rustle of dry leaves and limbs as the general's son stepped through the opening and released his hold on the bush. Slowly, aware of the soft grinding noise of loose pebbles beneath his boots, the Executioner started up the footpath into the rocks.

The course was more passage than path, rising at a steep forty-five-degree angle and spiraling past the rocky walls for perhaps thirty feet. Then, gradually, the grade leveled off. The voices remained clear as the two men climbed.

"You've got a headache?" a gruff voice said clearly. "You were drinking beer. How do you think I feel after downing that rotgut Lacie's brother-in-law makes?"

"It ain't rotgut, Bonner," another voice said. "That's the smoothest moonshine you'll ever see."

Bolan and Harsey moved along the flatter path until they came to another opening in the rocks. Unshielded by vegetation, both men pressed their backs against the stony walls and shuffled forward, their sound-suppressed weapons held down at the forty-five-degree ready angle. As they neared the mouth of the passage, Bolan saw an ancient rusted tractor surrounded by weeds twenty yards away. He moved closer, and from the new viewpoint he could see an abandoned shack beyond the rusty farm implement. The walls had rotted decades earlier and the roof had fallen in.

The voices—Bolan could tell they came from above them now—suddenly quieted. He moved back into the passageway between the rocks and they resumed. But when he stepped toward the tractor once more, they disappeared again. He nodded silently to himself. The acoustics in these mountains were strange, all right. In some places sound traveled as if propelled along radio waves. But they were in a dead zone at the moment.

The Executioner couldn't help wondering if his and Harsey's own quiet footsteps might be magnified and transported through the mountains.

Cautiously, Bolan stepped out of the passage into the valley where the tractor and ramshackle shack stood. He stayed close to the rocks, indicating with his hands that Harsey should watch their backs as he searched for another route upward. Moving along the mountainside, he hadn't gone far when he came to a break in the rocks. Through the clearing he could see the Snake River flowing by a hundred feet below. But what caught his eye next caused him to pause.

Etched into the rocks on both sides of the opening were several series of ancient petroglyphs. The Executioner could tell by the faded markings that they had been carved centuries ago. He wondered briefly what forgotten tribe of Indians might have done the inscriptions, and what they meant. But he wasn't there to do research for a history or archaeology textbook, and his mind moved back to the mission at hand.

From where he stood, the voices above could be heard but not their words. Bolan circled a large boulder which stood between him and the river, then worked his way between it and the mountain wall to its side. The voices were clear again.

"Suppose we ought to get up and around?" one of them asked. As he quit speaking the distinctive sound of a beer can popping open echoed down from the rocks.

"Hell, we ain't going to see nothing," answered another voice after another can had opened.

The two voices had been different than the first two. And by the laughter earlier, the Executioner knew there had to be at least a half-dozen men camped out somewhere overhead. Were they Handsmen? He didn't know yet. They had said nothing to help him decide but, at this point, they could just as easily be a bunch of good old boys escaping their wives for a few days on a camping trip.

The sounds and voices that came next erased that possibility.

"Jerome, get your ass over there and take a look." The metallic clink of a rifle bolt closing echoed through the rocks. "Harsey and that big bastard could be coming down the river right now for all we know, and Fred'll fry us for supper if we miss them."

"That's Colonel Moreland to you," came another new voice.

"Not since Russell showed up. He's back to just plain old Fred."

More laughter.

The Executioner paused. He remembered General Harsey mentioning Fred Moreland, the self-appointed Colonel of the Hands of Heaven. But the name Russell was a new one to him, and he wondered who the man might be. Someone who had overthrown Moreland for the seat of power among the Handsmen? He didn't know. He would, however, file the information away for future reference.

Bolan turned and motioned Harsey to stay and continue to watch the valley. He climbed on the boulder next to him and turned to face away from the river. He raised his head to peer over a ridge.

It came back down twice as fast as it had risen.

Just as his eyes came over the crest, Bolan saw a pair of black paratrooper boots shuffle forward toward the edge of the rocks. Ducking to a squatting position, he saw a man clad in well-worn camouflage standing over him, peering out over the canyon. The man hadn't seen him; his vision was glued to the water beyond. But that had been nothing more than a stroke of good luck—luck that wouldn't last forever. All he had to do was look down.

Without hesitation, Bolan dived away from the opening onto the ground. He hit as lightly as he could, but keeping complete silence under the circumstances was impossible.

"What the hell was that, Frank?" came a voice from above.

"Damned if I know," said the man at the edge of the rocks. "Want me to go down and check it out?"

There was a long pause, then the other man said, "Nah, probably a deer or something. Just yell down and tell it to be quiet. Noise hurts my head this morning."

Another round of laughs issued from overhead.

Bolan retraced his steps to where Harsey was scanning past the rusty tractor to the valley. "They're right above us," he whispered.

Harsey kept his eyes on the clearing as he answered. "Any idea how many?"

Bolan shook his head. "Half dozen I've heard. Could be more."

"You're sure they're Handsmen?"

The Executioner nodded. "Sounds like they were dropped off to watch the river for us." He paused. "Which means they'll have some kind of radio contact with their base."

Harsey took a deep breath. "What do you want to do?" he asked.

"Take them," Bolan answered. "But we still need at least one of them alive." He nodded toward the opening in the rocks and turned back, making his way silently back to the boulder. Risking a glance under the overhang, he saw that the man's boots were no longer visible. He might have gone back to the group. Then again, he might well have simply taken one or two steps back.

There was only one way to find out.

Bolan climbed the boulder again, the Beretta 93-R ready in his right hand. Again, he slowly climbed to the ridge where the man had stood. As soon as his eyes had risen over the rocky ledge, he realized his second guess had been the right one. The boots stood less than three feet away, and above them he saw a man wearing camouflage clothing, mirrored sunglasses and holding an M-16 in one hand, a can of beer in the other.

The man saw him.

Bolan could hear Harsey climbing onto the boulder at his side as he raised the Beretta and pumped a lone round into the man's lower abdomen. The near-silent 9 mm bullet caused the Handsman to double over and take an unsteady step forward.

"Frank...?" a voice called out from somewhere behind the man.

The man called Frank was less than a foot from the edge of the ridge, and Bolan aimed the Beretta. Another 9 mm round coughed through the barrel and out the suppressor into the Handsman's right knee.

Which was all the man needed to take another stumble forward and go sailing off the edge and down to the shoreline below.

"Son of a bitch!" shouted another voice from above. "Dumb fucking drunk fell off the ridge!"

Harsey stood next to the Executioner now. Rising to full height, Bolan jammed the Beretta into his pants and swung the

SIG from behind his back. He flipped the selector switch to full-auto and sprayed a volley of 5.56 NATO rounds over the ridge and into the leg of a Handsman trying to rise from his place beside the campfire.

But even as he fired, the Executioner realized that the chances of taking any of the men alive were slim. There were at least a dozen of them rather than the six different voices Bolan had heard speak.

And all of them were lunging for weapons.

7

The Executioner swept the SIG-551 across the men around the campfire, taking out three of them before they could grab for their rifles. Next to him, he heard Harsey open with his identical assault weapon. A fourth and fifth man fell to the ground.

From where they stood on the boulder, the ridge hit Bolan and Harsey chest level. They couldn't have asked for better cover—by leaning forward, they could use the ridge itself as a bench rest with only their heads and arms exposed.

But that didn't mean much, considering the fact that there were still six to eight men who had scooped up their weapons and were swinging them into play. Bolan knew they'd be lucky enough to get all the men with the easiest of shots, let alone take time for the selective targeting it would take to ensure that one of the Handsmen lived through the battle. He had shot the first man, at least, in the legs. Unless a stray round killed him now, the fallen Handsman would be alive a long time before he bled to death.

Bolan turned his rifle onto a tall, reed-thin Handsman wearing black plastic military-issue glasses. Sometime during the cold night, the man had slipped his hands into a pair of ski mittens.

The mittens might have saved him from frostbite the night before. But this morning, they cost him his life.

As the Handsman's clumsy fingers fumbled with his rifle, the Executioner tapped the trigger and sent a burst of 5.56 rounds through the parka the man had also worn against the cold. The NATO rounds ripped through the goose-down insulation, passed through the camouflage shirt beneath it and into the man's chest. A shriek escaped the Handsman's lips as he dropped his weapon and slithered to the ground.

Harsey had opened up full-auto and was cutting a figure-eight back and forth across the camp area between the rocks. Some of his rounds hit flesh. Others ricochetted off the stone walls of the mountain to zing back and forth around the clearing. Bolan felt one of the ricochetes fly past his head as he opened up on a Handsman wearing a fake sheepskin-lined denim jacket. Another burst from the Executioner's rifle turned the yellow lining red.

"Give up!" Bolan shouted above the gunfire. "Drop your weapons and you'll live!"

His words either went unheard among the clamor or were ignored.

A Handsman who had chosen insulated camouflage coveralls instead of a BDU got his M-16 around into play. But he was scared and fired blindly, using neither his sights nor the more effective close quarters technique of point-shooting. Bolan and Harsey both happened to choose him for a target at the same time, and a double burst of rounds struck his body from shin to nose, causing him to dance like a marionette before sliding down onto another dead body.

Bolan shouted again, pausing in his fire as he did so. "Drop them! You'll live!"

Again, his words went unheeded.

A Handsman in olive drab pants and a black sweatshirt also wore tight leather shooting gloves. The gloves had been a better combative choice than mittens.

But they weren't good enough.

Bolan swung the assault rifle toward the man as he tried to swing the AK-47 toward him. The Handsman began firing as soon as his leather-covered finger found the trigger, and the first few rounds struck the rocks ten feet in front of him, moving out until the last pair of 7.62 mm slugs skipped across the stone past Harsey and the Executioner.

Bolan dropped the SIG's smoking barrel to the man's chest and pulled the trigger.

Only two of the Handsmen were still on their feet, and Harsey changed that to one as the Executioner's soft-point rifle rounds continued to penetrate the black sweatshirt. As he turned his attention away from the falling gunman, he saw the final Handsman drop his rifle and turn to run.

"Stop!" the Executioner cried. "We'll let you live!"

He might as well have been talking to the wind whistling down through Hell's Canyon.

Swinging the SIG back across his shoulder, the Executioner pulled himself the rest of the way over the ridge and scrambled to his feet. The fleeing Handsman was making his way through the rocks, dodging outcroppings and short stubby trees. He disappeared around a curve in the trail.

Bolan knew he could catch the Handsman. The man was vastly overweight and didn't have that much head start.

"Stay here and make sure nobody shoots us in the back!" Bolan yelled to Harsey. There was always the chance one of the men was playing possum. And the Executioner was reasonably sure that the man he'd shot first in the legs would still be alive.

Bolan took off, dodging the same obstacles that had slowed the Handsman. He paused briefly at the place where the man had disappeared and drew the Beretta from where he'd jammed it in his belt. Although he doubted it, there was always the chance the fleeing Handsman had stopped just on the other side to set up an ambush. He waited, listening. When he heard no breathing or other sounds around the bend, he dropped low and let the 93-R lead the way around the turn.

As he'd suspected, the Handsman was no longer there. He had disappeared again in the rocks somewhere ahead.

The Executioner sprinted forward, running as fast as he could on the narrow trail through the mountains. He rounded the next bend and came out away from one of the mountains, looking down to see a drop of perhaps two hundred feet. He stayed close to the side of the mountain to his right as he raced on. Although he still couldn't see the escaping Handsman ahead, he heard the hard clomp of feet in between his own lighter footfalls.

When he'd rounded another of the many twists in the mountain path, the Executioner saw the man fleetingly as he disappeared around a corner twenty feet ahead. The pained sounds of wheezing echoed through the canyon as the man tired and gasped for air.

"Stop!" the Executioner yelled. "I don't want to kill you!"

Again, his words weren't heeded.

Not that it mattered, Bolan knew, as he ran on. The overweight man's breathing had grown increasingly labored. He had him.

The sudden scream echoed through the rocks like something out of an Alfred Hitchcock movie. The Executioner slowed. And while he would never know for sure, the scream might have saved his life. At half pace, Bolan rounded the next curve in time to see the Handsman run past a hairpin turn in the pathway and straight off the edge of the mountain. His forward momentum took him several feet out from the rocks before he began to fall.

Slowing further to keep from meeting the same fate himself, Bolan jogged to the edge of the bluff. Halfway down the side of the mountain the Handsman's arms were flailing like a windmill, as if he thought trying to fly might at least be worth a shot at this point. Another deathly scream proved that the man had realized such tactics were impractical.

A second later, the Handsman hit the side of the mountain near the bottom of the valley, crumpled into a ball and disappeared into the thick trees below.

The Executioner stood at the edge of the precipice for a moment, looking down to where the man had disappeared for the final time. There was no sense wasting time trying to find a way down to check and see if the Handsman had survived. It was impossible.

He had probably broken his neck. And every other bone in his body, as well.

Dropping the partially spent magazine from the Beretta, Bolan jammed a fresh box into the grip and holstered the weapon. Quickly, he retraced his steps back through the mountains to where Harsey sat on a rock waiting. The general's son heard him coming and raised the rifle in his hands, then lowered it. He answered the Executioner's question before it could be asked, looking at the men on the ground, then shaking his head.

"How about the first guy?" Bolan said. "The one I shot in the legs?"

"Bad luck," Harsey said. "Take a look."

Bolan moved to where the man had fallen and looked down. The camouflage pants were soaked a dark black from blood. A rip in the fabric pointed to the spot where one of the Executioner's rounds had drilled through the femoral artery—the only place below the waist that would have brought on such a fast death.

"Doesn't look like the gods are smiling on us today," Harsey said. He took a canteen from his belt, chugged half and extended his arm to Bolan. "Want some?" he asked.

Bolan shook his head. Combat brought on dehydration in most men. But he had seen so much of it over the years, it had lost its effect on him.

Harsey chuckled. "Should have known," he said as he replaced the canteen on his belt. "A man who doesn't eat or sleep probably doesn't drink water, either."

Bolan didn't answer. He knelt and began checking the men on the ground for any clues that might lead them to the Hands of Heaven compound. He wasn't particularly surprised when he found none. He took special note that unlike the other groups of Handsmen he had seen, there were no dark-skinned faces among this bunch.

Dropping back over the edge of the ridge to the boulder,

Bolan led the way past the tractor toward the shack in the valley. Again, he was hardly surprised when he found no leads to the Handsmen.

"What do we do now?" Harsey asked.

"Same as we've been doing."

The two men made their way back down out of the mountains to the *Norma*. Bolan lifted the anchor as Harsey started the engine and pulled them away from shore. The Executioner lifted the binoculars to his eyes.

The two men remained quiet as the *Norma* cruised down the river. Finally, Harsey broke the silence. "Tell me something, Mike," the general's son said.

"What?" Bolan asked as he swept the binoculars along the Oregon shore.

"Well, you don't eat, sleep or drink water, apparently. But I know you drink beer. I've seen that back at Dad's."

"Sometimes."

"You smoke?"

"Rarely," Bolan said. He kept the binoculars to his eyes. "Is there some point to this?"

To his side, the Executioner saw Harsey grin. "Just trying to figure out what you do for fun," he said. He paused, then a mock expression of sudden thought covered his face. "Hey, I know. You must spend all your free time with the ladies, eh?"

"I don't remember the last time I had any free time," Bolan said.

The Executioner suddenly focused the binoculars several hundred yards downriver. Something was moving. He squinted into the lenses, straining to make out what it was as his battle instincts went on alert.

Harsey, without the aid of his own binoculars, couldn't see it. But he had watched Bolan's body suddenly go rigid, and he immediately cut the engine, twisting the *Norma* toward shore.

The Executioner dropped the binoculars and reached for the SIG-551LB.

THROUGH THE NIGHT she ran. As if her life depended upon it.

As the sun began to rise over Hell's Canyon, Samantha Bass's body felt as if people had been beating her arms and legs with baseball bats throughout the night. There were differences between running up the rises and down into the valleys of Hell's Canyon and running the quarter mile on a flat cinder track. One of the main differences was footing. A track was secure; track-shoe spikes bit into it. But in Hell's Canyon, one step might find her on solid rock, the next on loose gravel and the third sinking to her ankles in mud.

Another difference was that there were no obstacles to dodge on a cinder track, and Samantha was beginning to wish she had specialized in the hurdles or the steeplechase rather than the quarter mile. So far, she had run headlong into two trees and skimmed the top of her head along the underside of a low overhang, missing being knocked cold by a matter of inches. As it was, she only had a sore scalp.

She supposed she should be grateful. If she'd knocked herself out, that would have been the end of it. She could also have sprained, or even broken, an ankle on this uncertain terrain, and that would have halted her flight as quickly as unconsciousness. In addition to the scrape burn on top of her head, she had cuts and slashes from tree branches on her arms and neck.

Suddenly Samantha Bass hit something. She fell to her knees, then rolled to her back on the ground, trying to catch the breath that had been knocked out of her as she stared painfully up at the stars shining down into the canyon.

Tears formed first in the corners of Samantha's eyes, then overflowed down her face. They were followed by a sudden jerk in her chest, which quickly became a constant, rhythmic series of sobs. Samantha couldn't take it anymore. She didn't even care if Moreland or the Hands of Heaven were nearby to hear her. Then she realized that if that were the case, the damage had already been done so she allowed herself to cry openly, loudly and without restraint. The crying lasted for a minute or two, then slowly began to subside.

The air finally returned to her lungs. Samantha Bass rose to a sitting position. In the moonlight, she saw the strange object. A machine of some type—an ancient, rusting machine.

"It's not fair," Samantha sobbed under her breath. "My life is just starting. There are so many things I want to know, want to learn. So many things I want to do, to experience." She clamped a hand over her mouth as soon as she realized she'd been speaking out loud.

Do something constructive, Samantha told herself. She had learned that in the trekker's club. Relax. Don't panic. Panic was the great killer.

Tears began to fall from her eyes again as Samantha Bass realized how foolish she had been to think the trekker's club had prepared her for this. She had been taught how to survive when lost in the woods, all right. But her training had been as much preparation for such a possibility as it was dealing with it. She had been taught to make sure she had matches, compasses, water-purification tablets and other gear. Well, she had none of those things—not even a pocketknife. And the trekker's club had never anticipated the possibility that while you were trying to fight off death in the wilderness, you might also be pursued by a bunch of crazy madmen wearing camouflage.

After another five minutes, Samantha had composed herself to the point where she believed she could go on. She took off at a brisk walk rather than a run. She had put some kind of distance between her and the Hands of Heaven camp. How much, she couldn't be sure. By now, even an imbecile like Moreland would have mounted a search. She could only hope she was far enough away that they wouldn't find her.

Samantha walked on through the night, up and down the crests and peaks. Hours—how many she couldn't be sure—went by. Her energy drained, both from physical exertion and mental stress. But just as she was ready to give up and lie down to cry once more, she saw a flickering of light through the rocks and trees. Her spirits suddenly rose with new hope, and she began to jog toward the light.

The vice president's daughter could make out more detail as she neared the light. It was a camp of some sort. Some kind of tourist place? Maybe a mining camp hidden away in the canyon? It didn't matter what it was. The people there would help her, she knew that. Even if they weren't the kind of people who helped human beings out of generosity, they'd be anxious to gain recognition as the ones who'd saved the vice president's daughter.

Samantha Bass's hopes soared further as she continued to near the camp. But something about it looked familiar. Had it been one of the places where she and her parents had stopped on their vacation in Hell's Canyon two summers ago? Was it one of the lodges where they had spent the night?

Reality suddenly struck Samantha Bass in the chest. She froze in her tracks and stared ahead in horror.

Of course the camp looked familiar. She had been in it only hours before.

All of the energy she had expended during the night had been a total and complete waste. She had run in circles through Hell's Canyon. And although she had returned to the other side of the camp from which she'd escaped, she was almost right back where she'd started—less than fifty yards away from the Hands of Heaven compound.

Samantha felt hot breath on the back of her neck as she heard a voice whisper, "Found you." The words were followed by a short muffled laugh.

BOLAN ADJUSTED the binoculars, concentrating on a small area downriver. It was a man. Tall and wiry, wearing desert camouflage pants and a black hooded sweatshirt with some kind of logo on the back, the man held a rod and reel in both hands, and as the Executioner watched he pulled a squirming fish from the river and dropped it into a net.

The Executioner lowered the binoculars, focusing on the

man's waist. He wasn't wearing a pistol. But the sheath of a huge knife was threaded through his belt, the tip of the sheath tied to his thigh with rawhide.

"Get her into shore as quickly as possible," the Executioner ordered Harsey. "He hasn't seen us yet."

Harsey required no explanation. He steered the *Norma* straight to shore on the Oregon side, dropping it skillfully into a small cove. Bolan continued to watch the fisherman through the binoculars. The man was preoccupied, grinning ear to ear as he reached into the river and pulled out a stringer dangling with more squirming fish, then turned to haul his catch away from the river and out of sight up an embankment.

The Executioner breathed a sigh of relief. It had been nothing more than a stroke of luck and timing that had kept the man's attention on his business. The *Norma* had been in full view for a good twenty seconds, and had the man not hooked the fish at that opportune moment he would have spotted them and sounded the alert to the other Handsmen.

Bolan and Harsey quickly anchored the speedboat and launched the Libra XT, then dropped over the rail of the *Norma* and into the kayak. The shore terrain between them and the spot where the man had been was thick with vegetation, and while that foliage would provide cover once they were near, it would slow their approach. It would also require using the Executioner's Hell's Belle like a machete—noise they didn't need. No, Bolan thought as he dropped his paddle into the water and began to stroke, they would be better off closing most of the distance by water, then switching to land for the final approach.

The two men kept the kayak hugging the shoreline, cutting visibility to a minimum from where the Executioner had spotted the fisherman. Was the Hands of Heaven compound up the rise where the man had disappeared? Bolan doubted it. They wouldn't build their camp in full view of the Snake River. More likely it was hidden farther back in the mountains, and the man had hiked down to the river to fish.

When they were fifty yards away, the Executioner motioned

toward shore with his hand. They angled the short distance to a bank of small boulders and, finding no place suitable to tie off the kayak, lifted it out of the water and set it on the rocks. Bolan scanned the immediate area. The trees were too thick to see through to the embankment where the fisherman had disappeared. But that didn't mean there weren't Handsmen concealed within those trees as sentries. For all he knew, he and Harsey could be in their crosshairs at that very moment.

With the kayak grounded away from the river current, Bolan unslung the SIG-551 and led the way off the rocky shore and into the trees. He heard Harsey's soft footsteps behind him as the general's son followed. The trees were thick, providing good cover for their final approach. But they also cut visibility as Bolan tried to skim his eyes across them, looking for any sign of posted guards. He saw none, and that fact disturbed him.

Something was wrong. Why were no men posted around the perimeter of their compound? That didn't seem to fit a group who appeared to have unlimited speedboats out prowling the river. Were the Hands of Heaven so sure of their hidden compound that they had grown too arrogant to post lookouts? That didn't follow either. Not considering the effort that had gone into the boat patrols.

Again, the Executioner heard the men's voices before he saw them. Muffled words and an occasional laugh came drifting through the trees. Bolan and Harsey dropped to their knees, slinging their rifles over their backs, then falling the rest of the way to their bellies and crawling forward.

Ten feet from the edge of the trees, Bolan maneuvered just to the side of a thick-needled pine tree. He waved behind him to halt Harsey. The general's son froze five feet to his rear. They were close enough, and the Executioner had a good view of the clearing. There was no sense in Harsey moving forward and taking the chance of being heard.

But what he saw beyond the trees brought another frown to the Executioner's face.

Perhaps two-dozen wood cabins stood in the clearing, and beyond them was a larger house. Another speedboat was moored beside the house. Bolan shifted slightly and cast his gaze toward the river. He could just make out the spot where the man had caught the fish. It was directly down the slope from the clearing, not twenty yards away.

The Executioner's eyebrows lowered. The cabins, the house, the training ground—the entire camp—was in clear view of the river. He'd been wrong about the camp being hidden farther in the mountains.

Bolan turned his attention back to the clearing. Closest to him, between the trees and the final cabin, was a large open grassy area, which was now being used as a training ground. Roughly fifty men filled the area, many dressed in camouflage pants like the fisherman had worn. Others wore brown or black Carhardt and Wall outdoor jeans of heavy canvas. But there were several common denominators in the men's appearance. For one thing, regardless of whether the men wore cammies or jeans, most, if not all, wore the same black hooded sweatshirts that the fisherman had worn. In addition, besides the rubber, wooden and aluminum training knives they held in their hands as they went about practicing blade drills, real knives of every size, shape and design hung from their belts. And the extra pockets afforded by the fatigue pants and outdoor jeans hadn't gone to waste, either. Folding knives from Spyderco, Cold Steel, Benchmade and Gerber seemed to be clipped into every available nook and cranny. Among them were almost as many high-dollar custom folders.

No, none of it made any sense, the soldier thought. While there looked to be a good hundred thousand dollars' worth of steel on the men, none of it had been formed into firearms. There were just knives. Not one gun of any kind was visible.

A militia that fought only with knives? Ridiculous.

Harsey started to move forward again but Bolan waved him back. He wanted time to figure out what was going on before he formed a plan of attack. Had the Hands of Heaven left their guns in the cabins while they trained knife techniques? If so, were there men armed with firepower hidden in the cabins and the house?

Where were Winston Bass and his daughter? Were they even there?

Bolan was close enough to make out the picture of the logo on the sweatshirts but not the words printed beneath it. The emblem was a takeoff of the age-old Jolly Roger skull and crossbones of pirate fame and featured a large skull wearing a flat-brimmed hat. Instead of bones, however, there were crossed Bowie knives.

Was it a logo for the Hands of Heaven? Were these even the Hands of Heaven, or some other paramilitary militia who just happened to have located in Hell's Canyon, too?

Bolan continued to watch the men train, but what he learned only led to more discrepancies and questions. For one thing, they each moved with a fluidity of motion that bespoke edged weapons skill far beyond what he would have guessed a rag-tag group of militiamen would possess. The fact was, these men as a whole were better trained with blades than most Special Forces soldiers or martial artists. And while the mood in the clearing was serious, it was hardly somber. The men were working hard but an occasional joke seemed to send them all into laughter—hardly the kind of atmosphere the Executioner would expect out of a bunch of militiamen holding the Vice President of the United States and his daughter hostage.

A door across camp slammed shut suddenly, and Bolan looked toward the house to see that a man had emerged. He looked vaguely familiar. The Executioner lifted the binoculars again to get a better look. The man was tall and wiry as the fisherman had been but if it was the same man he had changed clothes. The sweatshirt and cammie pants were gone, and in their place were a faded pair of brown Carhardt jeans, a matching jacket and brown felt, flat-brimmed hat. Wraparound sunglasses hid the eyes above a reddish-brown mustache and goatee. Shoved through his wide belt, however, was what looked like the same big knife the fisherman had worn. It was about the same size as Bolan's own Hell's Belle, but instead of the coffin handle on the Executioner blade, this knife featured some kind of hook at the pommel end.

But it was the way the man moved that finally convinced the Executioner he was looking at the same man he'd seen by the river. The man walked with the confidence of one who hid the strength of wiry muscles beneath his clothes. Yeah, Bolan thought, as he dropped the binoculars to the end of the strap again. It was the fisherman all right. He'd delivered his catch to the kitchen inside the house, and was returning to the training area.

What surprised the Executioner further was the reaction of the other men when the man arrived at the open area. All training came to an abrupt halt, and everyone turned to face him as if awaiting orders. It left no doubt in Bolan's mind as to who the leader of this group might be.

The man with the rust-colored goatee stopped at the edge of the group. He had opened his mouth to speak when a sudden sound from behind Bolan and Harsey echoed through the canyon. The sound was distinctive, unmistakable to anyone who had ever heard it before.

The slide of a pump action shotgun had just been racked forward along the barrel, then back into place to chamber a shell.

All of the heads in the clearing suddenly jerked up to squint past Bolan into the trees. Hands dropped to knife hilts.

The Executioner turned to see that Rick Harsey was still squatting behind him. But the general's son, too, had turned to look to the rear. Bolan looked up, beyond Harsey.

Behind the general's son stood a man with a Winchester 1200 12-gauge. He wore one of the now familiar hooded sweatshirts and plain khaki fatigue pants tucked into his black nylon combat boots.

Bolan's eyes stopped on the barrel of the shotgun aimed directly at him.

THE WINCHESTER pump gun had been fitted with a Choate folding stock but the man holding it had extended the stock and had it pressed into his shoulder. He glared over the barrel. Even from the distance he was at, Bolan could see his finger on the trigger. A thumb on the safety.

The man was roughly five feet ten inches tall, and Bolan guessed his weight at an even two hundred pounds. A lot of that weight was still muscle, and at one time the Executioner guessed it had probably all been. But now, in his midforties, he appeared to be one of those maturing warriors doomed to eventually lose the battle with middle age.

But the look in this man's eyes said he planned to extend that war.

Above the hooded sweatshirt, Bolan saw a completely bald head. It had the same pigmentation and shade as the man's face, meaning the shave job had not been recent. Bolan watched his eyes. They were greenish blue and had narrowed, telling the Executioner that the man was a hairbreadth away from pulling the trigger and would do so at the slightest provocation. Bolan remained still. This wasn't one of the bumbling-idiot good old boys General Harsey had said made up a large percentage of the Hands of Heaven. This man could kill. Would kill.

Then, just as suddenly as the shotgun slide had racked, a wide smile broke across his face. The man lowered the shotgun to his side and aimed it at the ground. "Dammit, Rick, are you trying to give me a heart attack?" he said. "What's the idea sneaking up on us like this?"

Rick Harsey rose to his feet and shook his head in disbelief. His quick laugh betrayed more anxiety than humor. "If anyone has a heart attack it's going to be me, Gary," he said. He walked forward to shake the man's hand. "I might ask you the same thing. What are you doing sneaking up behind us?"

The man called Gary shrugged. "I had to take a leak and the bathrooms are all the way over on the other side of the camp. So while I'm out there fertilizing the wildflowers I see these two diabolical forms creeping through the trees. It seemed to warrant caution."

"You always carry a shotgun when you pee?" Harsey asked.

Gary laughed. Then, glancing up at the mountains, he said, "Actually, out here we all do. It's loaded with slugs for bear, shot for snakes. Alternate rounds."

Bolan nodded. It made sense to him.

While Gary and Harsey had been speaking, the men training in the clearing had started pouring through the trees with Bowie knives, Arkansas Toothpicks, bolos and other serious edged weapons in their hands. A few had even drawn short swords.

Gary held up a hand. "Slow down, guys," he said. "Everything's cool."

The big blades lowered, but Bolan noticed they didn't get resheathed. Not quite yet.

Harsey turned to the Executioner. "Mike Belasko, meet an old buddy of mine, Gary Kirk."

The bald man extended his hand to the Executioner. He had a firm grip.

The leader of the group—the man with the red goatee—stepped to the front of his men. Bolan glanced down to the man's side. At close range he could now see that the big knife the man wore was indeed a Hell's Belle. And the strange "hook grip" was actually an intricately carved and decorated eagle head.

"Hello, Rick," the man said.

Harsey laughed again, and this time the nervousness in his voice was gone. "James Albert," he said. "Nobody's killed you yet?"

Albert returned a chuckle. "Nobody's even tried for quite awhile," he said.

As Albert and Harsey shook hands, Bolan finally got a look at the words beneath the skull-and-crossbones emblem on the men's sweatshirts. It read Edge Quest 2000: A New Millennium, A New World, and below that XLR8. The Executioner caught himself smiling. XLR8. *Accelerate*. He didn't know yet who the men were, but it was clear they weren't the Hands of Heaven. And they weren't some other far-out militia either, or Harsey wouldn't have been acting so friendly.

Albert's eyes narrowed slightly. He glanced from the SIG-551 slung over Bolan's back to the one Harsey wore. "So, Rick, I guess you're still mad about that little blonde in Walla Walla twenty years ago?" he said. The reference was obviously an inside joke of some kind. But what it really meant was that Albert was curious as to why the two men were so heavily armed.

Harsey laughed. "No, Jim, you paid dearly for stealing her from me by having to marry her," he said. He turned to the Executioner. "Belasko," he said, "our friend here is naturally curious about what we're up to. And several times over the past couple of days, you've offered to listen to me if I thought I had a better plan. I didn't." He paused and his face went serious. "But I think I just might."

Bolan nodded. He knew what it was and had already thought of it himself—as soon as he'd realized these men were friends rather than foes. But there were problems with the plan that would have to be resolved before, and if, they chose to put it into effect.

Without responding to Harsey, the Executioner turned to Albert. "Why don't you get your men training again? Most of them, at least. Pick one or two you trust and we'll talk."

Albert squinted in curiosity beneath the wide-brimmed hat. "Whatever it is, it sounds interesting."

"Oh, it has been," Harsey said. "And it keeps getting better all the time."

BOLAN FINISHED the last of his pork chop, scalloped potatoes and green beans and took a drink of iced tea. He looked across the table at James Albert. The man had eaten earlier and now sat drinking coffee.

The conversation had been light while the cook served their food. Bolan had learned that Harsey had known both Albert and Kirk for years, bumping into them now and then the way men of action occasionally crossed paths. From Albert, the Executioner had learned that Edge Quest was a four-day close-quarters combat school, which concentrated on the use of edged weapons. Sponsored by Albert's company, Edge Quest, Incorporated, it took place at the same lodge each summer. Experts at hand-to-hand fighting from all over the United States came to hone their blade skills as well as practice stick and other weaponry. All of the attendees were of instructor level themselves, and many were police or elite military trainers, or at least martial artists with decades of experience.

Interspersed with Albert's explanation, Harsey had made it clear that James Albert was considered by many to be the "best of the best," so it was to him the other experts came to further their own knowledge. While Albert had politely declined to tell Bolan that himself, the Executioner had seen no embarrassment on the man's face when Harsey spoke the words. But Bolan could tell it wasn't an inflated ego that kept Albert from blushing or arguing with the compliment. It was more as if he just accepted his abilities as the natural result of a life dedicated to the pursuit of close-quarters combat skills.

The Executioner liked the man's confidence. And the lack of false modesty was refreshing. Edge Quest, Bolan also learned, sponsored other seminars in everything from firearms to jungle survival. In addition, Albert had recently begun a computer on-line magazine for warriors, made combat-training videotapes and taught regular classes at a studio in Walla Walla, Washington.

Bolan drained the last of his tea and glanced across the table at Gary Kirk, who sat next to Albert. Kirk was a retired police officer from one of the Southwestern states whose specialty had been undercover work. A thirty-year martial artist, he had ended that career teaching weapons and hand-to-hand at the academy, then had been pressured into retirement for refusing to stick with the state certification board's politically correct party line.

Or, as Kirk himself had put it, "I got sick of teaching fancy crap that looked pretty but got officers killed on the street." Perhaps most surprising was how Kirk made his living. He had fictionalized many of his police experiences and become a novelist. Under a pseudonym, he penned a popular mystery series, which featured an unorthodox renegade detective.

Bolan had studied both Albert and Kirk intently as they spoke. His instinct told him they were good men and could be trusted. Which in turn meant he could put them to good use in his search for Winston and Samantha Bass.

Harsey was on his fourth pork chop when Bolan turned to him. "Rick, you might fill these guys in on what we're doing."

Harsey took a final bite, then did so. When he was finished, Albert and Kirk turned to look at each other in surprise. "We do lose touch out here," Albert said. "We hadn't even heard about the kidnappings."

The Executioner realized that the abductions had taken place during the first day of the Edge Quest seminar, after the men in attendance had already been far beyond conventional communication. Indeed, Albert had already told them the only contact the lodge had with the rest of the world was an emergency-only marine phone. The story of Winston Bass and his daughter might have made the headlines of every newspaper in the world but it was news to the Edge Questers.

"I've heard about the Hands of Heaven," Albert said, turning back to face Bolan. "Fact is, a couple years ago we had a bunch of cops show up here thinking we were them. They'd seen us wearing cammo and knives and such." His eyebrows lowered under the brim of his hat. "But from all I've heard, these Handsmen sound like incompetent idiots. How in hell did they ever pull off a job like kidnapping the VP and his daughter?"

"It's beginning to look like their strings are being pulled by someone else," the Executioner said. "I haven't put all the pieces together yet but my guess is the Hands have become cannon fodder for some more organized group."

Both Albert and Kirk leaned forward slightly, obviously interested. "What leads you to believe that?" the man with the red goatee asked.

The Executioner explained about the darker-skinned bodies, probably of Middle Eastern descent, he and Harsey had left in their wake, and how the men's presence seemed to contradict the racial bigotry attributed to the Hands of Heaven.

Albert and Kirk both nodded their understanding. "Prejudice is an indulgence of those in a position to indulge in it," Kirk said. "When it comes time for the action, most folks will use whoever is available to help them regardless of race, color or creed."

"So, Belasko," Albert said, "you wouldn't have told us all this unless you thought we had something to contribute."

"First, there are a couple of issues we need to iron out," Bolan said. He looked to Kirk. "If we don't find the vice president and his daughter before the FBI and ATF, there might be serious causalities." He paused a second, then asked, "You have any problem racing against your former associates?"

Kirk's eyes narrowed menacingly. Then his expression turned to one of deep thought. He lifted a hand and extended one, then two, then finally a third finger. "During my twenty years as a cop, I worked with maybe three Feds who didn't make me want to puke," he said. "And they were all DEA." He dropped his hand. "No, I don't have any problem."

Bolan concealed his smile. Such feelings toward federal law enforcement weren't uncommon among local and state cops these days. "Fine," he said. He turned to Albert. "You've got more knives in camp than the annual Atlanta Blade Show. But so far, the shotgun's the only firearm I've seen. On the *Norma* we've got a few extra—"

"The *Norma*?" Albert interrupted.

"Our boat," Harsey interjected. "It's anchored upriver."

"Ah," Albert said, nodding. "Love the name."

"We've got a few extra guns onboard," Bolan finished. "But not enough to arm everybody here."

A trace of a smile played at Albert's lips. "Officially," he said, "the shotgun is the only gun here." He glanced toward the kitchen but the cook was long gone. "Lodge rule." The smile spread. "But if you checked the cabins, I suspect you will find many pistols of some sort in the luggage."

Bolan nodded. These men were warriors, not just passing their time with wooden knives instead of golf clubs. They weren't troublemakers and they kept within the lodge's rules—at least on the surface. But the rules of common sense came before that of the lodge, and heading into backcountry like Hell's Canyon without firearms didn't fall under that heading.

"Item three," the Executioner said. "Who *don't* we want with us? There were roughly fifty Edge Questers in your camp, Albert. Anytime you get that many men together, no matter how elite the criteria might be, a few bad seeds sneak through."

Albert knew what he meant. "Only two," he said.

"Johnson and Baker," Kirk added. "Not bad guys, overall. But they spend most of their time in Walt Disney's Fantasy Land, if you know what I mean."

"I'll give them some important special assignment here at camp," Albert said. "I'll tell them we think the lodge might be attacked while we're gone."

"Oh, they'll love that." Kirk laughed. "Give them some kind of titles, too, Jim. That'll get their coffee percolating."

Albert frowned in further thought. "And if they've brought guns, I'll tell them we need the firepower with us. That'll keep them from shooting at shadows. Or us when we come back."

Bolan stood. "Then let's get moving. Go speak to Johnson and Baker and get them out of the way. Then get the rest of the men loaded on your boat. Harsey and I'll head back and pick up the *Norma*, then meet you a mile or two downriver past the lodge to explain things to the rest of the men. That way Johnson and Baker won't hear."

Albert and Kirk stood and headed out.

The Executioner watched them as the two Edge Quest men

left the dining area. He'd have preferred to have Able Team or Phoenix Force or some of the Stony Man Farm blacksuits with him on this leg of the search. But his gut instinct told him that these men could do the job, and do it well.

With no further words, Bolan and Harsey walked out of the mess hall and headed back toward the *Norma*.

The two speedboats—the *Norma*, and the Edge Questers' boat, which had been christened the *Rebecca*—sailed quietly down the Snake River in the midmorning sunlight. Like the *Norma*, it turned out that the Edge Questers' boat had also been rented from Rick Harsey's friend Tom Majors. Slightly slower than the boat Harsey piloted, it was nevertheless a top-of-the-line craft. Of course there was another reason the *Rebecca* wouldn't be slicing through the river with the same speed as the *Norma*, Bolan realized, as he scanned the shoreline with the Bushnell Yardage Pro 800 binoculars.

The boat carried somewhere between nine and ten thousand extra pounds of human cargo.

The Executioner dropped the Yardage Pros from his eyes and turned to catch a glimpse of the *Rebecca*, a good quarter mile behind them. All of the Edge Questers, with the exception of a couple who had come down from Canada, had produced various handguns from their luggage. James Albert had a CAR-15 in his equipment bag. Gary Kirk and a Quester named Rafe had smuggled in semiauto rifles, too. Mark Kane, a psychologist who had flown all the way from Pennsylvania to attend the seminar, had brought along a sawed-off shotgun. Bolan wondered if the man had bothered to get the tax stamp from the Bureau of Alcohol, Tobacco and Firearms. Probably. One of the first things he had noticed about the Edge Quest warriors was that they worked within the law.

In the distance, Bolan could barely make out the barrels of

four other rifles peeking over the rail of the *Rebecca*. Those weapons had come from General Richard Harsey's arsenal, as extra backup rifles he and Rick had brought along. There were two M-16s, one Heckler & Koch G-3 rifle and a Ruger Mini-14. The Executioner had commissioned Albert with the task of choosing which of his men should get the long arms, and had watched Albert's eyes narrow in thought as the Edge Quest sponsor carefully selected his riflemen. Bolan had smiled inwardly as all but one of the weapons went to men well over the age of thirty.

James Albert, the Executioner recognized, was a born leader of men. If there was to be limited firepower, he would put it into the hands of those who could make the most of it. Men who not only had training and ability but also maturity and experience.

Bolan lifted the Yardage Pros again and focused more intently on the other boat. Except for Albert and Kirk, all of the other men were on the bench seats. They had been placed under the command of two assistant instructors. Mabe Davidson was a short, lean-muscled man in his late-thirties with coal-black hair and a matching beard. The soldier remembered him leading the group during the training session he had watched from the trees, and the man's speed with a blade was almost frightening. The other assistant instructor was the only man in his twenties to which one of the rifles had gone. Josh Robertson was clean shaven, wore a plaid flannel shirt hanging outside his jeans instead of an Edge Quest sweatshirt, and showed maturity far beyond his years.

James Albert and Gary Kirk had been conscripted to ride with Bolan and Harsey on the *Norma,* and the Executioner's eyes now turned to the tall wiry man on the speedboat's port side. Albert's CAR-15 hung from the sling over his right shoulder, the barrel forward in assault mode. The Edge Quest sponsor was also armed with a Glock 20 10 mm pistol, extra magazines and his eagle-head Hell's Belle.

Bolan had first spotted Albert wearing cammies and one of

the now-familiar hooded sweatshirts while he fished. Then the man had switched to the brown jacket and jeans he'd worn during the meeting with Bolan, Kirk and Harsey. Now, Albert had changed yet again, and was dressed in black canvas Carhardts, another matching jacket and a wide-brimmed black oilskin hat, secured under his chin by a leather cord.

As the speedboat puttered slowly through the water, the Executioner glanced quickly to the bow of the boat where Gary Kirk sat scanning the Idaho mountains with his binoculars. The bald man had his AK-47 strapped to the handrail next to him. On his right hip, he wore an old Browning Hi-Power. The Browning—similar to Harsey's but in 9 mm rather than .40 S&W—held thirteen rounds in the magazine and one in the chamber. But two extra 20-round magazines extended high from a carrier on his belt. On his left hip, in a cross-draw sheath, Kirk carried a wide ten-inch Combat Smatchet.

Bolan turned back to the river and lifted the binoculars once again. Coming across the Edge Quest men had been a stroke of luck. Bolan was thankful for the brief period during which he'd been able to watch their training unobserved from the trees. Unlike many martial arts seminars, these men were training for reality rather than show. They weren't caught up in pretty-to-look-at-but-ineffective forms, and they weren't practicing their skills for competition.

The men at Edge Quest were training for combat, be it a street attack after they returned to their respective homes or all-out war right there in Hell's Canyon. They weren't artists or sportsmen. And they sure weren't a militia.

They were warriors, pure and simple. Which was exactly what the Executioner needed.

The *Norma* hopped over a short stretch of rapids along the Snake River. Ahead, just before the curve, the river narrowed and was surrounded by steeper rocky banks. The chirps of the birds in the sky overhead were all that broke the silence in the canyon. Usually, sound traveled well across water. But with all of the interference from the bends in the river and the mountainous banks, Bolan couldn't even hear the purr of the *Rebecca's* jet engines behind them.

That quickly changed.

A hundred feet or so from the curve ahead, the roar of another craft heading upriver abruptly filled the Executioner's ears. "Cut the engines!" he shouted at Harsey. "Pull toward shore!" Bolan's eyes skirted the shoreline for any available cover. The boat coming toward them might be nothing more than an early morning charter of sightseers. But his gut instinct told him it was another of the Handsmen's patrols.

With the jets off, the *Norma* slowed in the water. But the Executioner's directive to steer into shore had come too late for Harsey to comply. The boat glided silently around the curve, and suddenly the oncoming craft appeared, bearing down on them twenty feet ahead.

"Brace yourselves!" Bolan shouted. He lifted his hands from the outside rail and turned to grasp the railing that separated the passenger area from the steering deck. He had just looked back over his shoulder when the other boat struck the *Norma's* bow.

The screech of steel against steel echoed through the canyon as the two boats collided midriver. The force of the crash threatened to jerk the soldier's hands from the rail, sending streaks of seering pain up his arms and into his shoulders and neck. Harsey had braced himself against the steering column and looked as if he'd been pressed into the wheel with a steamroller. Bolan couldn't see James Albert but he heard something heavy come sliding along the floor between the two rows of seat.

The bewildered eyes in Gary Kirk's bald head looked up as the man suddenly slid to a halt on his back next to the Executioner. He was shaken and confused but looked otherwise unharmed.

Bolan twisted to see that James Albert had survived the crash by hugging one of the bench seats with both arms. As the boat continued to rock in the aftermath of the collision, the Edge

Quest leader let go of the seat and wrapped his hands around the CAR-15 tethered over his shoulder. Bolan released the rail and snatched the SIG-551 LB from where it was tied to the rail. He turned back to the other boat. There was no doubt in his mind that it was the Hands of Heaven.

The fifty to sixty men on board were decked out for war in cammies and other gear. As for rifles, the patrol boat could have passed for a National Guard armory.

Bolan swung the barrel of the SIG around. The bows of the two boats had locked together. A getaway was out of the question. And until the *Rebecca* caught up to them, Bolan, Harsey, Albert and Kirk were outnumbered fifteen to one. The crash had taken place out of the *Rebecca*'s sight. Had they heard the noise? Maybe. There was a chance, but it was slim. Bolan hadn't even heard the patrol boat coming until they were almost upon it. And the *Rebecca* was still a good quarter mile behind them. The other boat would have no reason to increase speed from its present crawl. It could be several minutes before they arrived at the scene.

Minutes in which all four men on the *Norma* could be killed several times over.

The Executioner aimed his rifle at the other boat and looked at the cammie-clad men on deck. They, too, had been shaken by the crash and were in total disarray. He, Harsey, Albert and Kirk had only one chance. They had recovered from the shock faster than the men on the other boat. If they could take advantage of that stroke of luck, they might survive.

Bolan pulled the SIG's trigger and sprayed a full-auto burst over the *Norma*'s rail. He guessed he'd have time to empty one magazine into the men before they recovered and returned fire. But when they did, he and his comrades would stand out like silhouette targets on a gun range. Their only chance, therefore, was two-pronged: Take out as many of the Handsmen as possible with the first round of fire, then close with the enemy, boarding the boat and fighting hand-to-hand so the Handsmen couldn't fire indiscriminately without hitting their own troops.

Then Bolan's men would have to try to stay alive until the *Rebecca* rounded the curve, saw what had happened and joined the fight to even the odds.

With his finger held against the trigger, Bolan emptied the rest of the magazine's 5.56 mm slugs. Cries of surprise, pain and terror shot up from the Handsmen in the seats and on the deck. As soon as the SIG ran dry, the Executioner dropped it and drew the Beretta in one hand, the Desert Eagle in the other. "Let's go!" he shouted at the top of his lungs as he stepped onto the bow of the boat and fired both weapons. He had no time to stop and explain his battle plan. But he had now worked with Harsey enough to be confident that the general's son would know what he had in mind. He could only hope that Albert and Kirk were just as battle savvy.

The Executioner continued firing with both pistols as he leaped over the locked rails of the two boats. He landed on his feet, his knees slightly bent to soften the fall. He had seen half a dozen men take hits from his autofire a moment earlier and he knew his pistol rounds had found Handsmen as well. Now, he sent a 3-round burst from the Beretta into the chest of a man with muttonchop sideburns. At the same time a .44 Magnum slug from the Desert Eagle burned through the face of a Handsman wearing a camouflage baseball cap.

Bolan stayed in his combat crouch, lifting both guns to eye level and pulling the triggers over and over. The Handsmen were so mashed together on the deck that there was no need to pick out targets.

To his side, the Executioner saw James Albert come over the rail and land on the body of a dead Handsman. The Edge Quest leader started to fall, checked his balance and raised his Glock in both hands. More men fell.

Harsey had kept the trigger back on his own SIG 551 until the magazine ran dry, before switching to his Browning Hi-Power. A second later, Kirk jumped to the top of the inter-locked rails, evidently recovered from his disorienting slide down the aisle. Instead of his own blue-battered Browning, the bald man held the wide leaf-bladed Smatchet in his hand.

As he fired the last rounds from both the Beretta and Desert Eagle, the Executioner smiled. He'd been right about Albert and Kirk. They, too, had realized that mingling with the Handsmen at close range was their only hope. And Kirk even knew that the time for all shooting had ended. It was time to close the gap and use the Handsmen as human shields while they killed them. And that fact had brought a grinning snarl to Kirk's face.

After all, knife fighting was the reason he and the other men of Edge Quest had come to Hell's Canyon in the first place.

Bolan emptied the Beretta and Desert Eagle, shoved them both into his belt and drew the Hell's Belle in his right hand. His left found the Applegate-Fairbairn dagger. He stepped quickly forward as a Handsman with a three-day growth of beard tried to lift the barrel of his M-16 into play. Bolan brought the big Bowie down across the man's left forearm. The razor edge slashed all the way through the bone, not stopping until it hit the steel of the rifle below.

The Handsman looked down in shock, his mouth gaping open as he watched his hand and half of his arm fall to the deck. The rifle barrel, no longer supported, tilted downward, away from the Executioner.

Bolan took another half step in and thrust the Applegate-Fairbairn over the falling barrel and into the man's heart.

In his peripheral vision, the Executioner saw why James Albert had come to be regarded as the premier knife guy. The Edge Quest leader had drawn a second edged weapon from somewhere under his jacket—a twelve-inch spear-point Crossada similar to the one Calvin James of Phoenix Force carried. Albert's arms looked like windmills as they began cutting figure eights through the flesh before him. Bolan recognized movements found in several of the Filipino blade systems. But just as he thought that must be the man's background, Albert suddenly halted the circular movements and lunged forward with the Crossada, executing a Western fencing thrust, which would have put the great Italian swordsman Aldo Nadi to shame.

A loud, animal-like roar sounded behind the Executioner. A split second later he saw Gary Kirk flying through the air. The bald man's Smatchet was held in a two-handed reverse grip over his head. Kirk came down on a Handsman with two-hundred pounds of weight and the added propulsion from his jump, driving the Smatchet into the man's chest up to the guard. His momentum took them both to the deck but Kirk was instantly back on his feet, ready to go again.

A glimpse of Rick Harsey out of the corner of his eye told Bolan that the general's son had realized he was underknifed for the current battle, having only his Livesay Air Assault. But Harsey was nothing if not an improvisor, and he pressed his Browning Hi-Power into service as a bludgeon. With the barrel gripped in his fingers, Bolan watched him bring the handle of the pistol down on top of the head of another Handsman trying to draw a blade from his belt. A sharp crack resounded along the river as the Browning's butt caved in the man's skull.

As the Executioner had hoped they would, the Handsmen had refrained from using their firearms, afraid they might hit their own men. And when Bolan, Harsey and the two Edge Questers had suddenly leaped on board a short second wave of shock occurred. The Handsmen found it hard to believe that four men would have the courage to close with sixty others bent on killing them.

But the Handsmen were recovering from their surprises, and knives appeared in their hands. They began to crowd closer, trying to corner the invaders at various points around the speed-boat. At least thirty of them still remained unharmed, and their plan was to kill the four men from the *Norma* with the sheer force of numbers.

And unless the *Rebecca* arrived soon, the Executioner knew they would do just that.

Samantha Bass felt what little resolve to escape she had left dissolve in one instant release. Suddenly, she felt no more fear, no more anxiety. Emotionally she was completely dead. Soon she would be physically dead as well.

The Hands of Heaven man who had snuck up behind her would kill her as punishment for trying to escape. Or maybe he'd drag her back to the camp, then throw her down into the hole with her father again. But if the man behind her was that foul-smelling Conway, he would rape her and perform all manner of sexual atrocities on her before she died. But she no longer cared.

Because it didn't matter, Samantha realized as the rough hands that had grabbed her rolled her to her back. She would not be going to college. She would never see Randy Holly again. One way or another, she was about to die.

All these thoughts raced through Samantha's mind without the terror she would have guessed would accompany them. The heart inside her chest felt like a lifeless rock, and her suddenly limp arms and legs could have been made of Silly Putty, ready to be twisted, smashed and molded into whatever shape the man above her might desire. But then, Samantha's mind fixated on the last of the thoughts about what she wouldn't have experienced before her young life ended—Randy Holly, and the fact that she would never see the handsome young Secret Service agent again.

Why had Holly entered her mind during these last moments of life? There could be only one answer. Her feelings for him were more than just a girlish crush. It was love.

Looking up at the man above her, half expecting to see Conway already pulling down his zipper, instead she saw the face of Randy Holly. Samantha Bass thought it was only a hallucination brought on by her thoughts.

Holly held his finger to his lips and whispered, "Shh, quiet." He reached down, gently taking her hands and hauling her to her feet. Samantha watched him wince in pain with the movement, and saw blood seeping through his shirt. It wasn't until then that she got her first hint that his sudden appearance wasn't just some stress-induced mirage. Was this real? Had Randy Holly actually found her?

"Come on," Holly whispered, taking her arm as soon as she was on her feet.

Samantha didn't speak. It all seemed too good to be true—and she still wasn't completely certain she wasn't experiencing some sort of illusion. But, she didn't care. If she could choose between the real world of the past couple of days and this sudden fantasy, she'd take this one, hands down.

So she let Holly take her arm, and whether in reality or her imagination, walked quietly off with him and away from the horrible reality of the Hands of Heaven compound in the distance.

THE MARINE HORN didn't sound like a police siren. But it served the same purpose, causing all heads on the Hands of Heaven speedboat to turn toward it as the *Rebecca* rounded the curve in the Snake River.

Using an underhand upward thrust, Bolan drove the Hell's Belle Bowie into the lower abdomen of a Handsman, then ripped the blade toward his chin, disemboweling the man. The two entangled boats were several hundred feet downriver from the point of the crash, having drifted with the current. They had also moved against the high rock walls of the steep shoreline, and banged into the embankment every few feet. It made for unsteady footing and an almost mass hysteria among the Handsmen.

The fight continued, with Bolan, Kirk and Albert ripping and slicing away with their double knives, and Harsey using his Air Assault to cut and slash and the Browning Hi-Power as an improvised war hammer. In his peripheral vision, Bolan saw the *Rebecca* pull up alongside them and cut her engines. Hands reached across the water to grasp the rail of the speedboat, and then the rest of the Edge Quest men began pouring onto the deck like something out of an old Errol Flynn movie.

Mabe Davidson came first, bounding over the rail and looking for all the world like a pirate with his dark hair and beard. In one hand, he held a Black Cloud short sword. In the other, a long Arkansas Toothpick dagger. With a vicious blow, Davidson slashed down through the fending arm of a Handsmen and sank the blade deep into the man's shoulder. The Arkansas Toothpick followed, penetrating the Handsman's chest, and a split second later four inches of its needle point came out the man's back, dripping with blood.

Josh Robertson was only a half step behind Davidson with a Cold Steel "Bad Ax" in his right hand. The Bad Ax—a modern rendition of the famous double-edged weapon of medieval days—slashed into the skull of a Handsman with a dull thud that reverberated along the river.

The sudden shift in the odds, combined with Robertson's and Davidson's decisive actions, broke the collective spirit of the Handsmen. A few turned to face the new oncoming Edge Questers but their efforts had lost fervor. They fell immediately to the more experienced knife experts.

Bolan and the original crew of the *Norma* finished the men they had already engaged, then stepped back as the rest of the Hands of Heaven shrank to the far side of the boat. Weapon after weapon clanged against the deck with resounding rings as the Handsmen let them fall from their fingers. Frightened whimpers and murmurs of despair tumbled from their lips.

One louder voice within the terrified mass summed up their feelings. "We give up!" The men's empty hands shot high in the air.

Regardless of how much the Hands of Heaven might deserve death, the Questers weren't about to butcher unarmed enemies who had surrendered. Bolan watched as the huge pieces of steel in their hands lowered.

But the men of Edge Quest stayed ready.

The Executioner herded the surviving Handsmen—there were roughly a dozen—to one corner of the boat. They undoubtedly had other hidden weapons but frisking them on board would be risky and would offer too much opportunity for a sudden sneak attack. Under such conditions, well-concealed hideouts might also be overlooked and lie in wait to create future trouble. No, he needed to get them to shore before the search began.

"Watch them closely," the Executioner growled to the Edge Questers as he moved toward the bow. Gary Kirk and James Albert joined him, and the three men jerked the *Norma* apart from the Handsmen's boat. Rick Harsey vaulted back onto the *Norma* a split second after the two boats had separated.

Albert fired the Handsman's engine back to life while Harsey did the same aboard the *Norma*.

"You," Bolan said, pointing to a tall well-built Edge Quester with a ponytail. "Your name?"

"Anton Zanna," the man said with a good-natured smile.

"Can you steer the boat?"

Zanna smiled wider. "I did it all the way here," he said. The Executioner recognized the accent as Hungarian.

"Then do so again," Bolan said.

Zanna jumped the rails to the *Rebecca* and slipped behind the steering column.

On Bolan's command, James Albert turned the Handsmen's boat in the water, steering it past the steep embankment to where the rock wall became flatter shore. Kirk dropped the anchor over the side, then he, Bolan and Albert herded the Handsmen off onto a pebbly stretch of coast.

Bolan stretched the Handsmen out on the ground in two rows, face down, with their arms to their sides. A few seconds later, Anton Zanna pulled the *Rebecca* in next to the Handsmen's craft, and a moment after that Harsey joined the fleet with the *Norma*.

Albert, Kirk, Josh Robertson and the Pennsylvanian psychologist, Dr. Mark Kane, were sent in to search the prisoners on the ground. Kane held his sawed-off shotgun on the men as the others patted them down. They came up with a multitude of tiny backup weapons, from Derringers and minirevolvers to boot knives.

When they were satisfied they had found the last of the militia's weapons, Robertson looked up at the Executioner and nodded. The searchers stepped away from the prone Handsmen and began dividing up the spoils of war. The Edge Questers kept the tiny guns and better hideout knives. Blades of lower quality were subjected to severe ridicule before being cast into the river.

"Sit up," Bolan ordered the men on the ground.

Slowly, they rose to sit on the pebbly shoreline.

Bolan studied them. Unlike the groups who had attacked them on earlier occasions, which had contained a few darker-skinned men, all of these Handsmen were white. They looked particularly pale in the morning sunlight, and Bolan wondered again at the strange descrepancies conjured by a militia such as this.

The Executioner let his eyes bore into the frightened faces before him. "I don't plan to waste a lot of time questioning you," he said. "I'll ask a question, you'll answer. Those are the rules." He paused, then said, "Are Winston and Samantha Bass at your camp?" His eyes fell on a clean-shaven Handsman in his midtwenties with long greasy hair. "You. Answer."

The man stared at the Executioner with false bravado. "You're going to get name, rank and serial number from us," he said. "Nothing else."

Bolan took a step in and brought his boot up sharply into the man's mouth. A loud crack echoed through the canyon as the young Handsman's head snapped back. A moment later, he lay on his back looking up dazedly at the sky. Blood drooled down the corners of his lips. He opened his mouth and blew several teeth out as if he'd just bitten into a handful of rotten popcorn.

The Executioner leaned over him. "I don't want to know your name, kid," he said. "And you don't have any rank or serial number because you aren't real soldiers. You're a bunch of misfits who like to dress up in camouflage and play army as if you were eight-year-old boys.'' He turned his attention to an older man with gray streaks through his hair who sat next to the youngster. "How about you?" he asked the man. "You in the market for a new set of dentures?"

The older man looked as if he were just glad to have survived the day this far. "No, sir," he said.

"Then I'll ask you. Are Winston and Samantha Bass at your base camp?"

"Yes, sir. The vice president and his daughter are back at camp, all right."

The rest of the Handsmen nodded their agreement.

"What's your name?" Bolan demanded of the gray-haired man. He glanced again at the kid who was still spitting blood and teeth, then back to the older man. "Now."

The man with the gray hair straightened the lapel of his camouflage jacket. "Spencer," he said, as proud as if he were a highly decorated prisoner of war. "Hiram Spencer."

Bolan scanned the men with some level of astonishment. The Handsmen—at least this group of them—were misfits, just as he'd said. Weak-willed, easily led, pliable and manipulable men in search of a leader. Men who would fall for the most simple of rhetoric and most outrageous of creeds as long as it had the word "patriotism" attached to it. "Well, Hiram Spencer," he said, "I'm giving you a new assignment. You're going to lead me and my men to your little playground fort. Think you can handle that?"

"Yes, sir," Spencer said.

The kid the Executioner had kicked sat back up. "You're a fucking traitor!" he mumbled through his broken teeth.

Kirk stepped in quickly and silently. Raising the Smatchet high over his head, he brought the flat side of the blade down with a crack on top of the young man's skull. The man returned to his back, eyes closed.

"Take a nap," Kirk said. "I don't think we need you."

Bolan thought briefly back to Jesse Davis, and how quickly

he had lost the man who had agreed to show them the route to the Handsman's camp. The same could happen to Spencer, and he wanted backups who could lead him to the Hands of Heaven compound in case it did. But taking them all along would be courting trouble. Even if they tried to be quiet, these untrained men in their Halloween costumes didn't know how.

"I want two more of you," the Executioner said. "Who's it going to be?"

Almost all of the remaining men's hands shot into the air to volunteer, and Bolan realized they assumed those not chosen would be executed on the spot. Good. Such thinking would promote good behavior. His eyes fell on another middle-aged Handsman in the back row of the group. "What's your name?" he demanded.

The man never got a chance to speak. Spencer had turned to follow the Executioner's gaze and immediately said, "You don't want him, mister. Nothing but trouble."

Bolan looked back down at Hiram Spencer. "What kind of trouble?" he asked.

Spencer shrugged. "Don't know. But he's always trouble, no matter where he is. Never satisfied with anything."

The Executioner drew in a breath of exasperation. "Okay, Hiram, I get the picture," he said. "Who do I want?" he asked.

Spencer swiveled to face the men behind him. "If it was me," he said, "I'd take that feller in the black Seattle Mariner's cap there."

"Why?" the Executioner asked.

"Well, he ain't going to make trouble like the old boy you just pointed out. That's one reason."

"There's another?" Bolan asked.

"Yeah. He's my bud," Hiram Spencer said. "Olin's his name."

Albert had moved up next to the Executioner. "Colloquial expression for brother, Belasko," he said.

Turning back to Hiram Spencer, the Executioner said, "Okay, pick one other man."

Spencer turned and his eyebrows lowered in deep thought. "How's about old Yulin over there?" he said.

Hiram, Olin and Yulin? Bolan thought. "Another brother?" he asked.

Spencer nodded.

Bolan turned to study the Edge Questers behind him. They had come in handy during the battle on the river. But the Hands of Heaven compound would be back in the mountains somewhere, and there were simply too many of them now to approach the camp unannounced. Still, he could use a smaller team—something about the size of Able Team and Phoenix Force combined. His eyes skirted the faces that had all turned his way.

"Okay," the Executioner said. "Albert, Kirk, Robertson, Davidson, Kane and Zanna. I want you guys with me and Harsey." He paused, then turned to James Albert. "Pick out three or four more good men."

Now it was Albert's turn to study his troops. He took only seconds before saying in a mock game-show announcer's voice, "Charlie Denton and John Crossett, come on down. You're the next contestants on *The Price is Right*."

Denton was a man in his early fifties, sturdily built and around five feet ten inches tall. He was dressed less extravagantly than most of the Questers, wearing OD fatigue pants and a faded denim jean jacket. He wore a blue .357 Magnum Ruger GP-100 on one hip and a medium-sized fighting knife on the other. Bolan squinted at the black micarta grips on the knife. They had been engraved in gold and read The Friend.

John Crossett was taller and wiry like Albert. He moved with the grace of a cat as he leaped from the speedboat and walked forward. His long hair was tied back at his neck, and a full black beard, beginning to speckle with gray, covered his face beneath wire-rimmed spectacles. His weapons of choice were a Glock and a large custom bolo knife.

Bolan saw Kirk say something to Albert and the Edge Quest

leader nodded. He looked out over the men. "Baggins," Albert yelled. "You up for a little fun, Buzz?"

A tall burly man with another full beard stepped out of the mass of Edge Questers. In his midfifties, he looked like an aging NFL offensive tackle. He wore a cowboy hat and boots, and carried a Colt .45 on one hip, another of the popular Hell's Belle Bowies on the other. In his hands was a .44 Magnum Marlin lever-action carbine.

"Moose!" Albert shouted. "You coming with us or you just going to stand around?"

The man in the tight black T-shirt, Bolan was about to learn, had actually been named T. Moose Roads—Moose wasn't a nickname and the initial T was the only first name he had. His head was covered in steel gray hair, and his beard matched. The simple gold earring in one ear, combined with the tattoos that covered every exposed area of skin except his face, gave him the look of a pirate.

"They're ugly," Kirk told Bolan as soon as the men had all stepped forward. "But they do good work."

Denton and Crossett sent burlesque scowls toward the bald man.

Bolan turned back to Albert. "You have any local cops here?" he asked.

Albert nodded. "Thompson," he yelled toward the group.

A short man who looked like he spent every waking minute lifting weights stepped out of the group of Questers.

"Sergeant, Lewiston P.D.," Albert said.

"Good," the Executioner answered. "Thompson, you and the rest of the men take the Handsmen back to Lewiston. Use their boat. Lock them up, then call the local FBI, ATF or Secret Service office. Make sure they find out you have these guys in custody, and who they are." It would probably have little effect, but it might distract some of the federal search teams for a while.

Like all good knife fighters, the Edge Questers carried bandannas as well as blades. Bandannas could be used as distractions or to tie off severed arteries if injuries were sustained. Many, Bolan had noted, had weighted the corners of their bandannas with fishing weights or other objects, making them suitable as whiplike saps as well. But the men of Edge Quest used these cloths for another purpose—they bound the Handsmen's wrists behind their backs before herding them on board the speedboat.

Bolan turned to Hiram, Olin and Yulin Spencer. "I'm not going to tie you up," he said.

Hiram squinted at him. In some strange way, the man seemed disappointed—as if he wasn't being shown the proper respect due a prisoner of war. "What if we try to run off?"

"You won't," Bolan said.

"How you know that?" Yulin asked. "We were all on the cross-country team in school."

Bolan drew the Desert Eagle and jammed the muzzle into Yulin's forehead. "Can you run faster than a .44 Magnum?"

The gulp going down Yulin's throat looked like something out of a cartoon.

As the Handsmen's boat pulled away and started upriver toward Lewiston, Bolan, Albert, Kirk, Kane and Zanna prodded the three Spencer brothers on board the *Norma*. They would lead the way, with Harsey, with the rest of the Edge Quest men chosen for the mission following in the *Rebecca*.

9

Webber Russell was fed up with the Hands of Heaven.

The leader of the United States Freedom Movement entered the door to the office building and saw Fred Moreland. The Hands of Heaven's self-appointed colonel was sitting with another of the endless chain of Diet Cokes that seemed to fuel what little ambition he had.

Moreland glanced up as Russell entered the room. He started to salute, then stopped.

Russell ignored him. At first, Moreland's almost compulsive need to be subservient in direct conflict with his desire to remain in charge of the Hands of Heaven had made Russell laugh. But the humor Russell saw in Moreland's behavior had begun to disappear as the man's stupidity, and that of the rest of the clowns who called themselves the Hands of Heaven, became a constant source of problems.

Russell walked to the cabinet where he kept his bottle of Scotch. He thought back on the pains he had taken to hire exactly the right men to create the fictitious United States Freedom Movement. He had known the men he chose must be more than good fighters—they had to be good actors as well. To find such men he had haunted all the bars catering to mercenaries in America, and half of those in Western Europe. He had hired only white men for the job, well aware of the Hands of Heaven's racial prejudices. But then, the man who had hired Russell had thrown in an addendum to their original agreement—he insisted that some of his own nation's agents accompany Russell on the mission.

Pulling the bottle down from the shelf, Russell twisted off the lid. He wasn't sure who he hated more at the moment, Fred Moreland or his employer. The man who had hired him had agents, all right. Good, competent agents. But they damn sure weren't *white* agents, and he'd had the devil's own time trying to figure out how he'd explain their presence to the Handsmen. Finally, he had decided that simple was best and had told Moreland and the others that the USFM had so many operations in progress that they'd been forced to hire mercenaries to assist them. In essence, he had simply switched the names for the whites and darker men within his group, calling the darker men the mercs and his real mercs "freedom fighters." Again, it had been nothing more than a low average intelligence on the part of the men who made up the Hands of Heaven that had allowed Russell to pull off such a preposterous ruse.

The leader of the USFM reached up into the cabinet and found a glass. Then again, he thought as he set it on the counter, extremists were extremists. Regardless of how smart or stupid they might be, they were always more inclined to believe the outrageous if it furthered their cause.

Russell lifted the bottle and poured whiskey into the glass, his thoughts turning away from the man who had hired him and back to the buffoon drinking the Diet Coke. He had divided his hired mercs and his employer's agents among the different units within the Hands of Heaven. His hope had been that their presence would create some structure within the rabble. But that hadn't been the case. Instead, rather than add a positive influence to the riffraff, his men and the Middle Eastern agents seemed to have become infected with the Handsmen's ineptitude. They had failed at every juncture to stop Rick Harsey and the big bastard with him. And a good number of them had lost their lives in the process.

Russell ran water from the tap into his glass on top of the whiskey. Yes, at first Fred Moreland had been a source of humor. But that time was over. Much like the man who finds the giggle of a woman charming on their first date, but after ten years of marriage swears to kill her if she ever laughs like that again, his familiarity with Fred Moreland and the Hands of Heaven had gradually bred the most intense contempt he had ever known in his life.

Taking a sip of the Scotch and water, Russell kept his eyes on the cabinet, away from Moreland. The man who had hired him for this job had known about the Hands of Heaven himself, and the reason he had chosen this militia to be the dupe for the actual operation was largely due to their incompetence and stupidity. But it had been a fine line his employer had been forced to walk in that decision; a delicate balance between a group stupid enough to be manipulated, yet smart enough not to completely blow Russell and his employer's plans.

It seemed now, Russell thought as he took another sip from the glass, that his employer had erred on the side of witlessness.

The leader of the fictitious United States Freedom Movement set the glass down on the counter but continued to look at the cabinet in front of him. Who would ever have dreamed that these Pacific Northwest hillbillies could have been this dumb? How could Moreland have ever organized or kept the Hands of Heaven together for the last four years, when he and all of his men were such fucking imbeciles? The Hands of Heaven had proved time and time again that their foolishness far outweighed his own men's professionalism. At General Harsey's house, at the Mountain Chief mine and other times along the Snake River, Moreland's bozos had showed they were no match for only two men—Rick Harsey and whoever that big bastard was with him.

Finally, Russell turned to look at Moreland. As far as he was concerned, Moreland deserved the title of History's Biggest Moron. Just hours ago, the fool had been outwitted by a seventeen-year-old girl. Now Samantha Bass was running for her life somewhere in Hell's Canyon, which meant he had been forced to further divide the men—both the Hands of Heaven and his own remaining mercs—to search for her. They'd find her eventually, he had no doubt. He had done his research before the kidnappings, and knew the vice president's daughter had received woodland training skills. But they were tree-hugger, pansy-assed skills—not true survival techniques. In Hell's Canyon, Samantha Bass would be lost without her Coleman lantern and a five-hundred-dollar water purification system.

"You know," Moreland said, breaking the icy silence between the two men. "I'd…like to try to explain."

Russell ignored him for a moment, then changed strategy. "Forget it," he said, taking another sip of his whiskey. "It could have happened to any of us." He paused a moment, then decided to lay it on a little thicker. For a while longer, at least, he needed Fred Moreland. "You're a compassionate man, Fred," he continued. "You're a patriot doing an unpleasant task for the overall betterment of the country. But that doesn't mean you enjoy inconveniencing people like Samantha Bass."

Relief spread across Moreland's features. "That's right," he said. "I guess I hadn't thought about it that way."

You haven't thought in any way, Russell wanted to say. Instead, he said, "Sometimes a man's got to do what a man's got to do." He laughed inwardly at the advance knowledge that the sarcasm behind this tired old cliché would be lost on the cretin before him.

He wasn't disappointed. Moreland nodded in agreement. "Yeah."

"We'll find her," Russell said. "It's just a matter of time."

Exhibiting a rare moment of insight, Moreland said, "I'm not sure how much time we have, Webber. Not only are Harsey and the big guy still alive, but our scouts say one of the Feds' search parties is getting closer." He took a drink of his Diet Coke. "And we've lost Boat Number Two. It just disappeared."

The federal search parties nearing didn't surprise Russell—that was all part of the plan. But this was the first he'd heard about the missing speedboat. "How do you know it's disappeared?" he asked.

Moreland shrugged. "They haven't radioed in for almost an hour. And I can't raise them."

A simple radio breakdown? Russell wondered. Maybe. But his gut instinct told him there was more to it than that. They'd probably come across Harsey and the big man and, as usual, the whole boatload of Handsmen had proved no match for the two skilled warriors. At least Boat Two had none of his own men on board.

Russell made the decision in a heartbeat. It was time to get this thing over. The vice president and his daughter had been captives too long, meaning they had milked the press for about all the publicity they could get. The entire world knew that a right-wing gun-toting militia had been responsible. When this was over, liberal gun control U.S. Senators and Congressmen would have more fuel than ever to disarm American citizens, and that was exactly what his employer wanted. That had been the real purpose behind the kidnappings.

Saddam Hussein knew that in a gunless America his terrorists, and agents such as those masquerading as USFM men now, could run rampant. And he could think of no better way to disarm the "Great Satan" than to murder Winston and Samantha Bass, then let an armed citizenry take the blame.

Yes, Russell thought, finishing his weak Scotch and water, it was time to get this thing over. Put the finishing touches on the plan by killing the Handsmen and making it look like some sort of mass suicide pact. Then and he and his remaining mercs would get the hell out of Hell's Canyon and collect their money. He turned back to Moreland. "Fred," he said, "it's time we moved out. How many men are left in camp?"

"About thirty-five of mine," Moreland answered. "Maybe ten or twelve of yours."

Webber Russell nodded. Considering the competency level of the Handsmen compared to his own men, he still had the advantage. But just to be safe, he'd pull in the rest of the mercs he had waiting in the wings.

"The enemy's getting too close," Russell said, taking another sip. "Get your men ready to move out."

Moreland frowned. "Move out? Where are we going, Web?"

Russell smiled. "Don't worry," he said. "The Hands of Heaven have done their part. Now it's time for the USFM to return the favor. There's a special place waiting for us."

Moreland still wasn't satisfied. "Where?"

Russell chuckled and patted Moreland on the shoulder. "I could tell you, Fred. But then I'd have to kill you," he said.

Moreland chuckled too at the worn-out joke.

"I'm going to call in some more USFM troops for security during the move," Russell said. "I don't know what we'll face on the way out. Maybe Harsey and the big guy, maybe the search teams. Maybe both."

Moreland nodded. "Makes sense," he said. He stood and set the empty Diet Coke can on the table. "I'll get the men ready."

Russell nodded as the leader of the Hands of Heaven left the office building. Yeah, he thought. They'll be just that much easier to shoot when the rest of my men get here.

The merc leader mixed another Scotch and water—stronger this time, now that the mission was about to come to an end. He sipped it and smiled. By the time he arranged the bodies, it would look as if there had indeed been some sort of Jim Jones-style mass suicide. He'd even scrawl some sort of note. *We killed the prisoners, then sacrificed ourselves.* Something like that, but with more off-the-wall, zealot-crazed detail.

Russell turned to look past the office to the back room where the cowardly Winston Bass was no doubt still feigning sleep. As soon as he finished his drink, he would kill the man himself both to make certain it was done right and because he had never killed anyone of such high rank before. He wondered how it would feel.

As for the vice president's daughter, one of his men had accompanied the Hands of Heaven who had left to search for her. And he had orders to make sure Samantha Bass got her little white throat cut the moment she was located.

BY THE TIME she half dragged Randy Holly out of the valley into the cave, Samantha Bass no longer held any delusion that she was dreaming. She had been found, all right. Holly had found her. But she wasn't sure who was rescuing whom at this point, or if either one of them was ever going to get out of Hell's Canyon at all.

Holly managed to make it three feet into the cave before he finally collapsed face up on the ground. The backpack he wore was beneath him, and as he panted his body swayed on the uneven platform, like a turtle overturned in its shell. Samantha saw that his eyes had glazed over. In spite of his heavy breathing, he looked more dead than alive.

The vice president's daughter fumbled with the canteen attached to Holly's belt, trying to get it off. But the fastening device baffled her.

The Secret Service agent groaned, and Samantha knew he was only half conscious. After another moment's confusion, she figured out how to get the top off the canteen. She held it to Holly's lips but the water only entered his mouth, then trickled down the sides of his face. "Randy!" she said desperately. "Come on, Randy! You've got to take a drink!"

Her words seemed to revive the young agent. He blinked twice, as if wondering where he was. But when Samantha held the canteen to his lips again he took a short, shallow swallow, then reached for the water with both hands.

Samantha let him take the canteen, worried that he'd drop it and they'd lose the precious liquid. She hadn't thought about water until that very morning, when she had realized just how dehydrated she was. But she had saved the canteen for him. He needed it more than she did. The wound in his shoulder had bled steadily ever since he'd found her, as they made their way from the Hands of Heaven compound to—

Where? Samantha wondered. Somewhere in Hell's Canyon not too far from the Snake River. That was the closest she could guess.

The water revived Randy further, and he sat up. Samantha looked at him. His shoulder, arm and most of the shirt he wore were completely soaked in blood. His eyes had cleared somewhat but his face was still pale.

Samantha felt a sob start in her chest but choked it off. Randy looked bad. Very bad.

When he spoke, the young Secret Service agent's voice could barely be heard. "Do you know where we are?" he asked.

Samantha shook her head. "Haven't the foggiest," she said. "How do you feel?"

"Like I just took on a whole tribe of Apaches," Holly said. "And they won."

Samantha forced a smile, more to cheer him than anything else. In actuality, the reference to Apaches made her wince as she thought of the injury to his shoulder which had started all of their problems. But she supposed the fact that he knew the source of his trouble himself was a good sign. It meant he could still think. She nodded to the canteen still in his hands. "You want some more water?"

Holly looked down, as if seeing the canteen for the first time. He raised it to his mouth and took another long drink. Samantha waited until he was finished, then took the canteen from him, replacing the lid.

The problem was, Samantha realized as she set the canteen on the ground next to her, she had training in how to survive in the wilderness but no actual experience. In short, she realized, she had no idea what she was doing.

But one thing she did know, and that was that it was time to change the dressing on Holly's wound again. Digging through the backpack still attached by straps across his chest,

Samantha found gauze bandages, adhesive tape and disinfectant. She helped Holly shrug out of his shirt, then went about peeling off the blood-soaked bandages as painlessly as she could. Still, she saw him wince. But she supposed that the fact that he could still feel pain might be a good sign, too.

Samantha wet one of the gauze bandages with water from the canteen and tried to clean the wound as best she could. The dried blood didn't make her gag as she would have guessed, and indeed, she found herself experiencing a sort of motherly feeling she'd never had before. "What happened?" she asked Holly.

The young man's speech was slightly slurred as he ran down the events that had transpired since Samantha's and her father's abductions. He had already told her of the crossbow that had sent the bolt into his shoulder. He told her of the interagency meeting in Seattle, the other search parties, how Singer had ordered him to return to the base camp after he'd been caught redressing his wound and how he'd chosen to disobey. The part about the kidnapping had come early in his narrative but one question had stayed in Samantha's mind throughout. When he stopped talking, she asked it.

"What happened to the other Secret Service men in the woods?"

When Holly didn't respond, she knew the answer.

"But if you decided to disobey Singer, your shoulder must have been all right," Samantha said, glancing at the wound, which was now freshly bandaged. "What happened?"

Holly looked down at the ground between them and chuckled sarcastically. "Pure, unadulterated bad luck," he said. "I lost my footing and tumbled maybe thirty feet down the side of one of the foothills. That was maybe an hour before I found you. I remember my shoulder hitting something hard during the fall but I don't know what it was. Probably a rock. Knocked me out for a minute or so and when I woke up all the stitches had ripped open. I haven't been able to get the wound to close since."

"You've lost a lot of blood," Samantha said.

Holly grinned weakly. "Tell me about it," he said. He was more alert than he had been since he'd first found her. His fall must have come shortly before that—before he'd had time to get really weak like he had as they'd moved away from the Hands of Heaven compound. During their flight, there had been no time to stop and redress the wound.

Samantha had pulled the leather strap that held his gun off his shoulder before she'd helped him remove his shirt and set the gun on the ground. Holly's eyes suddenly fell on the gun now, and he reached for it. "Do you know how to use one of these?" he asked.

The vice president's daughter shook her head.

Holly reached into the holster on his belt and pulled out a handgun. He handed it to her butt first and said, "Here. It's a Glock, and it has what's called a safe action. All you do is squeeze the trigger."

"Where's the safety?" Samantha asked. For some reason she had been embarrassed to tell Holly she didn't know how to operate the big gun he carried over his shoulder. But she was pleased that she could let him know she knew all guns had safeties. Her pleasure was short-lived.

"It doesn't have one."

"But—"

"Don't worry. It's safe without one." Holly said, smiling. "That's why they call it a safe action."

Samantha didn't understand but took his word for it. "But why are you asking me in the first place?" she wondered.

Randall Holly looked her in the eye. "Because like you said," he whispered, "I've lost a lot of blood."

It was at that moment that it first sank into her mind that Holly might die.

Holly must have seen the thought enter her head. "Don't worry," he said, reaching out to take her hand. "I'm not going to die. But I'm weak. And there's always a chance—" As if

ie had suddenly realized what he was doing, he let loose her
ingers and jerked his hand back away from hers.

Samantha stared into his eyes as she reached out and took
iis hand again. "I won't let you die," she said.

Holly opened his mouth to speak. "Samantha, I..." He let
:he sentence trail off, unable to finish it.

But Samantha Bass had known what he was about to say,
and she felt a warm feeling flood her body as the same unspo-
ken words made her head seem to spin. She continued to look
into the young Secret Service man's eyes as she said, "I know.
And I feel the same way."

Randall Holly grinned from ear to ear. "We're going to have
a lot of problems," he said. "Do you think it'll be worth it?"

"Yes," Samantha said, reaching out to take his other hand,
oo. "Oh yes."

Randy Holly's grin stayed on his face. "Me, too," he said.
"Maybe when I get fired I can still get a job as a security
guard at a hospital or something."

"You won't get fired," Samantha said. "I won't let them."

Holly laughed. "I'm not sure they'll listen to you," he said.
"You may be the vice president's daughter but you're only
seventeen years old. You're still a minor."

Samantha Bass returned Holly's laugh. "My birthday is to-
morrow," she said. Her smile narrowed to a coy grin. "The
shape you're in, I don't think you're going to be able to violate
:he law with me before then anyway."

Holly chuckled again. "I should be in jail just for what I'm
:hinking," he said. "But your age won't matter—"

Suddenly he heard footsteps outside the cave.

THEY HAD BEEN CLOSER to the Hands of Heaven compound
:han the Executioner had guessed. Even without the Spencer
brothers guiding them, they would have found it themselves
soon enough.

But that could have been too late.

Something was going on within the compound, the Executioner thought. Something that had the Handsmen running around the camp like ants who'd heard a foot about to come down on their den.

Bolan made his way through the trees, crawling on his belly across the rocky ground to the edge of the clearing. Stopping just inside the tree line, he stared through the face mask of the impromptu Ghillie suit. He, Harsey and Albert had formed an assembly line a few minutes earlier to quickly fashion the camouflage. Bolan had chopped small leafy limbs from the trees, then handed them to Albert who cut them down further with his eagle-head Hell's Belle. Harsey had then taken the pieces, supergluing them together, while the Executioner traded his blacksuit for a woodland BDU blouse and pants.

The Ghillie suit had holes in it. But it added the third dimension so needed for true camouflage, and with the irregularly patterned woodland clothes filing the holes, it seemed to be working just fine.

The Executioner rose to his knees slowly, concealed behind a short scraggly tree and a row of bushes just to its side. Looking down at the Ghillie suit, he saw that some of the leaves and twigs had been torn away by his crawl. It didn't matter. From here on in, the suit wouldn't be of much use anyway. He had every intention of just walking through camp as if he belonged there.

Staring into the clearing, the Executioner surveyed the grounds. There wasn't a lot to the compound. Only one building stood in the center, and it was no more than a hastily built modular cabin. But twenty to thirty tents—a mixture of military surplus canvas and nylon camping gear—circled the wooden edifice. Men dressed in the same camouflage the Executioner had seen on most of the other Handsman hurried in and out of the tents, their faces stern with purpose.

Bolan took in a deep breath. Yes, something was going on. He turned back to the wooden building. Were the captives in side? He couldn't be certain but it would be the most likely place to keep them—far more secure than any of the tents.

As he continued to watch the grounds, trying to get a handle on exactly what was happening, Bolan took a moment to reflect on the past few hours. The Spencer brothers had directed Bolan, Harsey and the Edge Quest warriors to within a mile of the Hell's Canyon Dam before they had pulled into shore. Bolan had been surprised to find that with the binoculars, he could even see the batching plant to the side of the dam in the distance. But that was where the easy part had ended and the hard part had begun. They had tied off and anchored the *Norma* and *Rebecca*, and began making their way up into the mountains. Hiram had explained the layout of the valley where the compound was located as they walked. It was hidden from aerial view by a natural overhang that more or less connected the peaks of two mountains, making them appear to be one. "What you got there, I guess," Hiram Spencer had said, "is a sort of a cave. Yeah, a sort of a giant cave."

The overhang of the mountains that concealed the camp from aerial view also kept the sun out much of the day, and the vegetation that grew below the rocks was stunted. That had accounted for the Ghillie suit, and Bolan's belly crawl forward. The overhang also kept the Handsmen's compound in an almost perpetual twilight.

Bolan had listened to Hiram Spencer with mixed emotions. He found it hard to conjure much sympathy for anyone who was part of a group who would kidnap the vice president and his daughter. On the other hand, Spencer and his two brothers had proved to have a combined IQ roughly equivalent to the rocks in Hell's Canyon. They were the kind of men who could be easily persuaded, influenced and tricked into following any sharp-witted leader. In this way, Bolan felt sorry for them and hoped they'd live through the rest of the mission and simply end up in prison.

In the eerie blue-gray twilight, the Executioner watched the men come and go from the tents, loading equipment into the back of several flatbed logging trucks. The trucks were pointed toward a ragged path that led out of the valley opposite Bolan, and to, he suspected, one of the many old logging roads that spiderwebbed through the mountains.

For all intent and purposes, it appeared that the Handsmen were moving out. Taking their prisoners to some other location. But something—he wasn't sure what—in the back of the Executioner's brain told him that wasn't necessarily the case. Was it the fact that some of the men worked more purposefully than others? He had noted certain apparent discrepancies within the ranks of the Hands of Heaven since the first attack at General Harsey's house where several of the bodies had been dark-skinned—probably of Middle Eastern descent. Then, in every later battle in which Middle Eastern men had taken part, they had fought far more efficiently than the average Handsman. He noted a pair of these men who appeared to be somewhat less enthusiastic about the preparations to leave the compound. They were carrying cardboard boxes but looked as if they were simply going through the motions rather than hurriedly trying to get ready. And as he watched, one of the men even elbowed the other in the ribs, then nodded toward a Handsman who was almost frantically stacking rifles on one of the trucks.

The Middle Eastern men chuckled.

The Executioner took a deep breath. He didn't know what it was, but something wasn't as it appeared. Which meant that the sooner he got Winston and Samantha Bass out of there, the better.

Slowly, Bolan dropped behind the bushes again and began shrugging out of his Ghillie suit. The cammo he wore beneath wasn't of the same pattern most of the Hands of Heaven wore, but he had observed a few exceptions among the men's uniforms during the past few days. He would have to hope anyone who noticed him took him for just another of the men with different camouflage.

The Executioner finished dropping the Ghillie suit, his mind flashing back to Harsey and the Edge Questers waiting a hundred yards behind him. They knew that as soon as he'd reconned the area, he might return for their help. If he didn't, it meant he had decided it was wiser to go in to extract the captives alone. In that case, they were ready to move in if he was caught in the act. If he was able to extricate the vice president and his daughter successfully, the Questers would stand ready to assist in their evacuation from Hell's Canyon.

Bolan waited until no eyes were turned his way, then quickly stood, shouldered his rifle and stepped from the trees into the clearing. He walked quickly and purposefully toward the wooden building, imitating the hurried pace of most of the other men in the camp. He passed a Handsman carrying a case of ammunition as he neared the door and nodded. The man nodded back, paying the Executioner no attention as he hastened about his business.

As soon as he reached the door to the wooden building, Bolan turned his back. He didn't want his face on display when he entered—his back would allow him a few more seconds of anonymity to anyone inside guarding Bass and his daughter. If they *were* inside—he still had no proof. But his instincts told him that this building did indeed hide the prisoners.

Reaching behind him, the Executioner's left hand found the doorknob as his right slung the SIG-551 LB over his shoulder. His hand closed over the grips of the Beretta. He opened the door and backed inside the building. From somewhere farther behind him, a voice called out, "Fred, that you?" Bolan didn't answer. Instead, he turned to face the room, the sound-suppressed 9 mm in his hand.

The room was empty. But a doorway in the far wall led to another room, from which the voice had come. The Executioner walked swiftly that way, the Beretta held in low profile against his leg. He sensed that the man who had called out was with the prisoners. He might even have a gun drawn, ready to kill them. Bolan would need to assess the situation the second he entered the room—before he was recognized as an intruder to the compound.

"Fred, you got your men ready?" the voice called out again as Bolan neared the door. "Come on back here. There's something you ought to see."

Bolan walked on, not trying to hide his footsteps. The man in the back room thought he was someone named Fred. Fred Moreland, the leader of the Handsman? Probably. That would also help give him an added split second to determine his course of action.

Gunfire flew toward him the moment he stepped through the doorway.

WEBBER RUSSELL was already mentally spending the money he was about to collect from Saddam Hussein's representative as he drained the last of his Scotch and water and drew the Colt Government Model from his hip. He pulled the small cellular phone from his shirt pocket and tapped in the number that would connect him to the rest of his thirty mercenaries who had set up camp less than a mile away. They had been his backup plan all along, ready to move in and finish off the Hands of Heaven in case Russell's men within the ranks dwindled. Well, thanks to the incompetency of the Hands of Heaven, that had happened. But the surprise attack would end the Handsmen once and for all.

As soon as the line was answered, Russell said, "It's time." It was all he dared risk over the easily monitored cellular. But it was all that was needed.

"On our way," answered the voice at the other end of the line.

Russell disconnected, shoved the phone back in his pocket and took a moment to glance through the window. The Handsmen were still busy loading the trucks. That was good. They'd be preoccupied when his mercs arrived in a few minutes.

He had mixed his last drink a little stronger than usual—not enough to affect his judgment but enough to keep the low-level buzz. With the cocked and locked .45 pistol in his hand, he moved through the doorway into the rear room, lifted the screen and looked down into the hole.

As usual, Winston Bass was pretending to sleep.

"Open your eyes, dammit," Webber Russell said. "I know you're not asleep."

The vice president did as ordered, squinting up at the hole above him. Mud, the product of the dirt in his underground prison mixed with tears, caked the wrinkles around his eyes. For a moment, he didn't speak. Then, finally, he asked, "Where's Samantha?"

"Don't know," Russell said, grinning as a light surge of whiskey hit his brain. "But my men are going to kill her when they find her. Unless they decide they want a little teenage pussy first."

Winston Bass closed his eyes again and bowed his head.

"Don't worry, Winnie," Russell said, raising the .45 and dropping the front sight down the hole onto the top of the vice president's head. "You won't be around to see it. In fact, say your prayers. I'll give you ten seconds."

Webber Russell had counted to five when he heard the door of the office building open. Dammit, he thought, just like that imbecile to come in at the wrong time. "Fred, that you?" he called out.

When he got no answer, he assumed Moreland hadn't heard him. "Come on back here, Fred," he said. "There's something you ought to see." He turned the Colt toward the door. The Hands of Heaven men were going to hear the shot that killed Winston Bass anyway, they might as well hear the one that took out their idiot leader, too. He'd put one between Fred Moreland's eyes, drop the bastard down the hole on top of Winston Bass, then be done with the vice president with one more shot. If any of the little boys playing soldier outside came in to see what had happened, they'd go into the hole, too. By then, his mercs would have arrived.

Webber Russell listened to the footsteps nearing the door. They sounded a little different than Fred Moreland's usual clomping stride, which caused the first flicker in his brain that something might be amiss. But before the thought could fully germinate, he saw the big man step through the doorway and suddenly knew exactly who he was.

Harsey's friend. The big Fed had found them.

The Colt was already aimed at the door, at a spot which would have been between the eyes of Fred Moreland. But the big man standing there was a good half foot taller than Moreland. Russell tried to realign the sights, but the sudden shock he felt from seeing that it wasn't Moreland and realizing who it was, caused him to overcompensate. Even as he pulled the trigger, he knew the shot would fly high over the big man's head.

As he fought the recoil of the Government Model, trying to bring it down for another shot, Webber Russell saw the Beretta 93-R rising in the big man's hand. Time slowed for him as he realized he was about to die. He saw the three 9 mm slugs that coughed from the machine pistol spinning through the air, one after the other. A moment later, they struck his chest.

BOLAN DROPPED to one knee, jerking the Colt out of the fallen man's hand. He pressed his index finger into the man's carotid artery but got no pulse. He was kneeling over a corpse.

Rising to his feet, the Executioner leaned over the hole in the floor. Below, seated against the dirt wall, he saw Winston Bass. The vice president's arms were folded over the top of his head as if they might shield his brain from bullets. Soft whimpers choked from his throat. "Please...." he whined.

Bolan's eyes searched the area. Where was Samantha? Had the Handsmen imprisoned her separately? Or was she dead?

"Mr. Vice President," the Executioner said. "Look up. I've come to get you out of here."

Winston Bass's face shot toward the top of the hole, a look of confusion covering it. Bolan could readily see the man was in shock. He knew he would have to give Bass the most basic orders if they were to get out of there alive. "Mr. Vice President, we're going home,'' he repeated. ''Now, rise to your feet and climb up the ladder.'' When Bass didn't move, the Executioner used a firmer tone of voice, adding, ''Do it now.''

Winston Bass obeyed, looking like a remote-controlled zombie as he climbed the rungs of the ladder. As soon as he was within reach, the Executioner grabbed his arm and hauled him the rest of the way up. ''Mr. Vice President,'' Bolan said, ''do you know where your daughter is?''

Bass shook his head.

Bolan blew a disgusted breath between his clenched teeth. Was she in one of the tents? If so, he had problems. There was no way he could haul a civilian with him as he searched the compound.

The Executioner was still contemplating his next course of action as he half dragged Bass out of the back room and into the office area. Through the window, he could see that a few curious eyes were turned toward the building. But the rounds he had fired from the sound-suppressed Beretta wouldn't have been heard—the .45 ACP from the dead man's pistol was the only sound that would have penetrated the walls. And while it seemed to have been enough to incite curiosity among the Handsmen, none of them were coming to investigate. If he waited a few minutes, perhaps even the curiosity would die down.

But even before completing that wishful thought, the Executioner saw a man start toward the door. He carried a plastic bottle of Diet Coke in his hand and took a drink as he neared the building.

Bolan pushed Winston Bass back into the other room. ''Stay here, sir,'' he said. ''Don't speak and don't move.'' His words weren't necessary. Winston Bass had become pliant. He would bend like a rubber doll when physically moved but would otherwise remain frozen in place.

The Executioner stepped back out into the office and trained the Beretta on the door. He watched the doorknob turn, then the man he had seen through the window suddenly stood before him.

"Come inside and close the door quietly," Bolan said. "Make any move to alert the men outside, and you're dead."

The man with the Diet Coke did as he was told, then turned to face the Executioner.

Bolan stepped in and pulled a Beretta 92 from the holster on the man's belt, shoving it into his own waistband. "You're Moreland, aren't you?" he asked. He remembered the man's face from General Richard Harsey's computer screen.

The other man nodded.

Bolan grabbed Fred Moreland's arm and ushered him into the back room with Winston Bass.

Moreland dropped the Diet Coke bottle from his hands. "Webber?" he said, looking down at the floor in dismay.

"Who is he?" Bolan asked.

"Web...Webber Russell...the head of the United States Freedom Movement."

Bolan wondered briefly what the United States Freedom Movement might be—he had never heard of it. But he had more immediate problems, and with his free hand he slammed the Handsman against the wall. Shoving the Beretta's sound suppressor under his chin, he said, "Where's Samantha Bass?"

The Handsman wasn't only confused, he was scared. He didn't hesitate to reply. "In a cave somewhere. She ran away. Some of the men just radioed in that they'd found her."

"Are they bringing her back?"

The Hands of Heaven leader shook his head. "Some guy— one of you Feds I guess—is with her. My men can't rush them without taking heavy casualties. But the Fed is wounded. My men are waiting them out."

Bolan glanced down and saw the walkie-talkie on the man's belt. He jerked it from its holder and shoved it into the Handsman's face. "Find out exactly where they are and exactly what's going on," he ordered.

Again, Moreland obeyed without hesitation. "Hand 1 to Hand 18," he said into the walkie-talkie.

"Come back, Fred," came the reply over the air waves.

"What's your 10-20?" Moreland asked.

"You know where Mitchell's Point is, Fred?" said the voice on the other radio. "We're about a klick and a half west."

Fred Moreland looked at Bolan and cleared his throat. "You have the girl with you?"

"Negative," the voice of Hand 18 came back. "They're still in the cave. Rogers went up to check a minute ago. We lost him."

Bolan pulled the radio from Moreland's hand to make sure the mike wasn't keyed. "Tell them to wait," he said. "Tell them you'll send reinforcements."

"Hold your position, Zach," Moreland said. "I'll send you some help."

"Affirmative, Fred," the voice said. There was a pause, then, "There's blood all the way into the cave, Fred. I don't see how the bastard can last too much longer."

"More men are on their way, Zach," Moreland said. "Don't do anything until they get there."

The Executioner wondered briefly who was in the cave with Samantha Bass. A member of one of the federal search parties, no doubt. He tore the walkie-talkie from Moreland's hand again, and turned it off. "What's going on outside?" he demanded. "Why's everyone loading up?"

"We're moving out," Moreland said. "Taking the prisoners to another loc—" His words were suddenly interrupted by a volley of gunfire outside the building. Another volley followed, and then suddenly the compound sounded like a Fourth of July parade.

Bolan twirled Moreland away from the wall, shoved the gun into his back and marched him back into the front office. Through the window, he saw confused Handsmen falling as they tried to bring their weapons into play. He frowned. Had Rick Harsey and the Edge Questers moved in to attack? Maybe.

Although he had ordered them to stay put until they heard from him again, they might have mistaken his long absence for capture and decided to take the initiative.

But moving closer to the window, Bolan saw that that wasn't the case. Emerging from hiding now, he saw armed men he didn't recognize firing into the Handsmen. Yet again, several had dark skin. One of more of the federal search teams? Bolan wondered. Again, maybe. But when he squinted at the men's shoulders, he saw no agency arm patches.

Moreland answered the Executioner's questions without being asked. "That son of a bitch!" the Hands of Heaven leader cried.

Bolan spun Moreland toward him. "What are you talking about?"

The fear Moreland had shown was gone now, replaced with anger. "Webber Russell," he said. "We linked up with his United States Freedom Movement for the abductions. But now that bastard's men are killing mine! I knew we shouldn't have trusted those damn sand niggers!"

The racial slur confirmed they were Middle Easterners to the Executioner, but he didn't have time to figure out their role in this. Not at the moment. But it did seem he had been right when he'd guessed the Handsmen's strings were being pulled by someone with bigger brains. A group that called itself the United States Freedom Movement. For whatever reason, it seemed the factions within the compound were now at war with each other, and the Handsmen were obviously on the losing end. They were dropping like flies to the unexpected bullets outside the building.

The entire battle didn't last sixty seconds. Suddenly, the last round had been fired and the rest of the men—the United States Freedom Movement, who evidently allowed foreigners into their ranks—stepped out into the clearing. Several of them began circling the grounds, checking pulses and adding the final pistol rounds to the heads of the few Handsmen who were only wounded.

The rest, rifles aimed in front of them, started toward the office building.

The Executioner waited, wondering what he would do when the door opened. He was far too outnumbered to hold his ground for very long.

RANDALL HOLLY knew he wasn't going to last much longer. He had begun to feel dizzy again shortly after they'd heard the footsteps outside. He had shot the man sent up by the Hands of Heaven to check the cave, and the Handsman had bled to death a few minutes later. He still lay in the entrance to Holly and Samantha's rocky fortress, and the young Secret Service agent looked at him now. Holly's own condition had been worsening since the shooting. The bleeding wasn't bad but it was steady. It had been going on for hours. And it was finally taking its toll.

Soon, he suspected, he would be lying on the floor of the cave next to the Handsman.

Holly looked down from the mouth of the cave at the men scattered through the valley, partially hidden by boulders and tree trunks. It had taken all of his strength just to lift the M-16 and fire a few more rounds to force them to cover. That had been over an hour ago, and since then he had heard the squeak of a walkie-talkie drifting up to the cave, but nothing else. He knew why.

The Handsmen sent to search for Samantha had seen his bloody trail. They knew time was on their side. They had no need to risk the shots he would send down at them if they charged. All they had to do was wait for him to bleed to death. Holly looked at the dead Handsman at the mouth of the cave again and wondered how long it would be before he did just that.

The young Secret Service agent turned to the girl next to him. Earlier, she had told him she loved him. He had told her the same. But he knew he wasn't getting out of Hell's Canyon alive, of that he was certain. But he was just as certain that he was going to do everything he could to see that Samantha Bass did.

"Samantha," Holly said, surprised at how weak his voice sounded even inside his own head. "Aim the Glock outside and pull the trigger."

"But—"

Holly took a deep breath and pain shot through his entire upper body. "Please, just do it. One time. I want to make sure you can."

Slowly, Samantha nodded. She gripped the Glock in both hands and aimed it over the body of the dead Handsman. Holly noticed she was using both index fingers on the trigger but he didn't suppose now was the time to worry about the finer points of proper shooting. What she was doing should get the job done at close range.

The Glock-21 exploded, threatening to deafen them inside the cave. When their ears had cleared, Holly heard excited voices below. The Handsmen were wondering just what the shot meant. Good—let them wonder.

"I did it," Samantha said.

Holly nodded toward the entrance to the cave. "I want you to keep that thing aimed that way," he breathed. "Shoot anything you see. Got it?"

"Yes," Samantha said, frowning. "But what are you—"

"I...think..." Holly said as his vision began to darken. "I'm going to...take a little...nap." With that, he closed his eyes and faded into unconsciousness.

The first three USFM men through the door of the Hands of Heaven office building expected to find Webber Russell holding a smoking gun, and a dead Winston Bass. So, while their M-16s were still slung over their shoulders, the pistol grips were only in their hands to aid in balancing the weapons. Their faces smiled—beamed, actually—reflecting the smugness of men who had done a job, were convinced they'd done it well and were about to see the final fruits of their labor.

But instead of their Russell and Bass, the face that greeted them was that of the Executioner. *Their* Executioner. And the smug expressions quickly turned to confusion.

A 3-round burst burped from the sound-suppressed Beretta 93-R, and the body of the lead man shook like a marionette gone mad as the hollowpoint rounds drilled through skin and muscle tissue. His eyes still perplexed, he fell forward on his face inside the doorway.

A whine of mixed confusion and terror escaped from the second man. It was cut off sharply as the Executioner swung the 9 mm machine pistol his way and pulled the trigger again. Another trio of lead slugs stitched new buttonholes in the man's BDU blouse. He went sprawling over his fallen companion.

The third man almost had time to recover from the shock. But not quite. He snarled, and Bolan saw his knuckles turn white as he took a firmer grip on his assault rifle and tried to raise it into play. But before his finger could find the trigger, yet another burst of sound-suppressed fire from the 93-R caught him in the throat and face. He slammed back against the door-frame, then pitched forward to add himself to the pile of bodies just inside the office door.

The three men hadn't been alone, however, and Bolan saw a collage of camouflage through the open doorway. But before he could fire again the patterned pants and shirts broke up like pieces of a jigsaw puzzle caught in a hurricane. The cammies darted to both sides of the opening a millisecond ahead of Bolan's next burst, and his 9 mm rounds blew harmlessly past them.

In less time than it takes most men to blink, the Executioner had dropped the near-empty magazine from the Beretta and slammed a fresh box into the weapon's grips. He slid the SIG assault rifle off the sling as he jammed the 93-R back into its shoulder harness.

"Webber Russell!" screamed a thickly accented Middle Eastern voice outside the building. "What's going on?"

Bolan turned to Fred Moreland. The leader of the Hands of Heaven was as frozen in place as the vice president. Briefly, the Executioner considered a bluff; a ruse in which he forced Moreland to call out, stalling the men and giving him a few moments to consider his options. Just as quickly, he discarded the idea. These men—the ones Moreland had called the USFM—had come to kill the Handsmen. All of the Handsmen, and that included Moreland. No, a bluff from Moreland would hold no weight. In fact, the time for subterfuge of any kind was over.

It was only the Executioner versus dozens of armed enemy.

A hard smile curled Bolan's lips as he readied the SIG-551 for combat. Death had been his shadow for too long to retain its sting. Should he die in Hell's Canyon, his only regret would be that he couldn't continue the good fight against men like the ones he now faced. His final hope would be for the safety of Winston and Samantha Bass to complete his mission.

Murmuring voices outside told the Executioner that the men

of the United States Freedom Movement were still confused. They hadn't expected resistance from within the building. What must have transpired between the USFM and the Hands of Heaven began to crystallize in Bolan's brain. Moreland and his Handsmen had believed there was an alliance between the two groups. But Webber Russell and his men had used the Hands for their own purposes. That answered two questions still in the Executioner's mind: How such a seemingly incompetent militia could pull off the elaborate kidnapping, and why a few men of obvious Arabic descent had been present in each group of professed white supremacists he had encountered. They had been guard dogs, positioned within the ranks to make sure the Hands didn't do anything too stupid. And to ensure that when the fall eventually came, the Hands of Heaven took it.

Bolan gritted his teeth silently inside his mouth. One question was still unanswered. What was the real purpose behind kidnapping Winston and Samantha Bass? What did Webber Russell and the men calling themselves the United States Freedom Movement really want?

He didn't know. But he intended to find out.

A rifle barrel suddenly appeared at the window to the side of the door. Bolan pulled the SIG's trigger and sent gunfire through the glass. The glass shattered, sparkling both red and white in the sunlight as blood struck the flying shards. The man and weapon both fell out of sight.

More murmurs, audible through the open window, followed the brief encounter. Then the Executioner heard laughter. A few seconds after that, a faint odor of smoke wafted into the office building.

Bolan caught himself nodding. Fire. It made perfect sense. They would simply burn the building. After all, they wanted everyone inside dead, and fire would be the easiest means to that end. Which presented the Executioner with a choice: He could take the vice president with him and try to flee, in which case they'd both be shot. Or they could stay inside the building and burn to death.

The Executioner moved cautiously to the broken window. In the yard he saw a man holding a broken tree limb wrapped with rags. Another man, his lips curled into a snarl of evil pleasure, tilted a five-gallon gasoline can over the rags, then pulled a cigarette lighter from his pocket.

Even as he raised the SIG-551 LB toward the torch bearers, Bolan sensed the futility of what he was about to do. Yes, he could shoot these two men before they set the building aflame, but behind them, around the compound, he could see dozens of other militiamen already at work constructing their own torches. Too many. He could never get them all before one of the flaming firebombs reached the building. Eventually, the Hands of Heaven headquarters building was going to become a fiery inferno no matter what he did.

The Executioner's jaw tightened. Still, he would try. The concept of surrender wasn't to be found in his personality profile.

Bolan sighted down the barrel and lined up the sights on the man holding the cigarette lighter. His finger found the trigger.

The Executioner was already squeezing the trigger when he saw the blurry object come flying out of the trees at the edge of the compound. A moment later, a sickening, wet-sounding thump broke the quiet. The man holding the torch stood for a moment, his mouth open in shock. Then he dropped to his knees, and Bolan saw the grip of a large knife extending from his chest.

The Executioner pulled the trigger and the man next to him turned a cartwheel in the air as a full-auto blast drilled into his head and shoulders. Then, for a moment, the entire compound quieted once more.

Bolan glanced back to the man still on his knees. His hands were wrapped around the hilt of the knife embedded in his chest as he struggled vainly to jerk it free. Then the struggling ceased. The man fell to his back and his hands splayed out to his sides. At this new angle, the knife was easily identified. An eagle-head pommel.

War whoops suddenly sounded from the trees. Then dozens of rounds of shot from the leaves and limbs, peppering the compound. The USFM men standing in the yard were as caught by surprise as the Handsmen had been only moments earlier when they had pulled the same trick themselves. As the roars of a variety of caliber rifle and pistol rounds boomed through Hell's Canyon, the men in the yard began falling.

Bolan opened fire through the window at the closest enemies, downing two USFM men with a figure eight of gunfire. As the hot brass casings flew from the SIG's ejector port, he saw James Albert step out of the tree line. The Edge Quest leader's leather Hell's Belle sheath hung empty at his belt. But he gripped his CAR-15 in both hands and pumped round after round into the USFM men.

Gary Kirk wasn't far behind Albert. The undercover expert's lips were curled in a grinning snarl as his AK-47 slung lead as fast as he could pull the trigger. Bolan swung his SIG to another cluster of surprised USFM men, emptied it, and six more of the enemy fell in death. As he stuffed a fresh magazine into the SIG, he saw that the Edge Questers had fanned out in a circle around the Hands of Heaven compound. Charlie Denton and John Crossett popped up from another area within the trees. Both men gripped M-16s captured from the Handsmen on the speedboat, and 5.56 mm NATO rounds glided through the air so thick they could almost be seen. More of the USFM forces were mowed down like a wheat field under a thrashing machine.

Some of the USFM men turned toward the trees and returned fire. But many more panicked. Some ran. The Executioner's well-placed rounds found homes between their shoulder blades. Other terrified terrorists sprinted irrationally toward the building where Bolan stood at the window next to the door. Those foolish enough to pick this route caught the Executioner's bullets in their chests.

Bolan shot a quick glance over his shoulder and saw that Fred Moreland was still terrified, unmoving. As he turned back to the window, a volley of rounds flew through the broken glass shattering the splinters that remained around the edges. The Executioner was forced to the floor. As soon as the barrage ended, he rose once more and stuck the barrel through the opening. Another half-dozen terrorists fell.

A face suddenly appeared less than a foot in front of Bolan's. One of the USFM men had crawled along the side of the house, then popped up. Between the Executioner and the SIG's barrel, the man brought up a Colt .45 Government Model and jammed it into Bolan's chest.

The Executioner twisted to the side as the gun exploded, feeling the heat as the big bullet penetrated his shirt blouse and skimmed across his bare skin. The odor of smoking cotton rose to his nostrils as he brought the stock of the SIG to the gunman's temple. A loud crack sounded as the USFM man's skull fractured, and he fell half in the window.

Bolan grabbed him by the hair and threw him out onto the ground where he began to flop spasmodically. A lone round to the head ended the flopping.

A multicolored flash appeared in the Executioner's peripheral vision and he turned to see that T. Moose Roads had worked his way around to the building to help him with the cross fire. Seemingly oblivious to the cool weather, Roads had stripped off his black T-shirt in preparation for the battle. His bare chest and back caught Bolan's eye, and the Executioner now saw that Road's entire torso was as blanketed with tattoos as his arms. The effect was that of war paint, and combined with the gold earring that sparkled in his ear, T. Moose Roads looked like a cross between a high-seas buccaneer and a Comanche warrior.

The Executioner had started to turn away again when another flash caught his eye. As Roads raised his weapon, a body on the ground ten feet behind him raised one as well. The barrel of the gun in the dead man's hand had already swung in line with the tattooed skin when Bolan pulled the trigger. More rounds from the SIG caught the face of the possum-playing enemy on the ground and made his fake death real.

T. Moose Roads continued to fire, never realizing that death had come knocking and that the Executioner had bolted his door for him.

As the melee continued, the Executioner caught a glimpse of Rick Harsey firing the other SIG-551 LB from the trees. Josh Robertson and Mabe Davidson flanked the general's son, and a few feet away stood Anton Zanna, blasting away with another of the captured M-16s. Dr. Mark Kane wasn't to be outdone by any of them, and the Pennsylvania psychologist pumped and fired his sawed-off 12-gauge so fast that the weapon looked like a full-auto shotgun.

Bolan ran the SIG dry for the third time, reloaded, then suddenly realized it no longer mattered. All of the enemy were down. The compound was filled with corpses now, both those of the Handsmen killed by the USFM and the USFM men who had, in turn, been killed by him and the Edge Questers. Smoke filled the air, and the smell of cordite was heavy in the Executioner's nostrils as he turned away from the window. And froze in his tracks.

Fred Moreland lay on the floor in a pool of blood. Bolan didn't have to ask what had happened. Either one of the rounds he had ducked earlier or the .45 slug that had burned across his chest had traveled on to find the forehead of the Hands of Heaven leader. Moreland lay flat on his back, his eyes staring at the ceiling.

The Executioner scanned the office for Winston Bass but the vice president was nowhere to be seen. Bolan found him thirty seconds later. The number two man in United States government had climbed back down into his hole in the back room. His arms were crossed over his bowed head, and he was pretending to be asleep.

Bolan led the zombielike vice president out of the building a few seconds later. James Albert had sent his men to search the tents for anyone who might be hiding. As the Executioner approached the Edge Quest leader those men began returning, shaking their heads. The Edge Questers were all smiles, their bodies pumping adrenaline. They had finally gotten a chance to put their training to use. Good use.

Bolan suppressed his own smile. If he'd had his choice on backup troops, he'd have brought along Phoenix Force, Able Team or a detachment of Stony Man Farm blacksuits. But the men of Edge Quest had held their own.

Quickly, Bolan explained to Harsey, Albert and the other men what he had learned about Winston Bass's daughter. "All of you guys have gone way beyond the call of duty," he said. "If you want to call it quits at this point, I understand."

The Edge Questers looked at him like a group of men who had just seen their first two-headed Martian. Anton Zanna spoke first. "Like Yogi Bear always says," Zanna said with his Hungarian accent, "'It ain't over 'til it's over.'"

"That's Yogi Berra," Dr. Mark Kane corrected. "But the sentiment is the same, and accurate under the circumstances." He turned to Bolan. "We're still with you."

"Okay," the Executioner said. He turned to face Albert. "You or any of your men know Mitchell Point?" he asked.

Albert nodded.

"Good. That's where some of us are going." He shifted his eyes to Harsey. "But I need a team to get Bass out of here. Rick, I'm afraid this is where we part ways. I need you to lead that team and make sure the vice president is safe. Turn him over to the first Secret Service people you can find." His eyes fell on the three men who had led them to the site. "Turn the Spencer triplets over to the cops. Let them drive the boys in blue crazy for awhile. And get a fully equipped rescue chopper ready to evacuate Samantha Bass and a wounded agent. Tell them to head toward Mitchell Point but to stay far enough away that they can't be seen or heard. I don't want them to know we're coming." He stared Harsey in the eyes. "Any questions?"

Rick Harsey grinned and shook his head. "Got it, Belasko. No problem."

IT WASN'T AN EASY trail they followed deeper into the mountains, but finally Bolan, Albert, Kirk and Zanna spotted Mitchell Point in the distance. They ascended a small rise, and from this vantage point the Executioner could see more of the mountain, still a half mile away. He pressed the binoculars to his eyes, adjusted the rings and suddenly the backs of men hiding behind the trees and boulders at the foot of the mountain came into focus.

Bolan raised the binoculars slightly. Perhaps forty feet above the closest Handsman, he could see the dark mouth of a cave in the face of the mountain. From Fred Moreland's last radio transmission, he knew that the Hands of Heaven sent to find Samantha Bass had cornered her and some unknown protector. This had to be the place. The Handsmen were following the orders Bolan had forced Moreland to give out—waiting for reinforcements before moving in.

Could he and the three men with him step in and play that part, passing themselves off as fellow Handsmen, as they walked openly toward Mitchell Point as if they had been sent by Moreland? If so, as soon as they were within rifle range they could open fire. But that plan had its flaws.

The Executioner took a quick glance at Albert, Kirk and Zanna. Zanna wore khaki pants and one of the black-hooded sweatshirts. Albert was dressed in his Carhardts, and while Kirk had on desert-pattern pants he wore another of the black sweatshirts above them. None of them looked enough like Handsmen, even from a distance. The possibility of approaching through subterfuge evaporated suddenly before the Executioner's eyes.

But Bolan didn't get a chance to formulate another approach. As he looked back into the binoculars, he saw the men hiding beneath the cave suddenly rise in unison and charge up the rocks.

The Executioner frowned as he gripped the binoculars tighter. He was still too far away to shoot, and couldn't even sprint forward into rifle range in time to halt the charge. So the best he could do was assess this change in the situation and reevaluate his plan of action. He wondered what had spawned the Handsmen's sudden action—had they simply grown tired of awaiting their backup? Had they tried to contact the camp again by radio and grown suspicious when they got no response? No matter.

Death for Samantha Bass and whoever was with her was the potential result, either way.

As he continued to watch, Bolan saw the man leading the charge reach the mouth of the cave. Then a lone pistol shot sounded in the distance and the Handsman jerked back out of the darkness, lost his footing and rolled back down the slope to the bottom of the valley.

But three more Handsmen had been on his heels, and after dodging his falling body they disappeared into the cave. There were no more shots, and through the binoculars Bolan saw the remaining two Hands of Heaven men slow their pace and enter the cave at their leisure.

Movement at the side of his field of vision suddenly caught the Executioner's attention. He swung the binoculars toward it. He saw the reason the Handsmen had decided to charge the cave before their reinforcements could arrive. Another group of men were descending a slope into the valley fifty yards to the west of the cave. The Executioner squinted into the binoculars, and saw the shoulder patches on their khaki shirts. The Handsmen had spotted them, and that had precipitated the impromptu desperation charge. The search team had then heard the pistol shot and were hurrying toward its source.

The Feds reached the valley floor and broke into a sprint toward the cave. What would they do when they reached it? Bolan wondered. Rush the slope and force the Handsmen to shoot their hostages? The Executioner cursed softly under his breath.

Still out of rifle range, there was only one thing he, Albert, Kirk and Zanna could do now: Get to the cave as quickly as possible and hope an assault by the Feds didn't take place in the meantime. Bolan turned to the trio of warriors at his side. The expressions on their faces told him they understood the situation too.

"Let's go" was all the Executioner had to say.

Bolan led the way, descending from the rise and taking off at a sprint across the flatter ground of the valley. Behind him, he heard the footsteps of his team. As he ran, he could see blurry movement at the mouth of the cave. One of the Handsmen had emerged. The Executioner watched as he ran. No, not one of the Handsmen—a dark-skinned man. One of the USFM terrorists who had been filtered into the Hands of Heaven earlier—before the final USFM attack.

Still running, the Executioner lifted the binoculars from around his neck to his eyes. Each time his foot hit the ground, he caught a glimpse of the scene developing ahead. The terrorist who had emerged from inside the mountain held a bolt-action rifle with a large scope mounted on top. As Bolan watched, the rifleman dropped prone and rested the weapon's fore end on a boulder in front of the cave. The barrel was aimed toward the approaching federal search team.

The Executioner shifted the binoculars just as the explosion echoed throughout the valley. He saw the lead federal man drop his own rifle, clutch his chest with both hands, then fall to the ground. The rest of the team halted in their tracks, raised their long guns, and blasted volleys of fire up at the mountain. But while their bullets sent the man with the rifle scampering back into the cave, they all missed their mark.

Bolan and his men raced on. They were only a hundred yards from the cave when the search party spotted them, mistook them for more Handsmen and opened fire. "Down!" the Executioner shouted, and he and the Edge Questers dived onto their bellies.

Prone, Bolan raised the binoculars again. Through the dusty

lenses he saw the search team halt, look up at the cave then back in his direction as if trying to figure out who was who.

"Here!" Kirk yelled from Bolan's rear. The Executioner glanced over his shoulder to see that the man had pulled a white bandanna from his pocket and crumpled it into a ball. The sweat-stained cloth flew through the air and into Bolan's hand.

Leaving the SIG on the ground, the Executioner raised the white flag over his head, then stood. He waved the bandanna as he walked slowly toward the team. He had gone only ten steps when one of the Feds broke away and began jogging toward him. Behind the running man, half of the search team kept their rifles aimed at him. The other half covered the cave.

They were fifty yards from the mouth of the cave when the two men met. Bolan had kept an eye on the opening in case the sniper returned, and the Fed had cast nervous looks over his shoulder as he ran. As he stopped in front of the Executioner he turned to keep the cave entrance in view.

"Who are you?" the federal man asked. He stared at the shoulders of Bolan's where patches would have been if he was with one of the other search teams.

"Justice Department," the Executioner said.

"Justice?" the man asked.

"Do you really want to waste time on details?" Bolan snapped. As far as he was concerned, Hal Brognola could cover any questions about his identity later. "Here's the situation— Winston Bass is safe and being transported back to civilization as we speak. But his daughter is up there." He nodded toward the mountain. "And I'm pretty sure one of your guys is with her. Wounded. Most of the men who just charged up the hill are Handsmen. But the man with the darker skin—the one who just shot one of yours—is with some group called the United States Freedom Movement."

"United States...what?" he asked, his face a mask of confusion. Then his eyes became suspicious again. "How do you know all that?"

"I'll explain later," Bolan said. "Who's leading your team?"

"It was Butch Singer," he said. "But he just went down."

"So who's in charge now ?"

"BATF man is next in line. Simon Donavan."

"What's his temperament?"

"He's an asshole," the Secret Service man said bluntly. "Real 'Kill them all, let God sort them out' sort of guy."

Bolan looked past the man to where the rest of the search team had begun cautiously approaching the cave, rifles aimed upward. They stopped suddenly when movement again appeared overhead.

The Secret Service man turned to see what had caught the Executioner's attention just as two forms appeared outside the cave. Samantha Bass came first. But right behind her, one arm wrapped tightly around her neck, the other jamming a pistol beneath her quivering chin, was the USFM man.

"Give me your attention!" the man behind the vice president's daughter screamed at the top of his lungs.

The valley fell into sudden silence, as if even the animals in Hell's Canyon understood that the moment of truth had arrived.

"This is Samantha Bass!" the terrorist yelled. "The daughter of the Vice President of the United States of America! And I will kill her if any of you disobey my orders!" He paused to let the threat sink in. "Throw down your weapons!" His English was good, but his Middle Eastern accent betrayed the fact that it wasn't his primary language.

The Feds waited for direction from Simon Donovon.

Bolan could see that the terrorist holding Samantha had his attention focused on the search team. It appeared the man hadn't yet noticed him or the Secret Service agent and Edge Quest warriors. From where he stood, the Executioner had a clear view of over half the man's head behind that of Samantha Bass. Too far away for a pistol shot. But he could end the threat with a rifle.

Bolan glanced down to the SIG still on the ground. Slowly, he bent forward.

But the movement caught the eye of the terrorist. He suddenly swung Samantha in front of him, and the opportunity was lost.

"You bastards out there, too!" the man shrieked. "Throw down your guns!" With two groups of rescuers to watch over now, Bolan watched his eyes dart back and forth between them. Timing it so that the man was looking at the federal search team, the Executioner quickly jerked both the Beretta and Hell's Belle from leather and hid them in his waistband behind his back. The Edge Questers and Secret Service man didn't move.

Bolan had just completed the transfers when the USFM man holding Samantha turned back to them. "Now!" he screamed. "Or I'll kill her!"

Slowly, the Executioner drew the big Desert Eagle and dropped it to the ground. "Do as he says," he told the other men.

The Secret Service agent shook his head. "Policy clearly states—" he started to say.

"Do it!" Bolan demanded, and something in his voice convinced the man that official Secret Service policy had suddenly been superseded. He dropped his M-16 and a SIG-Sauer 9 mm pistol. Lower, through tighter lips, the Executioner added, "The rest of you guys, take off everything that shows. Hold on to any hideouts you've got—at least for the time being."

Albert, Kirk and Zanna left their rifles on the ground, added their pistols and knives to the pile, then stood.

The man with the gun pressed into Samantha's neck shouted again. "You! Move forward, hands in the air! I want you all together down here! Where I can see you!"

Bolan and the Secret Service agent walked forward. The Questers followed.

The federal search team had still not dropped their rifles. The USFM man looked directly down at them. "I will count to three," he threatened. "Then, if every weapon is not on the ground I'll scatter this little whore's brains all over the rocks. One..."

Words of argument could be heard between the members of the search team.

"Two..."

"Any man who drops his weapon will be shot by me personally!" shouted a voice the Executioner had to assume belonged to Simon Donovan.

"Three!"

The search team apparently took the terrorist's threat more seriously than Donovan's. All of the rifles except that of their leader dropped to the rocky ground.

In a flash of speed, the USFM man holding Samantha jerked the pistol away and aimed down at the men. Another shot rang out across the canyon, kicking up dirt and gravel a few inches from the feet of the man who still gripped his rifle. "You too!" the USFM man yelled.

Bolan and his men were closer, and he could see Donovan's camouflage-painted face. Through the brown, black and green, angry eyes stared back at the man holding Samantha. But after a short pause, the final M-16 fell to the ground.

"Move away from the guns!" the man outside the cave screamed. "Right down here below me! Where I can see you!"

By that time, Bolan, the Secret Service agent, Albert, Kirk and Zanna had reached the other group of men. Together, they did as they had been ordered.

"Everyone sit!" ordered the terrorist. "Place your hands on top of your heads!" When the men below the cave had dropped to the ground, he added. "I'm taking her back inside. I'll return with a list of demands. So pick a man—one man—to come up here and receive your orders. And let me remind you one false move and there will be many tax dollars spent on this whore's funeral!" He paused for a breath, then added. "Do not forget that one of your own men is also inside. He, too, will die!"

With that, he and the vice president's daughter disappeared into the cave once more.

As soon as they were out of sight, the men turned to face one another in a circle. Simon Donovan didn't waste time. "I want to know what hideout weapons everyone has," he said in a voice that was obviously used to giving orders. "As soon as that son of a bitch comes back out, we're going to—"

"No," Bolan said.

Simon Donovan's head snapped around to face the Executioner. "Who in the hell are you?" he demanded. "You're not in charge here!"

"Yes," the Executioner said, "I am."

"Bullshit!" Donovan said. What little skin was visible through the makeup on his face now turned purple. "I'm in charge, and if I hear one more word of dissent out of you or anyone else—"

Bolan was sitting less than two feet from Donovan. He leaned slightly forward, and his fist shot out in a hard right cross to the man's jaw. The crack produced by the punch sounded almost as loud as a gunshot, and Bolan's knuckles came back wearing camouflage face paint. Simon Donovan closed his eyes and crumpled to the ground.

Next to the Executioner, undercover cop Gary Kirk chuckled. "Now that's what I call cutting through bureaucratic red tape," he said.

"Cuff him," Bolan said to no one in particular. Donovan, he soon saw, wasn't a popular leader. Several pairs of anxious hands, the faces above them grinning with pleasure, competed for the task.

The Executioner considered their options while they waited for the terrorist's return. He had known a negotiation like this was inevitable as soon as the man had emerged from the cave with Samantha in tow. Which was the reason he had hidden the Beretta and Hell's Belle behind him. But knowing that he would be forced to go up into the cave to receive the Handsmen's demands, he realized they would be of little use. He could pull his shirt out over the weapons but even a cursory search would uncover them. The pistol and knife were both far too large to conceal.

No, he would have to enter unarmed. Slowly, his eyes glued to the cave overhead, he slipped the pistol and knife out of the back of his pants and handed them to James Albert who was seated on his other side.

Albert took the weapons and stuck them out of sight in the small of his own back. But Bolan was surprised when the man reached into the pocket of his heavy canvas jeans and came out with a strangely shaped piece of plastic.

Bolan grinned as the tiny weapon was placed into his hand. It was a Combat Technologies Stinger. A small, inconspicuous little punching device that concentrated the force of a blow on a point half the size of a green pea, increasing its power a hundredfold.

The Executioner was almost as surprised when he felt a hand from his other side pressing something else into his. He turned to see the black handlebar mustache above Gary Kirk's white goatee curling upward in a grin. When he looked down in his hand he saw a small Spyderco Rookie folding knife.

But that wasn't the end of the hideout weapons offered up to the Executioner. Anton Zanna pulled an American Derringer from a Kydex holster suspended around his neck on a paracord lanyard.

Bolan took all of the weapons and jammed them into his underwear beneath his shirt.

No sooner had the transfers been made than the USFM man reappeared at the mouth of the cave. The girl was nowhere in sight.

"Your representative!" shouted the USFM man. "He is to come up here now! And if I find so much as a slingshot on him, I will put a bullet in his head and send him rolling back down to you! Then I will kill the girl and your agent!"

There had been no vote to decide who would go. It had been implicit. The Executioner rose to his feet and began making his way up the rocks toward the mouth of the cave. If he could survive the search he knew would come first, he had a chance to rescue the girl. A slim chance, granted. But a chance.

As soon as he reached the top of the rise, the USFM man and two Handsmen in camouflage stopped him at the mouth of the cave. The leader of the group trained an M-16 on Bolan's head as he said to the Handsmen, "Search this Satan from your American government. Search him well."

One of the Handsmen started at the Executioner's boots, tapping the sides to make sure nothing was hidden beneath the leather. As he moved up to pat the pant legs, the other man ran his hands though Bolan's hair, then moved down his neck.

The Handsman who had begun his search with the Executioner's boots was young, probably in his late teens. Bolan waited until the kid reached his upper thigh level and was about to move his hands toward the Executioner's groin. Timing it perfectly, he said, "You look like the kind of kid who gets off on this part. So take your time. Have fun. Be sure to get a good feel you can think about later when you play with yourself."

This inference had the desired effect on the young man. His hand shot away from the Executioner's crotch as if he'd touched a hot stove.

"He's clean," the young man said.

The other Handsman ran his hand around the Executioner's belt line, then nodded agreement and stepped back.

Bolan looked past the men into the cave. In the semidarkness, he could see Samantha Bass sitting on the hard rock floor. Next to her lay a man wearing Secret Service patches on his shoulders. He might have been alive; he might have been dead. It was impossible to tell. To the sides of the captives were two more Hands of Heaven men. One gripped an AK-47, which he had trained on the Executioner. The other had a Colt .45 Government Model pressed against the girl's temple. The Executioner studied them momentarily. They knew nothing of the massacre back at their headquarters or that they were the only Hands of Heaven members still alive on the planet.

Bolan casually moved his hands to his belt buckle, hooking his thumbs inside his pants as the USFM man began to speak once more.

"Here is what you are to do," the terrorist said. "You'll call in a helicopter, which will transport me, my men and both of our prisoners of war."

"They aren't your men," Bolan said. "They're Hands of Heaven. You're USFM, whatever that is, and my guess is that it's nothing. A handy name to cover who you really are. Iraqi terrorists."

A flicker of self-doubt appeared in the dark eyes. In his peripheral vision, the Executioner saw the Hands of Heaven men turn toward the darker man with blank stares.

"He lies!" said the terrorist.

"Do I?" the Executioner asked. Casually, he began to scratch his stomach above his belt. When he was finished, he let his right hand return to where it had been—but this time his fingers were tucked inside his pants just below the waistline. The tip of his index finger brushed the grips of the Derringer. "I don't think so. It took a little while to figure out, and I still don't have all the details. But generally I know what happened." He looked from one Handsman to another until he had made eye contact with each one. "You've been played as patsies, boys," he said. "You've helped this man and others like him convince the American public of the exact opposite of what you want. Have you got any idea how many people are going to support stricter gun control laws after all this?"

Bolan watched mistrust begin to fog the eyes of the Handsmen. He hadn't convinced them of anything. But he had started them thinking.

And that thinking would slow them down.

"Enough nonsense!" the terrorist screamed. "The helicopter will deliver us to the Lewiston airport. You'll have a plane waiting." He stared at Bolan with the hatred of the true zealot.

But behind the hate, the Executioner could see he had broken this man's mental balance as well.

"If everything has gone as ordered, when we arrive at the airport I'll release this man." He turned and jabbed a toe into the ribs of the Secret Service man on the ground. As he did, the eyes of the other Handsmen all turned that way.

It was the moment the Executioner had waited for. He wouldn't get a better chance.

Smoothly, Bolan stuck his hand the rest of the way down the front of his pants and gripped the Derringer. As soon as the tiny weapon cleared his belt line, he turned the barrel toward the man holding the Colt on Samantha Bass, thumbed the weapon's safety off and fired.

The bullet drilled through the Handsman's brain stem and paralyzed his trigger finger. The Colt fell to the rocky cave floor next to the vice president's daughter.

Even as he had drawn the Derringer, Bolan's left hand had shot into his pants and located the Spyderco Rookie. As his right hand rode the recoil of the Derringer, his left thumb found the opening hole of the small knife and swung the blade out of the handle. He fired again. His second and final round went through the nose of the Handsman with the AK-47.

The young Handsman who had been too timid to conduct a thorough body search stood directly to the left of the Executioner. Bolan twisted the Spyderco in his hand and brought the serrated blade across the young man's neck with a vicious backhand slash, severing the carotid artery. The young man reached up with both hands, grasping impotently at the wound in a vain attempt to close it.

Pivoting to the other side, the Executioner thrust the Rookie's short blade out and up. The point caught the soft flesh beneath the chin of the other man who had searched him, then traveled upward. Through the man's open teeth, Bolan saw the shiny stainless steel blade appear inside the man's mouth. He dropped the empty derringer and reached into his pants for the plastic Stinger, at the same time jerking the Spyderco back out of the man's head and tracing the serrated edge down his throat. Another geyser of blood shot forth as another carotid artery sliced in two.

The USFM man was the only one left on his feet. And he wasted a precious second in shock. When it finally sank in to him that the impossible had occurred the M-16 began to rise in his hands.

The Executioner stepped in, and with the same right cross he had used to knock Simon Donovan unconscious, drove his fist into the terrorist's face. But in addition to the massive power of Bolan's arm and shoulder, this time his fist held the Stinger. All of that energy emerged between the man's thick black eyebrows, just above the bridge of his nose. There was an almost nauseating crack as the Stinger penetrated the man's skull and the hard plastic tip traveled through the bone into his brain.

The USFM man was dead on his feet.

The entire process, from start to finish, had taken less than five seconds.

Bolan reached down and pried the M-16 from the USFM man's dead hands. He made his rounds of the Handsmen quickly, like a battlefield doctor. But unlike a doctor, the Executioner was checking for death rather than life.

Finally kneeling next to the body of the Secret Service agent on the ground, Bolan began to search for a pulse. He was alive. He had been wounded in the shoulder and had lost a great deal of blood. But if he received medical attention soon he would recover.

The soldier turned to the weeping girl still seated on the ground. She looked up, and in her eyes, Bolan saw the horror that had been her life for the last several days.

Reaching down, the Executioner took her hand. "Miss Bass," he said. "Don't you think it's about time we got you home?"

The federal task force members and the Edge Questers entered the cave. "Damn, it's Buddy!" said the Secret Service man Bolan had already met. Several other members of the search team lifted the wounded man off the ground and gingerly carried him out into the sunlight. Bolan helped Samantha Bass to her feet, then took her arm to guide her out. As soon as they had exited the cave, the Executioner heard the blades of a helicopter and looked up to see the rescue chopper. The federal search team had evidently radioed in the information that they'd located Samantha—probably as soon as they'd spotted the Handsmen outside the cave.

As her shock wore off, Samantha Bass broke away from Bolan and ran to the men carrying the Secret Service man. "Randy!" she said through fresh tears, then turned back to Bolan. "Is he going to be okay?"

The Executioner nodded.

The chopper landed and the search team carried the wounded Secret Service man toward it. The vice president's daughter followed, waiting as he was transferred to a stretcher and taken on board. Then, the sounds of more rotating blades suddenly broke the air overhead.

Bolan looked up to see a second helicopter, but this one bore no markings. It hovered for a moment, then settled to the ground twenty yards away. Through the glass bubble windshield, the Executioner saw the familiar face of Jack Grimaldi. Without another word, he started toward the chopper.

A second later, he felt soft fingers encircle his arm. He stopped and turned to see that Samantha had sprinted after him. "You saved us," she said.

The soldier didn't reply.

The vice president's daughter glanced to the second chopper, then looked back up at Bolan. "Aren't you coming with us?" she asked.

He smiled and indicated the other helicopter with his head. "The guy flying that bird is a friend of mine. And the fact that he's here means I've got more work to do somewhere else."

Samantha was disappointed. But she nodded and dropped Bolan's arm. The Executioner started toward Grimaldi again.

"Thank you," Samantha called after him. "Mr...?"

When Bolan didn't answer, she called out, "Please, you can at least tell me what to call you, can't you?"

Bolan stopped one last time and turned. "I'm a friend," he said. Without another word, he boarded the helicopter.

"Hello, Striker," Grimaldi said.

Bolan nodded. "Jack," he said.

The ace pilot grinned as he pulled the chopper's skids off the ground into the air. "Hope you got some rest on this one, big guy," he said. "'Cause we're headed for—"

Grimaldi turned to face the Executioner in the seat next to him and realized he was talking to himself. The Executioner's eyes were closed, shutting out the world. For the moment.

A jungle threat...

STONY MAN™ 46

Hostile INSTINCT

The Stony Man team is called in to stop a disenchanted Congolese man from taking over a jungle region in central Africa. He is setting himself up as dictator and wields a great deal of power...including several vials of Ebola virus that he stole from a lab!

Available in April 2000 at your favorite retail outlet.

James Axler

OUTLANDERS™

SHADOW SCOURGE

The bayous of Louisiana, steeped in magic and voodoo, are the new epicenter of a dark, ancient evil. Kane, a renegade enforcer of the new order, is now a freedom fighter dedicated with fellow insurrectionists to free the future from the yoke of Archon power.

Shadow THE EXECUTIONER®
as he battles evil for 352 pages of heart-stopping action!

SuperBolan®

(limited quantities available on certain titles)

TOTAL AMOUNT	$	
POSTAGE & HANDLING	$	
($1.00 for one book, 50¢ for each additional)		
APPLICABLE TAXES*	$	_____
TOTAL PAYABLE	$	_____
(check or money order—please do not send cash)		

To order, complete this form and send it, along with a check or money order for the total above, payable to Gold Eagle Books, to: **In the U.S.:** 3010 Walden Avenue, P.O. Box 9077, Buffalo, NY 14269-9077; **In Canada:** P.O. Box 636, Fort Erie, Ontario, L2A 5X3.

Name: _____

Address: _____ City: _____

State/Prov.: _____ Zip/Postal Code: _____

*New York residents remit applicable sales taxes.
 Canadian residents remit applicable GST and provincial taxes.

GOLD
EAGLE®

GSBBACK1